J E

TRUTH

Ottery Books

Published in Great Britain by Ottery Books

First published 2019

Copyright © J E Hall 2019

ISBN 978 0 9955035 6 4

Typeset in Palatino

Cover picture by Jack Kerslake, cover design by Short Run Press

This novel is a work of fiction. The names, characters and incidents and
are the product of the author's imagination

website: jehallauthor.com

A full CIP record for this book is available from the British Library

Printed by Short Run Press, Exeter

To

Rosie with all my love

ALSO BY J E HALL

"If you're going through hell, keep going"

A quote attributed to Winston Churchill

*"the church exists not to adapt, survive and succeed;
but rather to be faithful"*

The Very Rev Martyn Percy, lecture at Salisbury Cathedral 13 July 2019

"I believe in the power of narrative"

Arundhati Roy in interview with Gary Younge, The Guardian 1 June 2019

1

It was 4pm, the last Saturday in August – a bank holiday weekend in England. Passing somewhere high overhead the roar of a distant plane could be faintly heard in north London as it took its turn in the queue to begin its final descent west to Heathrow. The pilot glanced at his controls constraining him within a precise flight path. He thought to himself, flying wasn't what it used to be, today there was no freedom in the air. It was about time he retired.

Nearby, five thousand feet below the Boeing 747, down to earth, the incessant whoosh and reverberating hum of traffic on the ever busy North Circular Road offered a noisy accompaniment drowning out all plane noise from above. In the roaring and the hissing of stop-starting lines of road traffic, those who could afford it were squeezing out the last drop from their summer holidays before the pressing routines of autumn all too soon re-imposed themselves. Drivers' faces gazed blankly forward wishing themselves the open road, but having to settle for an endless switch between brake and first gear, the customary restrictions that came with driving in London.

Unseasonably hot continental weather had dried the grassy lawn outside Holy Trinity Church to a pale yellow, like patchy stubble on a sick man's chin. Heat pulsed from the red-brick walls. The long day had worn everyone down with the heavy, dry afternoon air hanging perpetually still.

The Revd. Ruth Churchill's every breath as she stepped outside her church was a stifling cocktail mix of black diesel particles and assorted urban fumes. At her feet lay dusty confetti, thrown just an hour earlier without regard to the

1

prominent prohibitive notice displayed. It lay in unmoving drifts of dusty white and pink on the church path to the street. Someone would need to sweep it up later. Perhaps one of the churchwardens ought to take the old sign down for all the good it did. Anyway, who wanted to stop confetti throwing at weddings, she thought, only those who wanted to shackle freedom and fun.

Locking the west door of Edmonton's Holy Trinity Church behind her, Ruth was feeling so thirsty she feared her tongue would stick to the roof of her mouth; her mind became set on getting a cold drink in the vicarage next door. She pictured the glass jug of icy homemade lemonade waiting in the fridge. Having tied the knot, she'd sent the happy wedding couple and inebriated guests off with her blessing; all bound for a glitzy reception in Hertfordshire. A ghastly, white American limousine, looking like a floating meringue, had been hired to whisk the ever-smiling couple away to their evening in a hot marquee; there'd be more drinks, speeches and cavorting on the dance floor until the early hours. They'd enjoy it, she thought, but personally she didn't envy them one bit.

Her duty done, Ruth's clerical robes were slung over one arm, the remaining wedding service sheets tucked under the other. Her weariness was such that she noticed neither the planes above nor the nearby traffic. Taking care not to drop anything, she paused at the church door to close up, it was only with some difficulty she turned the large rusty key, finally hearing the the ancient mechanism of the lock clunk shut. The church was safe and secure until tomorrow, Sunday. Funny that, she thought, needing to lock everywhere up in order to feel safe and secure.

Her mind began to turn toward what she still needed to do for the next day's services. She wondered where she would find either the energy or the time to do it and even more importantly how she could seize some precious moments with her husband Phil and their two children, Olivia and Paul; what with today's wedding, she hadn't seen them since breakfast. Her busy schedule closed off what she really wanted to do as securely as the locked church door before her.

It was only a journey of twenty paces from the church to the vicarage door, but Edmonton is not the kind of place to take even a short walk for granted. Retrieving her key from the church door, she dropped the heavy item back into her bag. The sun burning on her back, a rustle in the dry grass from behind and Ruth suddenly became aware of a presence nearby. Instinctively, she slowly turned from the locked door to face the street. A young man in a red, Arsenal football shirt, black shorts and trainers was lying face down on the grass just feet away from her; he was perfectly still. How strange, Ruth thought, as her mind began to process what she was seeing. What was he doing there?

Then she tried to take an involuntary step back only to feel the old oak door preventing her. She hadn't seen it immediately but his hand was on a long bladed knife. His fist clenched around the handle, he was keeping it close by him, almost tucked under his body, parallel with his right thigh. The far side of his body was pressed hard against the low boundary wall of the church, metal railings above, hiding him from view to anyone in the street.

His head was turned away from her facing in the direction of the wall, his prone form lying in line with the low wall's rows of orange-red bricks that were topped by black and

3

rusting spiked railings. Ruth stood perfectly still as she tried to assess both him and her own situation. He was on her side of the wall. Just him with his knife and her with... with her God.

Though not moving, he looked alive, his skin pink and blotchy, his chest rising and falling as if he'd been running. 'Was he hurt?' She could see no blood. Should she go to him? Then she panicked thinking he could be dangerous and knowing she had no escape route. It wasn't as if she could slide back inside the church door behind her, she'd just locked it, her key buried in the depths of her bag. But what kind of threat did he pose, she asked, trying to reason with herself? What should she do? In her moment of indecision she just froze, like a rabbit caught in the headlights, snatching her breath in shallow pants, feeling palpitations within her chest, imagining this was when she should see her life pass before her. But she checked herself and resolved with God's help to summon up some inner strength.

Then it became clearer to her what was happening. A vehicle was approaching, the gravelly humming sound of tyres pressing tarmac, and to her left she saw a police car turn slowly into Windmill Road from Silver Street and cruise by at a snail's pace just yards away. Her eyes followed it round.

Two young officers, both in short-sleeved white shirts, a man and a woman were glancing this way and that, as if looking for someone. She thought she detected a brief smile of recognition in the young policewoman's face when, just for a second, their eyes met.

The car would soon be gone, so Ruth tried to move, but her arms were full and then the opportunity to do something had passed and the police car had accelerated away disappearing from sight leaving Ruth alone again with a young man and his knife. She looked this way and that for help, but today, when she needed someone, on this normally busy street there was no one else in sight.

Trapped in the walled church garden, her eyes fixed on him. Then there was a sudden movement as the young man rolled on the grass in her direction. He sprang up like a dog on a lead keen to go for a walk. She could see his white teeth. Once upright he stood tall, and spotting her he gazed down at her with a puzzled expression as if he'd only just noticed her for the first time. As Ruth looked him in the face, she didn't recognise him, but then there was no reason to, why should she? He could be from anywhere. She was cornered.

On first seeing her, she saw uncertainty written in his face; she thought she saw a trace of fear, maybe of panic. Then his eyes spotted her clerical collar, her hanging robes and he shrugged his shoulders dismissively as if assessing her as irrelevant. He turned his back on her, looked out on the street this way and that before striding energetically toward the church gate to make his exit. Perhaps silence was the more prudent course, but from somewhere within Ruth found her voice.

'Can you tell me what's going on? Why are you hiding in my churchyard?' she called out.

'So they wouldn't get me,' he replied in a barely audible voice, seemingly oblivious to the fact of the knife hanging low in his hand. His face was pasty, spotty, dirty and his expression one of wild desperation. Bits of dead grass had stuck to his cheek. He had none of the fluidity of movement a real Arsenal player would have had, he was more like a gangly teenager, the trappings of poverty self-evident.

Throwing more furtive glances this way and that, he added uncertainly, 'I need to be off.'

Springing up the couple of steps from the gate onto the pavement, he walked a few paces, still eyeballing Ruth, and then he turned and started coming back toward her. Her heart missed a beat as he gazed back at her through the railings. He looked so unpredictable, someone with little more to lose if he attacked, yet to her surprise he'd returned to simply pull the church gate shut after him and for a brief moment he smiled at his own act of courtesy before once again striding away, his knife now held vertically, lying almost hidden between arm and body. Ruth watched as he broke into a loping run and turned left into Silver Street. He disappeared from view.

Once again Ruth was alone, this time conscious of her now furiously beating heart, her clammy hands and the need to get to a loo.

As quickly as she could, she moved the few paces to the safety of her own front door and rang the doorbell urgently. Three times she pressed it before trying to fumble in her bag for her house keys. They were never to hand when she wanted them – where were they? In the chaos of flight she couldn't put her hands on them. She turned her head panicking, the hairs at the back of her neck pricking her; was he following her? Then Phil opened the door. He instantly read the distressed look in her eyes.

'What's happened?' he asked, peering out of the door, then leaning out, looking up and down the street. 'The couple you married want a divorce already?' he lightly quipped, before swift realising he'd badly misjudged the real situation.

'I'll tell you inside,' she said, pushing and shoving her way past her husband. He closed the door slowly after making a final searching gaze and as he turned to her she let out a sighing breath of relief.

'Thank God you've shut the door.'

Phil waited for her to speak again.

'A youth with a knife,' she added, as she threw her things onto the hall chair.

'What!... Shall I call the police?' he said, pulling his mobile from his pocket.

'I don't know. I really don't. I'm... I'm not sure I can take any more.' Her hesitation came as her mind told her that every action she took in this place seemed to generate more actions and endless incomplete tasks all competing with each other to be done first. Calling the police required time she just didn't have. Yet even as she was saying it, deep inside her she knew she really didn't have any choice in the matter.

'Did he look like he was going to harm anyone?'

'No, I don't think so. Thought so at first, but then, no... He went off down Silver Street. He's gone, I think. Suppose I'd better call the police, give them a description. Can you be a dear and fetch me a glass of water or better still cold lemonade from the fridge?' she said, more as an order than a request.

As Phil moved off to the kitchen she fumbled in her voluminous bag to find her phone. Once retrieved, she punched in the direct dial number for Edmonton police station, a number she knew all too well. Phil returned, glass in hand, hearing her get through.

'Hi, Ruth Churchill here, Holy Trinity, Windmill Road. Just want to report seeing a young man carrying a long knife. He's headed east from the church, down Silver Street. I think you must be looking for him as a patrol car narrowly missed spotting him as it came by here. It all happened just now, a moment ago...'

More details were requested and replies duly given. Ruth was told to wait whilst they made contact with the car in the vicinity.

A minute or two later when the duty officer came back she was told there had been an incident reported at the nearby corner shop in Silver Street, an armed robbery. The lad she'd seen seemed to fit the description the police had been given and she was thanked for her call. The police would send someone round, but there was no promise as to when that might be.

Ruth's attention turned to the lemonade, a mist on the outside of the glass telling her of its welcome cold contents. Sipping it carefully, she and Phil wandered into the kitchen to sit at the battered, plain, oak, kitchen table; it served as the focus of life in the house. Everyone gravitated toward the kitchen. For the past six years this bare wooden table had been where the family decided everything and where all their meals were taken. It was the heart of the home. The secrets it knew!

Strategically placed in the centre of the kitchen it was possible to see over the low fence separating the front garden from the street and they could observe everyone who passed by on the pavement outside. In turn they could also be seen and some people waved in greeting. Ruth liked it that way. She remembered how, when they'd first arrived Edmonton, she'd stopped the workmen in the process of erecting two metre high fencing palings. When asked why, they'd explained with a shrug, 'clergy like to feel safe.' She said, 'not this one,' and made them cut it down by half, but she now wondered whether she'd been right.

'Olivia and Paul, where are they?' Ruth suddenly shouted in alarm. 'They're not outside are they?'

'No, it's OK, they're upstairs playing in their rooms. Relax, you've had a heavy day,' Phil added, placing a comforting hand on her shoulder. She knew she was near the end of her tether and took another sip of lemonade. It tasted refreshingly good.

Then the door bell rang loudly startling both of them. They looked at each other's mimicking open hands indicating neither were expecting a visitor. Ruth nodded to show she ought to be the one to go and get it. It had to be someone for her. There was another urgent, persistent ring.

She pulled open the door with its brightly coloured stained glass art deco window, a shadow visible of someone outside. Screwing her eyes against the bright late afternoon sun, she saw it was him again, the youth with the knife. He seemed even taller than before and now, having stepped forward, he was standing too close, in her space and blocking her view. He was so close she feared he might push past and get inside.

'I forgot earlier,' he said threateningly, waving his knife loosely, with an air of deliberate carelessness, the blade just

9

inches from her face, 'I don't want you calling the police, right.' He stared at her and her dropped chin. He hesitated as he looked at her, his eyes couldn't hold a steady gaze, perhaps he didn't altogether like what he was doing, she wondered. He'd done enough, she thought, something told her instinctively he wasn't going to do more.

Having delivered his message, he stepped back, turned, and moved briskly outside the porch and in seconds was through the front garden gate. She heard him close it behind him with a loud metallic ping. Then she watched as he made off, holding the door just slightly ajar, her hand ready to pull it swiftly shut.

Her eyes followed the lad as he dragged his knife, metal railing to metal railing past the church, making a dreadful dull dinging sound. Ruth watched spellbound. Then there was silence. She sucked in a breath as she saw the knife thrown high in the air. It spun and spun catching the light, finally coming down to rest with a thud and a bounce on the hard church lawn. By the time her eyes looked up for the youth again, he'd gone.

Sensing something was up, Phil had moved cautiously from the kitchen toward the front door. He'd not known what to do. He hadn't seen the fellow, but he'd listened to everything. As he moved from the kitchen to be closer to Ruth, he heard her finally close the door, then the metallic rattle follow as she slid the little door chain in place. She turned to face him. By now Phil was moving to hold her and the two stopped still, ashen faced, staring into each other's eyes.

'I'd better call the police again and tell them about our visitor, and that his knife is in the church garden,' said Ruth reaching for her phone.

'Do you think that's wise?' asked Phil, 'He might come back. You heard what he said.'

'We don't have any choice. It's too late. I've already called them once. It's the only thing we can do, I'll tell them about his threat, ask them to keep an eye on us, passing patrols, that kind of thing. I had a closer look at him this time. He's got matching badly done tattoos on both his knuckles. I'll be able to give them a good description,' she returned, as she stepped inside the privacy of her study to make the call.

Phil stood there, rooted to the spot in the hallway waiting until she had finished, always surprised at Ruth's ability to find some inner strength. Then he said, 'We need to talk.'

Both moved back into the kitchen, Phil reaching for the kettle, Ruth about to sit down at the table. Her mobile phone rang. The ID of the caller showed up number withheld, nerves on edge, Ruth decided to take the call. Was it him again?

2

'Pauline Brown here. We've admitted someone who's asking for you.'

It was the familiar warm voice, spoken in the softest of Caribbean accents, of the duty matron in ITU at the nearby North Middlesex Hospital. Ruth felt immense relief. She'd feared it was the tall youth again. She waved a dismissive, 'it's alright' hand in Phil's direction. Leaving the rumbling kettle on in the kitchen, he moved off, heading upstairs to the children as Ruth hunted round for a pen and paper.

'Oh, who's that then, Pauline?' asked Ruth, her phone held between shoulder and cheek as she pulled a notepad toward her.

'Not usual this. He's Hindu and he's asking for you. I've double-checked and he's absolutely sure it's you he wants. So I said, I'd ring, especially you being the duty chaplain on call for the ward this weekend,' she quipped.

'Who is he?'

'Raj Chauhan. Know him now?'

'Why yes! Corner shop, Silver Street?' She paused, tried unsuccessfully to master her thoughts, 'He's a nice man. Wears horn-rimmed glasses? Very short-sighted. Lives with his wife above their shop.'

'Yes, the very same.'

'How's he doing?'

'He's got another problem beside his eyesight. Someone put a knife under his rib cage earlier this afternoon and he's got a punctured lung. He's not very well, lost a lot of blood. He's some difficulty breathing and he's been badly shaken by it all.'

Ruth paused, her mind now in overdrive, the injury could have been hers.

'It's not the first time he's been attacked. His shop's such a target, though it's the first time he's been seriously hurt to my knowledge.'

'He's more comfortable now he's here on the ward. We need to keep him in under observation, until any internal bleeding stops. He'll probably be here a few days at least. Need to stabilise his condition. He's worried about his wife and wants to get back to his shop. I've told him that's out of the question for now, but I promised him I'd call you.'

'OK. Tell you what, I'll call in to see his wife, Darshana. It's on my way to the hospital. Are you working a late shift today?'

'Yes, until eight.'

'I'll look out for you, Pauline. I'll be on the ward before you go.'

'Thanks Ruth. See you later.'

With that she'd gone, leaving Ruth to wonder just how, what was left of the rest of the evening, was going to fall into place. Too little time with too much to do, she tried to gather her thoughts.

First, she had to dismiss all thought of the young man and his doorstep threat from her mind, then secondly, think about the children's teatime, all before, thirdly, making her visit to the hospital via the corner shop and Darshana and get to the hospital by eight at the latest. That would mean Phil getting the kids to bed again, but she ought to tell him to be extra careful, keep his mobile by him just in case. Her heart sank as she realised that fourthly, another late night's work stared her in the face if she was to be ready for the Sunday services she had to lead in church next morning. Not for the first time she wondered how she would cope.

Too often her present life felt it was on the edge of chaos but there was nothing she seemed able to do about it. A feeling of being overwhelmed and helpless in her situation often assailed her. These days her self doubt in her abilities was beginning to undermine her self-confidence. The ordered, secure world she'd known when she was younger had dissolved into one where she forever found herself on the boundary between chaos and community, fear and family.

She knew the endless short cuts she was currently taking and the lack of preparation time to do things properly would soon catch her out; the all round pressures combining to leave her feeling she was failing and with that came the guilt. Her mood was spiralling downwards and in this latest dark moment, her mind was once more involuntarily drawn back, as it often was, to her greatest ongoing burden, something she'd never be able to put down.

In recent years she'd carried a deep sense of personal culpability for the way her Drop In Centre for asylum seekers and refugees had been used by extremists, terrorists, right under her very nose. The Church enquiry into it all had been very damning. She'd been found personally responsible for her failure of oversight and leadership. She'd been culpable – leading a church Drop In care scheme that had inadvertently supported the Islamist IS terrorist, Ali Muhammed. She recalled that her church had even provided him with safe accommodation from where he'd been able to launch his Armistice Day attack in Westminster.

But how was she to have known the threat he was? She knew it wasn't any good endlessly asking herself such soul searching questions, she had to face it, Ali Muhammed had been looked after, supported even, on her watch.

As a result she'd been required to do further training before returning to parish duties. The Drop In itself had had to close, it had not been allowed to continue in spite of repeated assurances that additional safeguards would be put in place. She'd also had to accept inspection reviews conducted by the new and exacting Archdeacon of Hampstead, the Venerable Stephen Nicholls, under whose jurisdiction she fell. She disliked the man, his heart ruled by his sharp pencil which he wielded with forensic precision.

It was as if she ran a school that had failed its OFSTED inspection and had been placed under special measures pending a possible shut down. Ali Muhammed may have robbed the Prime Minister of his life, but he'd robbed her of her self-confidence, left her with recriminations, feeling humiliated. The Church of England had found her to be the obvious scapegoat for its own failure. That the attack was three years ago and the Archbishop's Report two years past didn't make any difference. She still lived with it all, the blame, the notoriety, the sense she did everything as if in a glass cage, open to everyone's inspection and criticism. She felt she'd been placed in a cell rather than her parish; she was boxed in, contained, where, providing she behaved herself, she could be conveniently forgotten about until she quietly left the church.

Could she cope for much longer, she wondered, with the incessant stream of parish demands upon her and with so little support? She concluded it didn't do to dwell any longer on such things and she broke off her reverie to go upstairs to find Phil, to discuss how the coming evening looked with him and at least catch a brief sight of Olivia and Paul before she headed for the hospital.

In climbing the stairs Ruth realised her fitness was slipping away from her as her weight had gradually increased. She glanced at the mirror on the stairs, observing that her round face, at one time a picture of health and jollity, now looked saggy. She found she was breathing hard by the time she reached the landing and her right hip niggled at the strain. She heard the bubbling chatter of the voices of the others in the recreation room.

Having a five bedroomed Edwardian vicarage meant the children had a large room each. They'd allocated one of the rooms as a guest room and another as a recreation room, the latter being kitted out as an upstairs lounge complete with easy chairs, rugs and a big screen TV. With so many church visitors to the vicarage, the downstairs rooms, apart from the kitchen had been given over to serve them, their own family privatised area was to be found upstairs. The arrangement worked, she believed the upstairs was a safe and private space.

'Phil, I've just taken a call from the hospital. Raj from the corner shop is in ITU and he's asking for me. I'll need to pop in on his wife, Darshana, on the way.'

'Surely not! You're exhausted. Just look at you. Ruth... you can't carry on at this pace and after what's just happened outside no one would think any the less of you if you took a break, just a short one. Why not go in the week?' pleaded Phil.

'Can't. Darshana will be worried sick. Must go. Sorry. I'll try and get back before the kids go to bed.'

'Any other job you wouldn't be allowed to...', he muttered resentfully under his breath.

Ruth half heard him and followed his drift but chose not to respond. She saw Phil turn his back to head off to the kids. She made a mental note that Phil and herself would need to talk properly later as she grabbed her car keys from the hall stand and headed quickly out of the front door. He was so long suffering, never complained. And the kids, maybe after church tomorrow...

Today, her old blue Fiat Punto she'd left parked on the road right outside their Edwardian vicarage had acted like a heat storage device. The day's incessant sunshine had used the dark plastic interior as a heatsink and upon opening the driver's door a blast of hot plasticised air hit her. She flopped down heavily onto the driver's seat and immediately opened the window before starting up and moving away. Must clean it sometime, she thought, chiding herself, spotting the fast food drink cartons and assorted detritus on the floor. Children and clean cars are mutually exclusive, she thought. Phil had wanted her to get a more modern vehicle with self-locking doors, but she had resisted it, maybe her old car blended in better.

It was but a few hundred yards to Raj's shop and she swung in to park up off the now busy Silver Street, noticing the shop was closed as she passed it. Raj's corner shop, 'Sonnys', had been open a generation. It was always open, but not this evening. Set in the Huxley Estate, surrounded by Victorian era brick built workmen's houses, arranged in long terraces, Raj and Darshana lived upstairs, above their shop, which sold everything from newspapers and lottery tickets, to everyday groceries.

She'd been seen, and the side door opened as Ruth approached and a beckoning hand waved her inside.

'Oh Miss Ruth, so pleased you come. I get tea, yes? Please to sit down. Here please,' said a fussing Darshana in her heavily accented voice.

'Thank you, that's just what I need right now.'

She settled herself on the deep leather sofa as Darshana disappeared into the kitchen. Ruth noticed joss sticks burning beside the family shrine by the door. Clearly Darshana had been attending to her family Hindu deities. How ironic, she thought, though these protecting deities had so evidently failed in their duties they were still being attended to. Tea arrived.

'Here Miss Ruth,' she said, passing her a mug.

It was Chai tea, spicy, aromatic and surprisingly refreshing. Ruth looked down into the yellow stained mug as a silence fell between them. Darshana looked as if she was overcome with emotion and her lip began to quiver. Her lemon and lime sari shook. Ruth for her part found herself struggling to give her her full attention. She suddenly found herself fighting against an overwhelming tiredness that had come from nowhere and knew she needed to inject some fresh energy into herself. Desperate to show she cared the weariness assailing her was such it was threatening to overwhelm all her good intentions.

'I'm on my way to see Raj at the hospital,' she offered, pulling herself upright to perch on the front edge of the sofa.

'My brother's taking me later. Stupid Raj. Very stupid Raj,' she said, grabbing a tissue to dab her eyes. 'He should have let thief take money. But no, he try stop him.'

'Oh!'

'Raj grab his arm. Try to stop him, but man pull him to floor, man too strong, had knife, Raj say. Yes, big knife. He stand over Raj like this and Raj fell down to the floor. Man ran off. I call ambulance and police, say, they "come quick" and Raj very sick. Lie very still. He bleed and bleed. I close shop when policeman come.'

'I saw him, the man with the knife, wearing a football kit. He came past the church. I called the police too,' said Ruth.

'Raj has had so many people rob him. I guess something bad had to happen one day... it was too much for him this time.'

'Will you be alright? Have you someone to be with you, your brother maybe?'

'Yes. My brother says he'll send his son over to help with the shop tomorrow. I'll be OK. When Raj gets back from the hospital we'll be OK again. That is when he gets better from the telling off he's getting, she added, trying to force a weak smile.'

Ruth felt uncomfortable. She couldn't share the humour. Didn't Darshana know Raj was in the Intensive Care ward? What should she say? She chose to stay silent. She couldn't leave yet, her tea too hot to drink and she'd hardly begun it. Fortunately Darshana was glad of her company and kept talking.

'I keep telling Raj he needs to take a holiday, go home to our village in Rajasthan. Now he have to do it. I make him. You help me make him listen, yes?'

'I think that would be a good thing to do. I...'

Ruth jumped, there was a knock at the door.

'Wait, I think maybe my brother come,' said Darshana as she went to get the door.

Ruth heard hushed voices. It didn't sound like it was her brother. Then, a policeman and woman entered the room. It felt cramped and Darshana was looking flustered.

'They want to come in, talk,' she explained, waving her arms about her like a windmill.

The officers stayed standing, looked at each other, looked at Ruth, nodded politely in her direction, not an acknowledgement of her presence, more an introductory prelude to what they were about to say.

'Darshana, I'm glad you have the Reverend with you,' began the skinny young woman officer, her hat in her hand, 'because it is our sad duty to have to inform you that your husband Raj passed away in the hospital. This is now a murder enquiry.'

'Passed away? Murder?' whimpered Darshana, 'what you mean?' She said as she half fell against the door frame.

'They mean he's... died,' offered Ruth, moving off the sofa to help sit Darshana in her place. 'He died,' she said softly. As she moved closer to Darshana she sensed the police officers were keen to move away, to leave her to do her thing. She knew she wouldn't be getting home any time soon. What had things come to when even this sweet couple were not safe in their corner shop? Was it a robbery, but no one had mentioned the till or the takings? Was it a racist attack, but no one was saying that either? What was the truth behind tonight's sad events, and how were such awful things to be stopped? What was the answer, a check out counter with protective glass like a post office? And the murderer, he was still out there roaming the streets. The world was full of uncertainty, unquantifiable risks, and tonight it just was not a safe place.

After making more tea and sitting quietly with Darshana in her state of shock, Ruth's own thoughts turned to getting herself safely home again. Eventually she excused herself and warily headed from the flat above the shop the short distance to her car. Once inside she quickly ensured the car doors were locked before setting off.

3

It wasn't until late in the evening and dark when Ruth returned home, the children long in bed. She found Phil sitting in the lounge vacantly watching the TV. He looked tired and turned his head wearily from the screen in her direction when he heard her enter.

'Was beginning to worry. You might have called, messaged me...' he said, with a detectable tone of being hard done by to his voice.

'Sorry. Things didn't go as planned. Raj died.'

'No!' he said, visibly shocked at this.

'I was with Darshana when the police brought the news. She needed me... I've been with her all this time. She's got her brother coming to be with her.'

'That's another murder in the parish. The neighbourhood's sinking fast. We're becoming a no-go area, given over to knife carriers and where are the police when you need them, drinking tea?' he said in exasperation.

'I think I need to eat something,' Ruth said, her tiredness returning once more.

'I left you some shepherd's pie. It's on a plate in the microwave. Three minutes on full will do it... No, you sit down I'll get it. You look all in.'

'Thanks.'

Whilst Ruth waited, the TV commentator's chatty familiar style, wittering on as if sport was the most important thing in the world, began to irritate her. A good man had died and the TV could only broadcast this stuff. She wondered how many people simply gave up and curled up in front of their TV screens to be amused whilst in the relative safety of their own homes? Reaching for the remote she pressed and he'd gone. She had to check her welling emotion... anger... grief... tears... she couldn't be certain which and then Phil was back with a steaming plate of food on a tray.

'What do you know?' asked Phil. 'What happened?'

Between mouthfuls Ruth told him. Finally, her plate only half consumed, her stomach tight and full, she had to stop and pushed it to one side. She was beginning to cry and knew she had to just let the tears flow.

Phil moved over, removed the tray, sat himself gently beside her and placed his arm comfortingly over her shoulder. She pulled a tissue out, dried her eyes and slowly calmed. For a moment she felt Darshana's pain was her pain. It was raw and visceral.

'I can't go on, Phil, I really can't. A hard day, a face to face encounter with a knife and now the violent death of Raj. I've done nothing for tomorrow and I'm too tired to do it now.'

'Right. I'm going to run you a bath. While you're waiting you're going to have ten minutes in your study to outline your first two services for the morning. You're always up early. You can finish off then. You'll have to wing it, do it on a prayer. Don't you think that's best? OK?' he said, in a supportive, yet directive manner.

'Can't do any more. Yes... I'm a failure, Phil.'

'No you're not. No one could do more than you. But you do need to set some boundaries... you're... well... looking shattered,' he said, feeling his own ability to cope beginning to slip as he looked at Ruth, sitting all bent over, like a wilted flower.

'It's impossible,' she said, 'I've run out, nothing left in the tank.'

'You need to speak to someone, request help... the Archdeacon?'

'No way! You know what I think of him.'

'Just an idea, maybe someone else…'

'Was there any mail today? I've not even looked at my emails,' she said urgently, a new fear of having missed something important giving an edge of panic in her voice. Slipping control led to the worst fear.

'On your desk. Not much. I'll go run your bath.'

'Thanks. I need it.'

As she heard Phil's retreating footsteps heading off upstairs, she felt her earlier lethargy take hold of her once more. It was even a struggle to get up from the easy chair. She felt fatigue washing over her in waves and held on to the furniture and door frames for support as she trudged the few yards to her study. My, she was tired. She feared she might fall asleep in her bath, that is if she could get herself upstairs.

She gazed at the window straight in front of her, the other side of her study desk. It was dark outside, only it wasn't really dark. Floodlights cast an icy white glow over the orange-red bricks and grey stone of Holy Trinity Church. Even the parched lawn looked frosted white in the lamp light. Glancing at the grass again her mind became fixated on the long knife that had landed there – the knife she had seen close up, the knife that had killed Raj.

The thought terrified her even though the knife now rested in the hands of the Metropolitan Police. An image of the young man's face made her catch her breath. Then suddenly, as she was looking out, all the lights outside went out. It took her a moment to realise it was 10pm and the auto time-clock had switched everything off, plunging the street corner into total darkness.

Feeling exposed and vulnerable she hastily dragged the study curtains shut and sat down in her private world, her study. The floodlights had been her idea soon after she arrived in the parish. Some said they gave the church a visible presence, others that the lit corner of the street made them feel safer at night. Either way it comforted her that it had been one success to chalk up in a place of so many challenges and set backs.

The lights were there on the one hand to keep the church secure, no miscreant wanted to be seen vandalising or breaking in, they'd be deterred, but on the other hand, the lights meant people still felt they could be out on the street, come to church on dark evenings, they could see any danger, they felt safer. Ruth wondered if the lights themselves were enough anymore, perhaps CCTV cameras were also needed these days. Perhaps it was too late for any measures, the streets were already lawless, lost and left to aggressive predators. What was the true state of her parish now, was it beyond redemption, beyond her?

She could hear bath water running upstairs as she tried to concentrate on the items on her desk. The pile of unopened mail, her computer coming to life, her wedding service papers she'd so hurriedly discarded earlier. She reached for her Book of Common Prayer she'd need for the morning's 8am Holy Communion service in church.

Taking the book, she found the page, turned to her computer screen, opened a new document. Then turning to the Bible readings set for the morning's Sunday service, she prayed for inspiration. As she waited, the call of the email inbox pulled her into its grasp and, as she perused the long list of unopened mail, she realised there was just too much there to even glance through. Overwhelmed, buried by an electronic media flood, she found herself staring vacantly at the thin curtains in front of her. She stood up, as if a goldfish rising in its bowl to take some air.

Her trance-like reverie was broken when Phil called downstairs. She tried to collect herself, her eyes still fixed on the closed curtain in front of her. Something caught her attention. Was it her imagination or was there really a light, someone, outside?

Shutting down her computer and turning off the room light cautiously she tried to pierce the gloom allowing her eyes time to adjust. Was something or someone outside? She needed to be certain what it was. Leaning over her desk she gently pulled open the curtain just enough to stay hidden yet peer outside.

Yes, someone was definitely there, a light came and went in the churchyard, someone was waving it to and fro as if they were using a mobile phone as a torch. The light jerked as if they were walking this way and that. She watched curious as to what it meant. Late night goings on in the churchyard were sometimes reported to her by concerned parishioners, youngsters usually seeing if they could frighten one another, but this felt different.

The torch light steadied and seeing a brief silhouette on the church wall her blood froze. It was him again. Then a late evening bus approached and her fears were fully realised. A pool of light briefly fell across and she saw he was still in the same football strip. Cautiously she let the curtains fall closed; she stepped backward, retreating quickly into the hall. What was he doing there?

Panic rose within. It now felt somehow worse not being able to see actually where he was, what he was up to, but she dared not open the curtains again for fear of discovery. Maybe, she thought, he was looking for his knife, trying to cover his tracks, remove the evidence. He wouldn't find it. The police had it. What would he do if he knew she'd called them? She felt unwelcome palpitations well up in her chest and her hand reached for the wall to steady herself.

The lack of church funds meant the old sash windows had yet to be replaced. The windows allowed the noises of the night to reach her and when the iron gate from churchyard to street clanged shut, she knew he'd moved on in his search. There was no way of knowing which way he was headed next, away or toward her? Her ears strained to catch any sound. It was only yards to her front door. Her heart was in her mouth. Would he come for her? She took a step out of her study to cast an eye to check how secure she was behind her front door and glanced at the little chain she'd hooked across earlier. It looked so flimsy, the glass, like the old study window, so easy to shatter.

Creeping soundlessly and slowly, she moved upstairs, cautiously edging past the landing window and whispered Phil's name. 'Phil, Phil...' and there he was in his pyjamas and dressing gown, hardly her knight in shining armour.

'Phil, he's back, he was in the churchyard. Came out. Don't know which way he went next. We'd better call the police again. I think he's had second thoughts and is looking to retrieve his knife. He won't find it, I'm frightened he might call here...'

Phil nodded in agreement and Ruth's emergency call went swiftly through. Only when she explained who she was, did they promise a nearby patrol car would be there shortly. Meantime Phil had grabbed his shirt and trousers and was hastily dressing on the landing, awkwardly pulling them over his pyjamas, balancing and hopping on one leg then the other as he struggled.

Ruth couldn't help herself. She crept to an upstairs window with a view of the street and churchyard, pulled the curtain back cautiously to gain a view. At first she didn't see him, but there he was, standing perfectly still, hardly visible in the darkness, leaning against the railings. As she watched, something made him turn toward her gaze, his instinct, like that of an animal with a sixth sense. She knew he'd seen her and still holding the curtain back she took one step back from the window in alarm. Then she caught her breath as she saw him move purposefully toward the vicarage.

'He's coming this way,' she blurted. 'Phil, what do we do? What can we do?'

He had no chance to answer as there was a loud knock at the front door.

'I'll talk to him from the upstairs window,' offered Phil. 'You stay back.'

From the landing, she heard the sash window slide up and Phil, as calm as you like, call a firm, 'Yes?' She saw the ends of his pyjama trousers protruding as he lent forward.

'It's your missus I want to talk to. Tell her.'

'It's too late for callers tonight. Can I get her to call you tomorrow? Who shall I say?'

'Just fucking go get her. Won't take two minutes.'

'I suggest you go on your way.'

Then there was a great kicking and crashing from downstairs as the front door was repeatedly hit. Glass shattered. Further kicking and banging followed, accompanied by cursing. More glass could be heard breaking as heavy blows fell and shook their target. How long until he got inside Ruth wondered? Phil stepped back from the window and grabbed hold of Ruth as they embraced helplessly on the landing.

It was precisely then a police patrol car appeared, its blues and twos switched on briefly for all to hear, just long enough to signal its arrival. The incident was over in moments as Phil and Ruth, back at the upstairs window looked on. They gazed down as the now cowed young man, lying on the pavement, his arms behind him, resigning himself to receive a set of handcuffs. Finally, he was pulled none too gently upright and ordered to take a seat in the back of the car. The door was slammed shut after him. A second back up car, blue lights flashing then arrived, tyres losing traction as it pulled swiftly to a halt.

Words were exchanged between the four officers. Ruth glanced at the first car, inside the young man was gazing blankly up at them. She tried to read his empty expression but could not do so and returned her gaze to the actions of the busy policemen.

Moments later the first car left with its prisoner, leaving the remaining two officers conferring on the pavement. Seeing Ruth and Phil in the window they signalled that they should come down to open the front door.

Phil got to the door first. The officers came inside, stepping carefully over the shards of broken coloured glass, to sit in the kitchen with Ruth and Phil. Tea was made. One officer began asking questions, the other taking notes as to what had happened. Things were taken slowly and more tea was drunk before they finally departed. It was nearly 3am.

Forgetting the now cold bath, Ruth then took herself to bed whilst Phil did his best to clear up the debris on the door mat before screwing a piece of chipboard to the front door before finally crashing out himself. Doors, thin security chains, pieces of chipboard and police on hand at the end of a phone; none of these things seem enough to provide security, and Ruth's now alert mind was still buzzing with fear and apprehension. Surprisingly, in spite of all the noise there had been downstairs, neither Olivia nor Paul were disturbed in the slightest. Ruth checked their sleeping forms, wondering how they might be spared all the dangers there seemed to be right at their door.

As Ruth lay on her back in bed, her sleepless eyes in a fixed gaze on the bedroom ceiling, she thought about the face of the young man in the police car. She found herself thinking of him as so utterly alien to her and so hostile she began to think it would be no bad thing if stronger measures were taken by the authorities to remove such people out of the community. The young man would frighten any decent person like herself. He and those like him needed to be locked up for the safety of all before they could do anything more. How was it, she asked herself, that we let such hooligans roam the streets? Whatever happened to stop and search? Policing needed to be ruthless, not a stone left unturned in finding every last knife in Edmonton and any sympathiser needed to be taken out, removed, exited… Unaccustomed to entertaining such extreme thoughts Ruth's tiredness eventually overwhelmed her rampaging mind and she eventually crashed out.

4

Ruth woke with a scream on her lips but wasn't sure if the sound had come out. Phil moved closer beside her. Had she disturbed him? He didn't really wake up, only wriggled under the duvet and a moment later he was snoring softly. Perhaps she'd made an involuntary sound after all. She glanced at the clock. It was just after 4am, less than a hour of sleep and yet she was wide awake. Not good. This was happening too often. Maybe she ought to speak to the doctor. Tell of her tiredness too. Get some tablets.

There was no point just lying there. Whatever the nightmare she'd had, it had gone, elusively slipping ever further from her memory. Probably as well, she told herself. Creeping out of bed she grabbed her dressing gown from the back of the bedroom door and cautiously headed downstairs and back to her study, reminding herself the police had the young man in their custody. As she sat at her desk, she tried to tell herself, all that was needed was one big push and she could rise on top of things again.

An hour later she felt some relief. She had a notion where the day's sermons were headed and switched attention to her email mountain. There were now 358 showing up as unopened. That wasn't strictly true. Some she'd opened earlier, looked at cursorily and then marked them as unopened because she knew she'd have to return to them and give them more time later; these were messages she didn't want to miss. It was the sheer numbers of them that worried her and sent flutters of panic through her stomach. How had it got to be so many? Wouldn't it be good if her computer has some kind of fire wall that could sift out the dross, cull these attacking demands before they reached her. Dream on, she told herself. Even so, August was a holiday month, it shouldn't be like this. This felt like such a huge pinnacle to climb. Somehow she began to apply herself to them and make that final assault.

Half an hour later the number had dropped by about one third; she saw herself as having made significant inroads up the lower slopes. Feeling a little better about things, she lifted her head from the screen. Slowly her eyes re-focussed on the room, the desk, the curtains, the rows of books, the old filing cabinet, the disused feature fireplace with its shiny green Edwardian tiles, the family photograph above in a pinewood frame; the four of them, in the garden last summer, all happy and relaxed if their camera smiles were to be believed. And now…

She looked back toward the window, it was getting noticeably light outside, dawn was breaking. It was her favourite time. Early Sunday morning, and her thoughts turned to the smell of coffee, toast and getting started on a new working day.

As she strolled over to unlock the church door at 7.30am she couldn't help but notice how unusually light headed and jumpy she felt. She kept looking round, up and down the street; she even had the church door key ready in her hand before setting off from the vicarage. As she walked she recognised the previous day's events had shaken her right down to her foundations and her once unwavering sense of personal stability had been once more severely rocked, was still rocking her and the thought that she might be losing it further disturbed her.

Some of the faithful, regular, familiar worshippers began to appear, their presence reassuring. But even their good humoured chat was different this morning. The parish grapevine had been working as effectively as ever and their hushed conversation, focussing on the raid on Raj's shop and his alleged demise, was generating a nervous concern over and above everything else.

From what she could gather the troubling events were being set in a context of there being a general decline in the local neighbourhood and it being commonly understood that such things were the accepted state of things today. There was much shared lament at the widespread moral decline which seemed to parallel a fall in churchgoing. It was 8am and by this time everyone, minus a couple of absentees no doubt sheltering from the dangers outside who had remained in the safety of their homes, had made their way to their usual seats. Ruth began intoning the familiar words of the Lord's Prayer to begin the worship.

Once in the zone Ruth pressed on and thirty minutes later it was over and she was at the church door shaking hands as people headed off. Gladstone Harris was the last to leave, clearly hanging back in order to speak with her.

'Can I have a word?' he said quietly, politely.

'Sure…' she answered, not knowing what was coming next.

'Are you alright, Vicar? I mean, you missed out part of the service and you're very quiet today. Out of sorts maybe? Forgive me for asking.' He had a gracious manner, his message delivered in a Jamaican accent betraying his roots. He was waiting for an answer.

Ruth was thrown. Missed out what? She couldn't think what it might have been. In fact she recollected only her trancelike state. Gladstone was a kindly soul, but he wouldn't go without receiving some kind of answer.

'Lack of sleep… I lost a lot of sleep last night… Things can be 24/7 here sometimes… my apologies Gladstone. Glad someone was on the ball,' she stammered, not wanting to say too much when she couldn't for the life of her recall where she had gone awry. Yet she couldn't deny it, something told her, in his solid manner he never spoke a word wrong, he'd be the one in the right.

'Then do put your feet up later. Look after yourself. I find forty winks after lunch works wonders. The last Vicar, Charles, he swore by his catnaps. In fact he used to divide each day into three parts and never, never, worked more than two out of three parts – follow me?' he said smiling broadly, 'and to be sure, with the changes in the area for the worse, you've got a tougher time than ever he had.'

'Yes, but if it were only ever that simple…'

Having made his point Gladstone, feeling his years, was ready to let the matter drop and shuffled off to his car. At his age he really should have stopped driving by now, she mused, but it wouldn't do for her to tell him. After all he was one of the Windrush generation, deserved where he'd got himself to and that included his treasured old Volvo estate car.

In the short period of time she had in the vicarage between the two church services she tried, but couldn't for the life of her recall, which bit of the service she had inadvertently omitted. Was Gladstone mistaken? No, absolutely not.

She gripped her mug of coffee firmly between two hands, the conversation with Gladstone continuing to trouble her, the more so as her recollection of the service was unusually vague and fragmentary. No, Gladstone wasn't usually incorrect. His body may be frail, but his mind was sharp. Her omission was just one more unnerving sign left nagging at her crumbling composure – she'd made an error, of that she was certain, she was scared she might be losing it.

By now it was time to step forward and lead another service. She returned to the church thinking of herself like a castle. Not a strong impregnable castle, but one where someone had left the drawbridge down with the enemy baying for her blood right outside.

5

The next church service further ruffled her sense of being in control as, inexplicably, she came to a halt a couple of times, her mouth drying up. Momentarily her mind froze, being quite unable to place at which point precisely she'd reached in the proceedings. Back on track, she started using her index finger, pointing it at the text to help her follow the service booklet, determined to keep her place.

Each time she paused, somehow she managed to pick up again and push on through the pervading vagueness. However, in the moments of disjuncture she wasn't confident she'd held it all together.

Usually she felt the church architecture itself gave the air of an open, friendly space in which she and the congregation could experience a sense of spiritual presence and nourishment. This morning, she couldn't quite figure it out, but it felt different, she felt herself to be out of place in her own church.

There was a different atmosphere, one more of estrangement, even disengagement, as if the people in front of her had themselves switched off. Today the very walls hemmed her in, grey stone and red brick pressed against her. She knew the congregation weren't following her, they too were otherwise preoccupied. Was it the murder? Was it her? Where had all that warm harmony she was used to gone? She was appointed to lead them, but this Sunday she knew she was ill-equipped to do it. The only warmth and security the building seemed to offer today was that of an enclosing cold tomb.

Then it was over and she was at the door as people were leaving, once again offering her hand to everyone together with what Phil called, her "smiley face". She felt warmer and safer at the church door with all the people about, even if recent images of the young man and his knife kept flashing before her eyes. In the gaps between people her mind repeated a simple silent mantra of reassurance – "he's locked up stupid, he's locked up".

Service over, it was the custom for most to wander the few yards up the road past the vicarage and into the adjoining church hall for coffee and chat. As people ambled slowly for refreshment, chatting as they went the few yards to the hall, they left behind them a hard core of non-participants, those who, despite Ruth's every encouragement, steadfastly refused to partake and determinedly headed off for home. She knew they nonetheless needed their vicar even if they didn't need the rest of the congregation.

Once through the church hall door, a warm, stale, stuffy fug assailed her nostrils, the smell of a crowd of people in an enclosed space on a hot day in an inadequately aired space with no windows open. To greet them the utility green crockery cups and saucers and assorted biscuits on matching plates were already laid out in ordered rows on top of the folding tables. The coffee rota team with smiling faces were busy serving the hot brown liquid out to people on arrival. The buzz of conversation showed the beverages were working their usual magic.

Ruth joined the tea and coffee drinkers, a crowd of around fifty people, all busily chatting away in twos and threes. Phil had arrived ahead of her and she could see he was engaged in what appeared to be an animated conversation with half a dozen people surrounding him at the far end of the hall. She could read his defensive manner without being near and would ask him about it later. He could look after himself, she thought, as she took a hot drink for herself.

Coffee in her hand she headed straight for Flo and Bert – good, solid, now frail and elderly local people, two friends she counted amongst her most faithful supporters. Both increasingly struggling with infirmities, she knew little would prevent them ever getting to church. The couple were held in respect by everyone, they were the solid reliable sort and willing to help anybody out.

Until a couple of years ago Flo and Bert regularly offered their spare room to anyone who had need of it. Ruth could not help herself from thinking, even with the church's say so, to the terrorist Ali Muhammed!

The comfort she'd anticipated finding just seconds ago, in going over to speak to them, was being eroded and undone by the memory. It was as if all her bad encounters were coming back to haunt her at once. The recollection of Ali Muhammed, a now deceased IS terrorist, as a one time church hall user, drinking from these same tea cups assailed her; it was all so vivid; it made her shake involuntarily. Flo immediately sensed something was amiss and reached out a steadying hand.

'Lawd above! You ain't looking yerself today. Now what is it?' she asked, peering over the rim of her glasses. 'Come on, sit yerself down. You work too hard, take everything on yerself, sit, come on, sit down with us dear,' she said patting the vacant chair seat beside her.

Ruth hadn't the motivation or energy to resist and allowed herself to flop down between Flo and Bert, but said nothing.

How could she? She was the vicar. Expressing personal weakness, as she saw it, didn't go with the role. She tried to regain her composure.

Bert twitched the control lever on his shiny red new mobility scooter to draw in closer. With Flo the other side of her, Ruth felt she was surrounded; they were still looking to be taken into her confidence. Although she felt moved to respond positively to their kindness, she couldn't bring herself to be open with them.

Another insurmountable obstacle, she realised, was their deafness. Anything she said would need to be said really loudly otherwise they just wouldn't hear her. Furthermore, she felt anything she said might be misunderstood or require the kind of lengthy explanations which she wasn't prepared to provide. Indeed if she wasn't careful she might even undermine their well-being and faith. For the present, silence and discretion seemed to be the better part of valour. Maybe what followed was an act of God – for she was suddenly provided with a way out.

Standing at the hall entrance, gazing round with searching eyes, certainly looking for her, were the two policemen who had come to Darshana's flat the previous evening. Ruth rose quickly, squeezing past Bert with a loud, 'will you excuse me,' and headed off quickly to intercept them. The police officers spotted her and stepped toward her.

'Ah… good, we thought we might find you here. Is now a good time for a word?'

'Maybe somewhere quiet might be better,' offered the police woman.

'Sure, let's pop next door to the vicarage, its more private. I'll just tell my husband, Phil.'

In fact Phil had observed what was happening and a couple of, now routine, flashed hand signals up and down the length of the hall, were all that was required to be sure they understood one another. Phil nodded over toward Olivia and Paul with a look of resignation, the two were busy trying out a friend's computer game. That gesture was enough to say he'd also be keeping an eye on them.

As Ruth followed the two officers outside and walked the few paces to the vicarage, they had by now attracted a few curious glances from wary onlookers. It was a good decision to go next door. As they walked under the hot midday August sun, Ruth observed that the wearing, tired hot summer was still hanging on, surely autumn could only be round the corner? The weather created its own stress and needed to break and soon.

Ruth wondered what had brought the police back. Did they need a statement about yesterday's events? They waited until she had shown them into her lounge before they spoke. Before doing so, both removed their police hats in unison and then introduced themselves by name – a proper double act and well practised, thought Ruth.

'This may seem a strange request, but we've got a problem. The young man we arrested yesterday, thanks to your assistance, has now been charged with the murder of Raj Chauhan. He is currently being detained at Edmonton Police Station pending his appearance before magistrates in the morning,' began PC Alan Dallow. 'Trouble is, he isn't saying much and what he's saying is, well… odd, very odd.'

'How do you mean?' asked Ruth.

'He's into drugs,' offered PC Alice Such. 'But that doesn't begin to explain it.'

'We went to his home in Henley Road, spoke to his mother. It took ages before we entered. She wouldn't come downstairs to open the door to us. Their house is the strangest place,' added Alan.

'What do you mean by odd, strange?...' asked Ruth.

'More your department... spiritual, mystical, religious. She asked after you by name, which is why we've come round. Do you know her?' asked Alice

'What's her name?' Ruth queried.

'Lady by the name of Angela Morris, single parent, rents the house I think,' the police woman continued in a voice typical of the way police might give evidence. 'Do you know her?' she repeated.

'No, I don't think so. Which end of Henley Road?'

'The far end, almost at the Haselbury Road junction. Going from here on the right hand side.'

'No, doesn't ring any bells,' replied Ruth.

'Its dark, full of native American stuff, feathers, shields, mystical words on bark, religious books, artefacts and the like,' added Alice. 'Angela is, well... an unusual lady, strangely religious. I'm not easily spooked but she got to me! She told us she'd never been out of the house for over a decade and as far as we could ascertain she's telling the truth. She spends most of her time just lying on her bed. Treats it like a throne. Gives out orders all the time. Her son, Anthony or Tony as he's called, the one we're holding in custody; he did everything for her. I mean everything! The lad seems to have lived like her slave. We haven't been able to find any other family or friends to call upon. The neighbours either side want nothing to do with her... So we have a problem.'

'Which is why we've come round to you. Would you be able to make a visit?' Seeing Ruth's hesitancy, she quickly added, 'She's a needy soul. No immediate crisis. There's some food in, but who knows how she'll cope when it runs out?...'

'I'll call round. Leave me the number. Is she on the phone? Can I call her?'

'No phone. She said just call round and the front door will be open, always is. We told her that was not a good idea, to keep her front door unlocked, she needed to be mindful of her personal security, but she just laughed at the idea. Suppose she's at a point in her life beyond caring. She said she would be expecting you, like she knew you'd come.'

'OK, though it does sound like she might be in need of a professional social care package rather than my support. I'll call and see her this afternoon, then get on to the authorities.'

'Thank you. Here's her details,' said a clearly relieved Alan, passing across a piece of paper torn from his police notebook. 'We're very stretched at the station. It really is a thin blue line these days, so thank you. We need our partners.'

'Call us if you need more. There's a direct line number there, you'll be put straight through to one of us,' Alice added, pointing it out.

With that the two police officers stood up and were on their way, leaving Ruth wondering at the unusual pastoral request she'd just accepted. What was she walking into? A discomforting ambivalence was felt at having said "yes" to the police so readily, after all, Angela was the mother of knife wielding, threatening Tony.

Too late for second thoughts, she followed them out through the vicarage door, seeing them head directly for their car before walking back to the church hall where she rightly guessed there would still be a few coffee drinkers to be found.

Flo and Bert were just leaving for home, Flo with a supporting arm on Bert's mobility scooter to steady herself. A brief farewell was exchanged and before their earlier conversation could be revisited, Ruth stepped quickly back into the hall to rejoin Phil and the two children. Flo and Bert hadn't asked what the police visit was all about, after years of working in the church, they instinctively knew the meaning of confidentiality.

'What was that all about?' asked Phil, never being one to hold back.

'The guy with the knife. His mother, bed-bound, needs a visit,' she explained.

'As if you haven't got enough on. Couldn't you say "no"? When are you going round?'

'I'll go straight after lunch. If I leave it, you know what happens, I'll get another call and I'll never fit it in.'

She spied a couple of parishioners she really ought to speak to before they left for home, nodded in their direction by way of communicating the same to Phil and walked over to speak to Julie Brown the longstanding Church Secretary. Julie was deep in conversation with Stephanie and Lionel, both fondly described as pillars of the church; all three were on the Parochial Church Council. It looked like a meeting of conspirators.

'Hi you three. Hope I'm not breaking into anything?'

'No, we're glad you've come over. In fact we've got our heads together and we've got something to say. We're all agreed – we all wanted to say that we think you ought to look into having a sabbatical some time soon. It's a way of giving you a significant break from your duties, a chance to recharge your batteries. Making yourself stronger for the battles ahead, you know…' offered Lionel.

Ruth stammered, 'Yes, but it's not that straightforward.'

'But you will consider it, seriously think about it,' pressed Julie. 'You've been under such pressure and well, we're worried for you. It's a few years, but the Ali Muhammed business took its toll and the report the church did recently, it hit us all hard. You've been on the receiving end of such, well, such blame. Can't you have a word with the Archdeacon or someone? Make a case for purposeful time out, we'd back you…'

'You have to have been in ministry for seven years, then make an application, so I'm not yet eligible. But thank you for your concern,' she replied, not really feeling very thankful.

'Inadvertently harbouring that terrorist Ali Muhammed let everyone have a go at us. But onwards and upwards I say. Time to prepare Sunday lunch,' Ruth parried, as she half-turned, trying to make as confident an exit as she could muster. She wanted to be conciliatory and offered some final placatory words of thanks for their thoughtfulness before heading off quickly to rejoin Phil, Olivia and Paul whom she could see out of the corner of her eye heading off for home and lunch next door.

Escaping from their ambush, she ambled back the thirty paces to the vicarage to be with her family. Realising how badly exposed and vulnerable she felt in the face of the coordinated approach to get her to take time off, she saw the picture of a castle once again in her mind's eye, this time there were tunnels being dug under the walls in an effort to undermine and collapse it.

Did she really look that worn down? She recalled the pale self she had seen in the landing mirror. Or did they want to get rid of her? Surely they were well meaning, but could she be certain of that?

The damaged front door reminded her that she'd need to call the diocese first thing in the morning, Monday. On second thoughts tomorrow was a bank holiday, it would be Tuesday then – this, yet another task in a long list of tasks she could well do without.

In that instant she spotted the last of yesterday's confetti, dry and dusty in the gutter, gathered in a heap, and pictured herself lying there, being buried by her pastoral and administrative workload, a hot wind blowing still more burdens down on her, this time the confetti falling down on her as shards of coloured glass.

6

Sunday lunch was uninterrupted by any further calls and proved to be a welcome space for them to take their family meal, all sitting round the kitchen table together as was their custom. Phil had done much of the preparation earlier in the morning whilst Ruth was over in church. The spread included roast beef and Yorkshire pud much to the delight of the kids. The flavoursome provision of a generous helping of gravy made from the aromatic beef juices was a fine finishing touch. Eating as a family gathered round the old kitchen table felt safe, comforting, evocative of nostalgic warm memories.

Food consumed, Ruth was feeling warm inside and more relaxed as she made a cafetière of coffee whilst Phil made a start on the dishes and the kids disappeared upstairs to play. The orderly family homeliness of it all was a tonic she had desperately needed and now all too soon it was very nearly over. Her pending visit to see Angela Morris began to weigh heavily on her mind. She judged now to be the time to mention it to Phil.

'Think I'll take my coffee into my study, grab a few minutes for reflection, then make that visit to Henley Road,' she said as she poured out two steaming mugs. Glancing at the kitchen window facing the street she looked twice. The hot glare of past weeks was giving way to something different, she could see the weather looked set to turn. The dusty heat haze was slipping into a more active mood. Dusk would soon be coming earlier, surely autumn couldn't be far away? Some of the brightness had gone from the hot summer day. Above the school opposite there were some high, grey-white clouds. Change was definitely in the air. Phil nudged her to gain her attention.

'Leave mine on the table. I'll have a look at the Sunday paper when I'm done at the sink,' he replied, interrupting her skyward thoughts. His eyes returned to the sink full of suds and he stepped across to tackle the task before him.

Ruth heard the children in conversation upstairs as she walked through the hallway to her study. They were talking animatedly about going back to school after the holiday, psyching themselves up for it, she thought. It was all reassuringly normal in what felt to her to be an unsafe world. They should be safer once back at school, she told herself.

She heard Olivia telling Paul that he shouldn't have eaten so much beef. 'It's not right when the planet is under threat,' she teased. Ruth was reminded that Olivia was rightly pointing to bigger issues out there facing the planet than anything she might be addressing in her little corner of Edmonton. Pulling her study door to, she shut their banter out behind her. Ruth placed her coffee mug on a mat on her desk and sat back in her chair gazing through the window in front of her at the church building. This was her own space.

Then her eyes rested on her bookshelves. To her left she had collected several books about her parish. The distinctive thing about the Church of England was, that it still tried to operate on a geographic parish based system. Holy Trinity had some 17,000 souls living in a geographic area called quaintly a parish, an area whose boundary made little sense today. It wasn't a community with any specific centre to it, rather it was just more of the north London sprawling urban metropolis, comprising houses, corner shops and occasional factories, cut through by the ever busy and polluting North Circular and Great Cambridge arterial roads together making a criss-crossing of the patch.

The roads defined boundaries. Virtually impossible to cross on foot without taking one's life in one's hands, they divided people from people, hemmed them in, locked them down in small neighbourhoods. Escape was invariably only by car or bus.

Strange, she thought, how it was that most people passed through her parish on arterial roads without stopping, all on their way somewhere else. They probably never cast insignificant Edmonton a second thought. If it wasn't the junction of two main roads, maybe it was the church that lay at the geographic centre, the heart of the patch, she mused, before reading something spiritual into the thought – the realisation that the two main roads formed a cross in the centre of her parish.

To most eyes Holy Trinity Church sat in an unremarkable corner of Edmonton where those two huge multi-lane roads met in an ever busy roundabout and underpass. It was an area now subsumed, in local government terms, into the London Borough of Enfield. But talk to people locally as Ruth had done, look at a few books and some historically interesting data on who'd lived nearby, draw out the local stories, then some historic sense of community could be re-discovered.

People need to know their place, the truth about themselves and their sense of self- identity, to know what it meant to be rooted in a parish, she thought. A sense of belonging gave people strength and resilience, a feeling of community, and she saw it as part of her role as a priest to recover the often hidden local history of her community and give her parishioners an added sense of pride in belonging here. As her eyes followed along her line of books, she realised her bookshelf pointed the way.

At one end of the local history shelf she had placed books about two women with a religious connection. The first, Dorothy Kerin, a woman who lived from 1889 until 1963. She'd lived a remarkable, self-assured religious life. It was based around her healing ministry, begun after her stay and a mystical experience in the early days of this very vicarage.

Then to the right there were more books. These told the story of the life of Gladys Aylward, born 1902, died 1970. Gladys' father, a local postman, had also been a churchwarden here. The amazingly determined Gladys had single-handedly taken herself off from Edmonton to China as a missionary. Both Dorothy and Gladys were women who were to Ruth's mind every bit examples of faith and empowerment. Ruth couldn't help but admire their strength, women who were ahead of their time – one a healer, the other a missionary. But who knew of them today? Their names were but faint memory. Communities still need their role models, she thought, their heroes.

They were so different from her. Gladys and Dorothy both, in their day, had the touch of saintly greatness and public recognition, the one stepping out on her own with a one way ticket to China, the other, into healing, the first Anglican to have carried the stigmata, the nail marks of Christ, on her own hands. The two of them had faced enormous challenges in their time and not a little suffering, even so, both had won through, they'd escaped the confines, overcome their protagonists and obstacles in their path and made it – big time!

As Ruth sipped her coffee reflecting on the lives of these two inspirational females, she wondered what shape her own ministry might take and immediately felt inadequate. It would certainly be nothing like those two, she concluded. She didn't even see her own Christian beliefs sitting squarely with theirs. For her part she'd had a most ignominious start, her life dominated by the recently concluded church enquiry into her role in harbouring an IS terrorist. The Church Drop In for the needy had offered, albeit naively, a warm welcome to all, including Ali Muhammed, the terrorist. The scandal itself would take some getting over, damage done, the reputational flack had stuck to her like glue, offering no way back, no escape. She was a tarnished priest, damaged goods, a wounded and scarred leader.

What if any chance did she have of making a significant contribution to the church? Her vocation had been tainted, her future uncertain and her daily acts of ministry subject to continuing close scrutiny by the Bishop's fixer – the Archdeacon.

Her eyes then fell on the slip of white paper so recently handed her by PC Alan Dallow. It read simply, 'Angela Morris, 23a Henley Road, N18.'

She turned it over in her hand, wistfully wondering if there was more on the other side. It was blank. Putting it into her bag, she thought she'd walk the five minutes to Angela's house, anticipating it to be one of the last in the long row of uniform Victorian terraced houses that stretched the full length of the road on opposite sides. These had been built for artisans in the late 19th century when the railway opened up what was still mainly farmland. These houses, once filled with white working class families, were presently undergoing a fundamental change in occupancy as the whole world in all its diversity seemed to be coming to live in Edmonton. If Gladys had had to go to China to find the world, today the world was coming to Edmonton and not everybody liked it. Stranger danger; migrants and asylum seekers stoked and fuelled the fears of those unable to put a hand out in welcome to others, rather, seeing them as a threat to life and well-being. Them and us. Us and others. The world around her had fallen into two opposing camps.

Prayer came naturally to Ruth. She placed her folded hands on her desk and let her head drop. In the silence she asked God to help her and give her the right words to help Angela Morris whose son Tony was now in police custody. What else, she wondered, was there to tell the almighty that he didn't know already?

In her mind's eye, she thought Angela would be distressed at her son's predicament. It should be a straightforward pastoral visit, but something nagged and unsettled her. She wasn't quite sure what it was, but the strange looks in the two police officers' faces had stayed with her. Her prayer gave her no answer to her uncertainty, no calm to her anxieties. She threw in a prayer for her own safety as she walked there and back before finally she lifted her head and opened her eyes.

At least if she couldn't be a Dorothy Kerin or a Gladys Aylward she could try to be a good listener. And with that energising thought she got up, grabbed her bag, called out loudly, 'See you later' and headed off on foot the half mile to Angela Morris' house.

She'd only walked two minutes to the next street corner before she felt her right shoe pinching uncomfortably. Her thoughts turned, as they so often did, to the question of her increasing weight and decreasing fitness. It was not easy to see a solution. Her pace slowed to accommodate the pain, even so she began to feel hot and then wished she'd taken the car. Since she was only half way, perhaps she ought to turn back? Hearing footsteps ahead she lifted her eyes from the pavement.

Three young men were approaching and taking up the full width of the footpath. She couldn't turn round now, it would look like she was afraid. Then she realised she was actually fearful and beginning to take her breaths in rapid succession. Maybe this is what a panic attack felt like? The lads got nearer and looked so much taller and bigger than herself. At the very last moment, just as she was about to slow, the lad in the middle stepped to one side and let her pass. Her breathing eased and she felt her foot hurting once again. On the one hand fear can stop one feeling things, she mused, and yet on the other lead one to make a fool of oneself.

She turned the corner into Henley Road and began counting down the house numbers. A few minutes further, there it was, looking slightly less well cared for than the houses either side and with all the curtains, upstairs and down drawn shut. Turning five paces off the pavement to her right and she was standing at the badly painted front door. She paused.

An old rusting horseshoe shaped knocker was the only way to signal her arrival and she lifted and let it fall with a sullen thunk. That made enough of an impact for the door to shift inward ever so slightly. It clearly wasn't locked, not even held by a catch, open, just as the police had said. Pushing the door inwards with an outstretched arm, she couldn't quite see into the hallway so she reached for the knocker again, let it fall, calling out as she did so, 'Hello, it's Ruth Churchill from the church. Are you there Angela? Is it alright if I come in?'

There was no reply and as she stepped inside, the door rolled back flush with the wall of its own accord to reveal a gloomy corridor. It wasn't inviting. A stale, musty incense-like smell teased her nostrils. She could sense someone was inside, somewhere in the back of the house, maybe upstairs. She definitely wasn't alone. Taking one step further in she called out again, this time more loudly, 'Angela, Angela, are you there? Is anybody in?'

This time a reply came back. A woman with a shrill Cockney accent, 'Shu' door will yer and come upstairs if yer don' mind. And can yer stop all that hollering.'

With the door shut, the hall corridor was almost totally dark. Her way lay past the living room, first on her right, from which there was a little light, then next right was an empty upward void where the steep staircase rose before her.

She moved slowly and cautiously upstairs, her arms held out either side to touch the walls lightly, her fingers feeling her way in the darkness, only for her to quickly pull them back close at one point as they brushed something like feathers. Then some unseen creature brushed past her leg, maybe a cat, almost unsteadying her, as it headed silently downstairs.

Her nose signalled that somewhere ahead there was incense burning, far stronger than simply a fragrance, this was more heady, pungent and all-pervading. The place reminded her of somewhere she'd been before, yet for the moment she couldn't quite recall where it was.

'Hello Angela, it's me Ruth,' she said, this time more softly. 'The police officers asked me to call and see you, to see if you were alright. I'm on my way up. Is there a light switch?'

'No, me electrics don't work, aint got no dough, know what I mean?'

'Oh, OK, nearly there,' she said, her hands following the line of the wall to the top of the stairs. She heard a sound in the front bedroom and gently pushed open the door not knowing what she would see. At first her eyes couldn't make it out, but between her and the closed curtain was a large bed, a heavy wooden headboard obscuring most of the window behind it with what looked like a very overweight woman facing her, propped up by several pillows. It wasn't light enough to make out her facial features. She had a white lace cap, Victorian looking, on her head. How very strange, she thought.

'C'mon in,' Angela said, imperiously.

She could see a raised hand beckoning her in with a gesture as if she were summoning something or someone up. The room felt cold, the atmosphere oppressive and Ruth felt an inner reluctance to step any further inside. Then she noticed there was the familiar, warm yet unmistakeable smell of urine, that even the incense was failing to completely hide.

On second glance the woman on the bed looked to be little more than a giant spectre. Her eyes adjusting, Ruth was beginning to make out her features. For a moment she wondered whether what she was encountering wasn't a real person but some imagined malign spiritual presence, an evil alien. It was so odd to have stepped from the hot pavement outside into such a cold place. How could it be? It felt unnatural, other worldly, that the walls of houses hid such strange and hidden worlds.

At that moment Ruth felt unsteady on her feet as if something seemed to be making it hard to get her breath, crushing the life in her. The dark, the presence on the bed, the heavy smells and what she took to be strange mystical powers were conspiring to work against her. She fought to control herself and silently called upon the almighty before speaking.

'I'm Ruth, Ruth Churchill...' she stammered. 'Come to see how you are. Are you unwell? It's very dark in here.'

'My boy Tony. He see's me right. But he's inside, done it this time, he 'as. Don't know what I'll do. Don't like the ligh'. Don' like neighbours seein' in me 'ouse. No-one understands.'

'Have you any other family?'

'No, just Tony, 'ee's good to me.'

Ruth's eyes had sufficiently adjusted to make out Angela shuffling herself, tidying her pillows and trying to pull herself into a more upright sitting position. Weirdly the resultant position she was in distinctly reminded her of someone seated on a throne. To Ruth's mind, her posture removed any doubt that this was where the power in the house lay and from where orders were issued. Son Tony was her lackey. She stayed within her four walls, Tony dealt with the outside and all outsiders.

Seeing more, Ruth glanced round the walls. There were so many religious pictures, churches, temples, mosques, pictures of pontiffs, native American chiefs and then there were framed religious texts and open books like Bibles and other scriptures on every available surface. There were old dolls in glass boxes and old books untidily scattered on every surface. There were burnt down white candles of various sizes, some stuck at crazy angles in candelabra; on the floor, there were cardboard boxes of new candles waiting to be lit.

She spotted the smoking incense sticks in pots and jam jars on the floor either side of the bed, fumes sucking the very life out of the airless room. In the corner to her left, creating some light, was a kind of Hindu shrine with a flickering candle in front, a tableau of small idols of Hindu gods. The moving light behind seemed to make them dance, bring them alive somehow, incense smoke adding to the theatre of it all.

Her eyes fell to the floor where she could see another strange light. Drawn to follow the pattern she realised the bed lay inside of a large luminous hexagon outlined in white. A similar white pattern had also been painted on the far wall, two end on triangles inside a white circle. Whatever all this signified, Ruth couldn't conceive. It felt like she was in the middle of a religious nightmare and she didn't like it one bit. The hexagon was a way of containing, bounding as a wall. Angela was inside one, a spiritual protection for her in a dangerous world. What did it all mean?

'Have I got it right? Tony looks after you?'

'That's righ'. Ee's my righ' hand.'

'And forgive me for asking, but what's wrong with you?'

'Been in bed like this since Tony was born, I 'ave. Not been righ'. Unsteady on my feet. Tony's been good to me, 'ee 'as.'

'But the police are holding him for… a serious crime. I can't think he'll be home for a while. What will you do?'

'Come back later and I'll give you a list, things I'll need. Alrigh'? I'll manage. Know what I mean?'

Ruth saw Angela shake her head dismissively, her whispy, straggly white hair shaking too. She could now make out Angela's facial features. She'd never seen a face so waxy and pale, dark pin prick eyes darting this way and that, like those of a crafty yet dangerous wild animal. The folds of hanging skin on her cheeks and neck had something porcine about them. But it was Angela's eyes, piercing, powerful and controlling that were most unsettling. Angela was a paradox, confined and powerless in the wider society she hadn't been into for years, yet influential and all controlling in her private sphere, sitting up on her bed-throne, protecting herself with an eclectic mix of mystical powers.

Then Ruth sensed deja vu, finally identifying and recalling a similar past feeling. It was when she was deep underground in the catacombs of Rome, in a burial space where people had lit candles and left wilted flowers. There on holiday, she'd come off the hot streets of Rome into those cold claustrophobic tombs. And here she was again, in what felt exactly like a living tomb surrounded by strange religious artefacts and smells of decay. Only here in front of her was a spectre, a living ghost of a woman, someone whose life was so strange the police had seen her, Ruth, as the only one to deal with her. Now she understood. Now she began to feel afraid and wanted a way out.

'Shopping list. No problem. Jot it down. Myself or someone else will call by later. Anything else?'

'You want to go. Yer all the same. I want you to stay for a minute, 'ear me out. I don't bite,' she snapped loudly. This paradoxical cry of reassurance fell on deaf ears.

Ruth felt trapped. She glanced around her for somewhere to sit, she was once again feeling a little light headed. There was nowhere. So she remained standing at the foot of the bed as one summoned, waiting for instruction and she imagined Tony doing just the same, day in and day out, always at his Mother's beck and call.

There was a cracking and groaning from the bed as Angela again adjusted herself. With a pale bare arm outstretched she reached amongst the detritus resting on the grey bedspread and tugged a crumpled piece of paper and from somewhere magicked a biro.

''Ere, take this. Write!'

Ruth took an involuntary step toward Angela and almost immediately recoiled at the odours emanating from her unwashed body. An old plastic washing up bowl with a flannel in lay on the floor, suggesting washing had taken place, but who knew when or how often the water had been changed?

Pen and paper in hand, Ruth began writing down a simple list of wants. Digestive biscuits, white sliced bread, a pot of raspberry jam, full cream milk, dry cat food and a 12 pack of Dewey's sausage rolls.

'Is that it? Any fruit or veg?'

'Don't get smart with me. I live simply, in touch with the earth, like everyone should. No extras, no waste. Take this.' A ten pound note appeared which Ruth took warily along with the list. 'Be sure you check and bring back the right change. See yourself out will yer.'

Ruth needed no second bidding. 'I'll see you get them later today. But what about Tony?'

"E's done it now. 'E's a man now. 'Ave to stan' on 'is own feet. Police say he stabbed the man at the corner shop. After all these years, what did that man do to so upset my boy? Expect he'll be home soon. 'E's a good lad. Does everything I tell 'im. Never been a day's bother. Know what I mean? You got family? I see you 'ave. Boy and girl, aint it? You worry about them don't you. I can see that. I can see…'

Ruth felt thoroughly unnerved. Angela's comments felt like a violation of her space. How did she know about her family? Had she some gift of second sight? She wanted out and now.

'I'll see myself out then… I'll leave the door how I found it.' With than she stepped out of the room and felt her way down the stairs to the hallway. Then she stopped.

A large black cat stood between her and the door. It seemed to look at her, or even through her and wasn't intending to move. Maybe Ruth should reach over and let it out. Maybe it was a house cat and never went out? What should she do?

Ruth froze. There was a stand off and the cat was winning. It seemed like an age, but then the cat moved first, passing by her heading for the kitchen at the back of the house. What horrors lay there Ruth could only imagine. Now seeing better in the gloom, all she could see was the accumulated dirt of decades and a mystical, extensive, eclectic collection of religious items buried in dust and grime. It reminded her again of being buried in a tomb. It was time to get out, escape into the light, get some fresh air on the street. She desperately needed to breathe.

7

Pulling the door shut behind her, the sudden contrast between the dark interior and the bright afternoon daylight made Ruth screw up her eyes. She felt such relief to have re-surfaced safely on the pavement.

Drained by her visit, it took her a while to get on her way home. Before setting off she glanced back at the decayed front door, then up at Angela's bedroom window with the closed curtains. Of the mysterious secret world ruled by Angela Morris from her bed throne inside nothing here on the outside could be discerned. Once walking, Ruth was mightily glad to be out of that dark place and with every step she willed herself ever further away.

Half way along Henley Road she realised she was clutching the crumpled piece of paper that was the shopping list along with a ten pound note. Stopping briefly, she pushed them both into her bag. To her mind, every pastoral visit led to yet more things needing to be done. Maybe she could delegate the shopping task to one of her parishioners. She thought she'd ring Julie Brown.

Five minutes later she was back at the vicarage. By then her foot was throbbing furiously and she was once more feeling hot and uncomfortable. The afternoon itself was not so much hot, but sultry and sticky, the building clouds looked even more threatening, the late summer air hanging heavily as if the weather would soon break. Maybe rain would bring some relief. Throwing her light jacket top, bag and keys on to the hall cloak stand, she listened out for the children. There was not a sound. It was then she spotted the note.

Gone to Pymms Park with the kids.
Two of their friends have joined us.
Back by 5. P x

A wave of sadness swept across her and she felt the warmth and wetness of unexpected tears. Not usually given to much emotion it caught her by surprise and she reached for a tissue to dab her eyes as she tried to regain her composure. As was increasingly becoming her custom she dived into her refuge – her study and closed the door.

The experience of visiting Angela's home wouldn't leave her mind. She kept getting recurring vivid pictures, like watching an unsettling film extract. The gloom, the smells, the religious gloss, the throne-like bed and then Angela's eyes and face flashed before her causing her to shudder. She tried to concentrate, focus her thoughts in a moment of mindful reminiscence deciding to consciously reflect on the experience of her visit as a means of putting it to rest.

Often being needed when people were in a time of crisis was very affirming, but it had not been like it this afternoon. What exactly was it that had so unsettled her? It wasn't the evident poverty, neglect and dirt. She'd seen that kind of thing on innumerable occasions. No, it was something entirely else. It was the spiritual aura, the threatening sense of power that emanated from Angela and her home. It was as if she'd encountered a throwback to some past age, a seer, a wise spiritual woman, who in aeons long gone had with her sisters maybe ruled the world. Somehow Ruth had come to feel she was being pushed by Angela into being a subject and a follower. The whole experience made her feel as if she'd contracted a virus that had got inside her. Somehow she'd been contaminated and rendered... powerless. She'd have to wait to see how bad it was affecting her before, hopefully, she'd recover and get over it.

The vicarage phone rang startling her reverie. Lifting the handset, she immediately recognised the precise intonations of the archdeacon's voice and her heart sank. It was the way he made himself sound so self-important and assured which always left her feeling incompetent and deflated. Not now, she thought, I don't need this.

'Stephen here. How are we today? All tickety boo doing the Lord's work on the sabbath day?' he cheerfully, but annoyingly asked.

'Not been the easiest of days actually...' she found herself saying, but instantly wished she hadn't been so transparent. That man would be looking for any indication of stress, any hint of her being under pressure. Then he'd probe to find out why she felt life was all so harassing and feel further vindicated in his view that she was less than competent, an opinion he'd consistently held since the Ali Muhammed enquiry. She'd long ago concluded he was just looking for any excuse to see her go and the sooner the better. Thankfully he was based several miles away, in Hampstead, rarely venturing over to Edmonton in person.

'Do tell me about it, I'm all ears. Please put me back in touch with the nitty gritty of parish life.' How his obsequious voice annoyed and grated on her.

'Oh, just another pastoral visit,' she replied, trying to close down the conversation, 'you know the kind of thing, a troublesome son who can't help his Mum at home, a disabled woman needing her shopping done... that kind of thing.'

'Oh, oh. The poor dears.' He seemed satisfied with that and changed tack. 'Tell you why I called. One of your flock called me…' He paused, leaving Ruth feeling exposed, betrayed even. His instinct for making her feel vulnerable was so attuned, if he could help her fail and fall, she believed he would.

'It's so touching how people care, support you,' he added.

'That's good to know,' she said, not believing a word he said.

'Want you to think of taking a sabbatical, a three month break should do just the trick. Give you time to rethink direction, recharge the flat battery, that kind of thing.'

So that was it. Ruth let all his assumptions pass unchallenged, recalling the gang of three after the morning service – Julie, Lionel and Stephanie, and then it all made sense. Only Julie would have taken it on herself to call the archdeacon. Julie never let the dust settle on an idea. Now she was reaping the whirlwind.

'Yes, it was suggested to me earlier today. I think they know that in a parish like this there is considerable wear and tear on the vicar. You know how it is, All kindly meant I'm certain of it,' she said.

'Oh, to be sure, absolutely. Believe me, I only think they ever had your well-being in mind.'

'But I'm still standing upright, doing what needs to be done here and now, speaking frankly, the time's not right for a sabbatical, and besides, I'm not due to be considered for one for another twelve months.'

'Ah, but in your case, I think a little discretion might be exercised. I'm sure I might be able to help there. We all know what you've been through. No doubt a word in the right place and the time line could give a little in your favour. Rigidly applied rules are not always helpful are they?' he added, hoping to smooth talk her into agreement, getting her to put one foot out of the door of her office before finally seeing her leave for good.

'But it's amazing what you can come back from,' she replied. 'The human being bounces back like a phoenix from the ashes,' she said confidently, trying to coax her voice into sounding on top of things.

'Hmm. But do one thing for me, Ruthie...' How she hated his use of the patronising over-familiarity, 'Think on it for a day or two and let me know what you decide. Give it some serious thought, will you, for me...? In fact drop me a line with your final word on the matter before the end of the week. Just remember, I'm sure an immediate sabbatical is yours, it's there just for the asking.' And with that he'd gone.

Ruth felt furious. 'That man!' she exclaimed staring into the handset on her desk as if it were poisonous.

Thinking to prove her competence to herself she immediately picked up the handset again and keyed in Julie Brown's number, realising as she did so she was gripping it so tightly her knuckles were chalky white. On reflection, perhaps it would be sensible to calm herself before making the next call and spend a moment carefully choosing her words to Julie. It wasn't a time to be creating more enemies and fighting battles on every front. She gently laid the handset down on her desk. A couple of minutes later and having recovered her composure she was ready. She pressed dial and Julie picked up.

'Hello Julie. I wondered if you could do me a favour?'

'Why, what is it Ruth?'

'I've just been round to see Angela Morris in Henley Road. Her son Tony was the lad picked up with the knife and charged with Raj Chauhan's death.'

'Oh yes. Can't say I know her. Everyone's talking about it. So very sad.'

'Angela's confined to bed... I popped to see her and I've got a short shopping list here and some cash from her. Any chance? You know how hectic it's been...'

'No problem dear. I'll be round in a few minutes.'

'Oh, and I just had a call from Archdeacon Stephen. He says someone called him suggesting I took some time out, a sabbatical...' she paused and waited.

'That was me, following up our chat earlier. I did right didn't I?' said Julie, annoyingly sounding quite unperturbed, genuinely well-meaning and every bit as if she believed she'd done the right thing.

'Well, I'm sure it was well meant, but please leave me to manage my sabbatical arrangements Julie. It makes life less complicated that way,' she said, the anger by now having almost entirely dissipated.

'Well, tell me, what did he say? Did he offer you the chance? I won't tell…'

'Julie, this isn't the right time for a sabbatical and I'm not taking one. It would help if you make that clear to Lionel, Stephanie and anyone else who might have the wrong idea about it,' she said forcefully.

'Are you sure about this? It could be just what you need.'

'Certain, and I don't want any rumours circulating round the church about either my fitness to work or my commitment to my parish duties. It unsettles people. Alright?'

'Yes, only wanted what was best for you… I'll pop round right now to collect the shopping list.' Her cheerful demeanour was unstoppable.

Handset down, Ruth breathed a sigh of relief. The calls were sorted, the immediate shopping task delegated. Managing things felt reassuring good. She told herself, she hadn't lost her touch.

However, the feeling was short lived as she realised her family were down at the park with Phil and she wasn't with them. Perhaps there was sufficient time for her to go and join them? Then she realised Julie would be round any minute to collect the list and cash and then she'd need to drop Angela's shopping back at the vicarage. She was trapped in the house. Perhaps the delegation to Julie had been a mistake after all. Now she was stuck in the house, waiting to perform her next pastoral task.

The phone rang.

'Stephen here again. I've had another thought. I'm off to the Walsingham Shrine in Norfolk for a few days after tomorrow and well, being away, I didn't want to depart leaving you feeling all high and dry, without some hope.'

'No,' said Ruth waiting to hear what was coming next.

'I might not agree with your judgement, but I hear you loud and clear, you're not keen on a sabbatical, so why don't we get someone to join you in the parish? Give you an extra pair of hands to lighten the load... I had in mind a student from a theological college. The autumn term starts soon. Strike while the iron's hot. Sound them out, get your name down. Do you like the idea, Ruthie?'

'Give me time to think on it Stephen, if that's alright,' she said, in effect giving herself space, kicking the can along the road.

'Sure, sure thing. I've made a note. I'll call when I'm back and get something sorted. Can't have you feeling under resourced. Must dash. Bye.'

As she closed the call, Ruth was feeling so angry with the man she was almost shaking. She took a deep breath to help herself deal with her fury. Every time Archdeacon Stephen called he left her feeling more isolated, more under threat than ever. Underneath his ostensibly caring exterior, she knew his Anglo-Catholic theology had no time for her, her a woman priest and one with a chequered past.

Every encounter with that man left her feeling he had no time for women in the church, but he was cunning enough never to give cause for action against him. She could do nothing other than hear out his dutiful offers of support. To her mind they sounded every bit as hollow as the local drug addicts' promises were to stay clean – entirely vacuous and empty, with a soul-less voice behind them.

No, it was more than that – he was deliberately undermining her and deceitful with it. He was just waiting for her to collude with his view that she was incapable. She admitted it to herself, the truth was, the Venerable Stephen Nicholls just wanted her gone, out of the parish and out of the church. OK, she concluded, he was but another problem in a long list of end of August problems yet to be managed. She realised that once more she was feeling incredibly thirsty, she glanced at the time and decided she needed a cup of tea.

The large vicarage felt empty with only her in it. The largest house in the parish, it conveyed an image of faded past grandeur with hints of the Arts and Crafts movement in its design. It was a house built on ideals. But far too big for today and far too expensive to run. In itself it was impossible to keep on top of. Sometimes she didn't even feel she could manage her home – everything conspired against her.

Since the beginning of the summer they'd had no help with the vicarage chores. Anne Chigowe, her Zimbabwean home help had gone, a better paid cleaning job in the city luring her away back in July. Joseph, the gardener, had also given up work around the same time. It had felt better having people around in the house. Right now she began to feel herself vulnerable again and hoped it wouldn't be long before the others returned. Perhaps she ought to ask Phil about finding extra help?

As she glanced around she realised the end result of no Anne or Joseph was that here and there chaos was showing the upper hand over order. As she filled the kettle, she noticed a dirty kitchen sink in front of her, a once white but now dusty grey linoleum floor lay beneath her feet and outside the kitchen window the untidy spikes of green privet waited for an overdue clipping. It made her wonder how these two vital helps were to be replaced and reminded her again of the emptiness and powerlessness she felt in controlling her world. All that early energy she'd set out with at the beginning of her ministry had led to this – today she found it disconcerting that she didn't know how to set about tackling even basic things.

The kettle boiled and she made the tea. There was still no sign of Phil, Olivia and Paul. The tea was left on the kitchen table as the door bell rang. Increasingly it unnerved her these days to get callers at the door, the more so when she was alone in the house. Peering round the boarded panel and through what remained of the panes of painted coloured glass in the front door she was unable to make out who it was. She knew that she had no choice. She had to see who it was.

She opened the door cautiously. A skinny man, probably in his early twenties, scruffy jeans and black top with the words emblazoned on it – *Barbados Rocks* zipped tight up under his chin turned to her, his face full of agitation. He had really bad body odour and he wasn't even standing right next to her. Ignoring her he began bouncing on his toes on the second step, glancing skyward and then up and down the road.

'Hello, can I help you?' she asked him calmly, recognising a troubled personality when she saw one.

'They're here,' he whispered confidentially, bending toward her, with wild alarm in his flashing eyes. He was leaning toward her, closer than before and she saw his teeth were badly decayed. Bad breath combined with bad body odour making her want to recoil.

'Who's here?' she enquired gently standing her ground.

'Look!' He waved his arms in an expansive gesture to include, she thought, the roofs of the surrounding buildings.

Her eyes followed his arm. But what was she supposed to be seeing. A black crow lifted off the school roof opposite.

'The crow?' she said pointing her own arm.

'Can't you see? It's them,' he muttered, his eyes leaping and betraying a certain terror. His mind became more troubled, his actions less predictable, as she failed to follow him.

'Tell me, what you see,' she asked working hard to keep her cool and to keep him calm.

'Aliens…. aliens! They're using those ariels and dishes to communicate. They're taking over. We're being invaded. We'll all be dead. It's the end…'

'Oh, I see,' she said, 'I see what you mean,' she answered, realising that either the man was in the midst of a drug high, mentally ill or both. The man stopped talking, but had no intention yet of going. Disconcertingly, he spun and twirled on his toes ending up facing her.

'My name's Ruth Churchill, what's yours?' she asked.

'Leroy,' but the man was no longer listening. He was set on leaving. He turned and was as if gliding away on dancer's footsteps, heading toward her gate, spinning and pirouetting as he glanced skyward. Momentarily he bent down behind her fence out of sight as if hiding, only for his face to reappear again, his anxious, contorted facial expression leading him to twist this way and that as if to escape his imagined foes. Suddenly he sprinted awkwardly, on his heels not his toes, to the corner of the road thinking no doubt he could escape that way, hide behind the church building and then he'd gone from sight.

Ruth closed the door. She got all kinds of strange callers. Weekends and bank holiday weekends like this were always the worst times, when the health community support services were on minimal or non-existent staff levels. That's when the vicarage became the last port of call for marginal, magical and mental people. Pulling the front door shut, she found herself beginning to chuckle, then laugh at the scene she had just witnessed. 'Leroy,' she voiced and made a spinning turn. It reminded her that there were times and moments she wouldn't miss what she did for the world. Yes, archdeacon Stephen could stuff his sabbatical.

Returning to her tea in the kitchen, she sipped the cold liquid, the skin from the milky surface sticking to her upper lip. My goodness, she was tired. Leroy, she thought, was as much a prisoner of his aliens tormenting him, as she was afflicted by her archdeacon. Flopping down on a chair, her elbows resting on the table to take her weight, her head slipped down and turned, resting on her now folded arms. Before she knew it she was fast asleep.

A sudden crashing and calling of children brought her round. She couldn't work out were she was, when it was or what she should be doing. On each elbow she saw Olivia and Paul looking into her opening eyes with puzzlement.

'You were asleep, yes you were,' said Olivia, 'but it's not your bedtime yet, Mummy.'

'Are you alright Mum?' asked Paul quizzically.

Not waiting for a reply he spotted the biscuit tin and reached in for a handful of chocolate digestives, seconds before Olivia did the same. Then they were off running, taking the tin with them and disappearing upstairs.

'Hello love,' said Phil, bending to kiss the nape of her neck. 'I've been worried about you...'

'I've been waiting for you to come home,' she said and upon that she found she couldn't hold back her tears. They flowed like a torrent and wretched at her inside. What made it worse was the shocked look she saw on Phil's face.

8

Ruth had been woken by her returning family whilst she was in the midst of a weird dream. Once she'd entirely come back into the present moment, the kids having appeared in an instant and then just as quickly disappeared upstairs there was just Phil alone beside her. She couldn't explain her tears, but she felt a need to talk about her dream. She felt sure Phil would help sort things.

'Phil, bear with me. When you came back I was asleep and I was dreaming.'

'You were right out of it. You never even heard us come in!' he chuckled, 'you never do that! What a way to spend a Sunday afternoon!'

'Well, I was dreaming. You know I'd been round to see Angela Morris earlier. My dream was somehow connected with that visit. Her house is… really strange, hmmm…. It was like meeting a kind of Dickensian Miss Havisham in a gothic setting. This living ghost of a woman was upstairs lying, no, sitting on her bed as if it were a throne, ruling the world from her private religious museum – really, really weird… I've never seen anything like it before. It was like entering a forbidden, hidden world, most unsettling. I dreamt… no, it was definitely a nightmare, I was very frightened.'

'I have to say you did wake with a shocked expression on your face.'

'In my dream I was a beautiful blue butterfly trapped in her dark room and there was no way out, no way to escape to the light. As I fluttered this way and that, a black cat tried to catch me with its paw. It jumped up and with all the effort I could muster I kept dodging it, yes, she really did have a black cat.'

'And what do you make of that? Did my little butterfly escape?'

'No, I was still shut in there and whichever which way I tried, there was no way out. I did find a hiding place though. There was a Hindu shrine in the corner. I had to be so careful that the candles and incense sticks didn't set my wings on fire. I got behind one of the figurine gods and kept as still as I could. As I rested I realised the statue was none other than Raj, Raj Chauhan. Either side of Raj were two Hindu deities, Shiva and Vishnu. They seemed to be arguing with Raj who was turning first to face one then to face the other. He was twisting and turning in a religious dance. It got really heated.'

'What were they arguing about?'

'The two gods were telling Raj he should do more to care for creation, but Raj was saying he was too busy with his shop and trying to make ends meet. This just made the two gods angry and they were arguing about what to do with him. Shiva wanted to destroy him, kill him there and then and began waving sword blades, but Vishnu said he wanted to preserve Raj's life. That was when you woke me. As to what it means. You know I don't hold with over-reading meaning into dreams, but sometimes, just sometimes, when we're asleep don't you think we get insights, moments of true reflection?'

'Personally, no. I go out like a light and rarely recall any dreaming moments. Never give it a second thought. But did you, did your dream actually gain you an insight into your mysterious Angela Morris?'

'It's just a notion I've got, maybe an idea that I dreamt up. She did seem to be spiritually connected. I'm not saying in a good way, certainly nothing mainstream like being a Christian, but she seemed to me to be linked to something ancient, as if she were the last of the Edmonton witches. I was rather shaken when she seemed to have some knowledge of my family situation when I hadn't told her anything about us.'

'More like either the police had told her or she'd heard about us through someone. It could have been anyone, I wouldn't go reading too much into that, even though what she said obviously surprised, shocked you.'

'You might be right, but it shook me. Made me shudder. In fact the place felt unnaturally cold.'

'You were unnerved by it and you're overtired – an understandable bodily response.'

'And I'm left thinking about Raj. In my dream he offered me shelter but was the victim of the wrath of his god. He died because he didn't help save the planet. It was nothing to do with a corner shop robbery.'

'Now you really are reading too much into it,' said a vexed looking Phil. 'Time for more tea vicar?'

'Maybe. Let's put the kettle on.'

Tea making under way, there was a ringing at the front door. But neither Ruth's mind nor her body wanted to face more work. Pushing her hand back through her hair to try and make herself look presentable, nonetheless she slowly made her way to see who it was this time, opening the door to find a smiling Julie standing there with a brown paper bag of groceries clutched in front of her as if it were a baby.

'Job done,' she said cheerily, 'Got everything on the list and here's the change and till receipt.'

'Thanks Julie, I'll pop it round and drop them in to her,' she said, reaching for and taking the freshly bought supplies. 'Thanks again.'

'Might look in again to see you later,' offered Julie, 'been having some ideas. Hope you'll like them,' she said with a mysterious twinkle in her eye as Ruth faltered.

'Bye,' she pronounced. Before Ruth could think of anything further to say, Julie had turned and was off.

She's so energetic that girl, thought Ruth as she used the weight of her body to push the front door closed before returning to the kitchen, dropping the grocery bag on the kitchen table. Meantime, Phil with his back to her was pouring boiling water into two mugs.

'Phil, I'll just take these round to Angela. Won't be long.'

'Tea before you go, surely?'

'Sorry. Must do this now,' she sighed.

Leaving Phil standing forlorn clutching two mugs, she grabbed her handbag and swept up the bag of groceries from the table and headed out. This time she went straight to her car which looked battered, tired and dust covered. It's overdue a clean, just like the house, she thought, as she struggled to get herself and her bags inside.

Five minutes later she was back at Angela Morris' home and conveniently managed to park right outside, just in front of an old white Transit van. The van looked vaguely familiar but she couldn't place it. As before, she found the front door unlocked and she went straight inside loudly announcing her presence in as friendly and as booming a voice as she could muster.

'Angela, it's me, Ruth. I've got your things from the shops. I'm coming up. It's Roooth...'

Ruth could hear indistinct sounds indicating someone, presumably Angela, moving upstairs. There was still no verbal reply.

'Hello-o...' she called, even more loudly this time. Realising as she did so the climb up the stairs had left her breathless.

'Don't stand on ceremony, come on up,' she heard Angela eventually say with an edge of impatience in her tone.

Ruth took the final steps more slowly. She felt the spicy sweetness of the burning incense closing her windpipe and it was getting harder to breathe the thick musty air. The lack of light made her slow and reach for something to grasp on to, with the result she almost fell into the bedroom. It was not a dignified entry.

'Got them then?' asked Angela.

'Yes, everything you had on your list and here's your change.'

As Ruth leant forward to give the money over, she misjudged the distance and stumbled into the end of the bed bumping a protruding foot. At this Angela let out a piercing scream as one in pain and Ruth involuntarily moved quickly backwards.

'You clumsy woman, just leave me my things and get out.'

'Sorry, it was an accident. I had no idea…'

'No, you have no idea. I suffer from fybromyalgia, life is painful for me, I can't bear to be touched and I can't stand the light,' she explained, wincing in pain as she spoke.

'Have you had it long?'

'Since Tony was small. He helps me. I don't know what I'm going to do with him away-ee. Ow! O—w!' she cried, clutching at her foot under the bed cover.

'Can anyone else help you out? Family? Friends? Neighbours?'

At each suggestion, Angela shook her head. 'I'm all alone. I have no one,' she asserted plaintively, gently adjusting the bedding.

'Then I need to see what I can do to help,' offered Ruth.

'I don't want any strangers helping me. Leave me be.'

Ruth didn't know what to do for the best. Should she go? Or maybe Angela was just testing her, seeing if her offer of care was genuine, in which case she should stay. It was then she sensed something wasn't quite right, the incense smelt different and in the background there was a faint roaring and then she discerned a crying of alarmed voices coming from somewhere. They were outside. Ruth wanted to part the curtain but just looked at Angela who didn't seem to have noticed anything untoward.

'Can you hear it? Shall I look?' she asked.

Now there was more noise. Without waiting for Angela's say so, she parted the curtain slightly to peer out. There were people gathered in the street outside. The roaring noise grew louder and was followed by an explosion, a bright flash penetrating even the gloomy room, bright enough to alert Angela too that something was very much wrong outside. Ruth grabbed and pulled the curtain further back to stand in the window and look out.

'It's the white van, it's on fire. My car it'll be damaged. I must call the fire service,' she cried.

However, even as she reached for her bag and her phone she heard the approaching sound of sirens coming from the direction of Edmonton Green and then she saw the red beast pull up, blue lights winking, siren now off, uniformed firemen jumping down from the tender and running every which way to their different tasks.

Transfixed, she saw a hose deployed and the van doused with water, clouds of hissing steam rising high. Even as she watched she could see the blue paintwork on her Punto's bonnet steaming. It had already blistered.

She looked round at Angela who hadn't moved from her bed. It was as if she had no interest in things on the outside. Her world was her bed, her bedroom. Out there didn't matter. Only she herself mattered.

In the instant she'd turned from the window to look at Angela, Ruth remembered the van – it was Raj Chauhan's.

9

'It's a fire. The white van outside. It's burnt out, a total wreck. I think I know whose it is.'

Angela said nothing, simply stared straight in front of her, defying any interest in events in the other world beyond her room. A few minutes passed whilst Ruth looked again through the window at the scene below.

'I'd better go down and talk to the firemen. They seem to have everything under control now,' said Ruth. Angela remained impassive, propped up by pillows and cushions sitting upright in her bed without making the slightest effort to take a look for herself.

'Then you'd better do that,' she replied curtly.

Ruth made her way carefully down and out of the front door, standing well back from the action. One of the firemen nodded as he saw her and spotted her vicar's dog collar.

'Keep clear, go back inside or move quickly down the street please ma'am. We don't know what's inside the van,' he said, raising an outstretched arm to gently guide her where he wanted her to go. She chose to walk into the street.

'That's my car,' she said.

'Sorry we couldn't have got here earlier. It's a bit scorched, paintwork will need seeing to,' he said sympathetically.

'Can I drive it?'

'Not right now, no… Please move down the street, keep well back for your own safety, ma'am,' he insisted.

'What happened here? I think I know whose van it is.'

'Really! We believe this vehicle was deliberately set alight. The police are on their way. Who's the owner then ma'am? Do they live locally?'

'I think I'll talk to the police when they arrive,' she said, walking away from the still smouldering van.

The fireman moved away, smelling heavily of acrid smoke, walking over to rejoin his colleagues, the crumpled wreck of the van showing little of its former white paintwork. It sat lower on the ground, like a dying beast, its burnt tyres in a pool of black water slushing down the gutter, marking the street with a dark stain. The distinctive rounded padlock on the back still held the two rear doors shut.

Two of the firemen were obviously having a discussion about how to get inside. One went off to re-appear with a mammoth sized bolt-cutter and the two worked together snipping through the metal lock as if using scissors on paper. Then the two of them pulled the doors back, the resisting metal creaking and groaning as a fresh grey smoke cloud and white stream hissed and rose into the early evening air.

'My God!' she heard one fireman exclaim. The other stepped forward, shielding his eyes, to try and see what had been discovered, before also recoiling back grabbing the arm of his colleague as he did so. Ruth, a safe three cars away down the road tried to see for herself what it was and stepped in as near she dared.

As she watched, another fireman played a hose into the van's dark interior as from inside fresh flashes of orange flame lit and licked the air. She thought she could make out the blackened shapes of two people but they were so contorted she wasn't sure what she was seeing. Perhaps they were just tailor's dummies, or not... The smell, it was her nose that gave her the answer. It was two bodies.

One of the firemen was throwing plumes of white vomit into the black slurry beside the van. His colleague had grabbed a phone and was obviously making a call as to their shocking discovery. There was now no doubt to Ruth's mind what she had seen.

Ruth's attention had been so taken up by the unfolding events, she never heard or saw the police car arrive. It pulled up beside her in the middle of the road and PCs Alan Dallow and Alice Such stepped out, both putting on bright yellow high vis jackets as they did so.

They were intercepted by the fireman at the back of van who gesticulated, beckoning the two officers closer to his gruesome discovery, the two then trying to peer inside. Immediately, Alice was calling for back up. As she ended her call Ruth stepped into the road and called her name. She looked up in friendly recognition and raised the palm of her hand to say, hold on a moment will you.

'It's Raj Chauhan's van,' she said, the instant Alice looked her way.

'I know. But what's it doing here in Henley Road? Sorry, I've work to do Ruth. Please can you help us keep this gathering crowd of onlookers back. Reassure them and please keep from seeing what's in the back of the van. We'll move them

86

all over there I think,' she said pointing away down Henley Road toward Windmill Road. For all her apparent professionalism, even Alice seemed to Ruth to have been unnerved.

Ruth helped out and chatted to the gathering crowd of the curious and the voyeurs. One or two she knew and rather more knew who she was. Some already had their mobiles out and were taking selfies before the final flames and drama had past and she knew she would also be splashed across social media in the coming minutes and hours.

Ruth kept what she had seen to herself but her mind wouldn't let her forget or stop asking who the poor people were in the back of Raj's van. What were they doing there and what did it all mean? She realised that the other onlookers were the wrong side of the van to have seen what she had seen. To them it had simply been a vehicle fire. For her, there was the disconcerting matter of the two burned bodies she'd seen in the back.

She must have stood there waiting on the pavement about an hour. By which time more police cars had arrived and white police vans with people in white forensic suits had moved in.

The road was formally closed to traffic and a traffic officer was placed at the Haselbury Road end to re-direct traffic. A second officer stood in front of a blue and white tape line to prevent traffic coming any further up Henley Road from from the opposite direction. Large screens were erected to block off, protect and privatise the site together with a white police incident marquee. The police were going to be around for some while – so, not just a vehicle fire, thought Ruth.

Ruth was told her car was part of the crime scene and she would have to leave it where it was for now. She left her details with the police who said they may want to interview her later as to what she had seen.

So, feeling weary and puzzled, Ruth walked slowly home. When she arrived she opened her much in need of repair, front door and called out, 'Is anybody there?'

She was desperately wanting to talk to someone, to share the horror of what she thought, but couldn't quite believe she'd seen.

10

'I'm back!' Ruth called out, looking at herself in the hall coat-stand mirror before recoiling at the grey image she saw there. She tried to pat her out of control hair back into line and pulled off her dog collar as if to tell herself she had finished work for the day. There was a noise from upstairs and Phil's head leaned over the bannister.

'I didn't think you'd be so long. The kids have settled to doing some homework for me and they're just getting ready for bed.'

'There was a vehicle fire and more, right outside Angela Morris's house in Henley Road. The van I parked next to totally destroyed. Had to leave my car and walk back. My car's paintwork's blistered. Wasn't able to check if it still drives. Something wasn't right about the fire. Thought I saw two dead bodies in the back of the burnt out van before police hustled us away. Who could they be? What's that about do you think? I'm certain it was Raj's van, so what's it doing there, outside Angela's?…' she blurted out, before finally pausing long enough to take a sharp intake of breath.

'I'm beginning to think I should come out of the house with you – it feels like every time you step out of the front door something happens! Well, I expect the police will soon get to the truth of it. Are you alright? You look all in.'

'I know, I know, it's been a long day. Just so sorry you've had the kids all weekend again.'

'They're fine. Why don't you nip upstairs and see them, we can talk later. I'll start putting some left overs together for a light supper. It'll be all we need.'

Ruth nodded and climbed the stairs wearily to find Olivia and Paul already in their pyjamas. She found each in their own room preoccupied with a book and an electronic game respectively. She went to Olivia first. Olivia looked up with a serious, yet earnest expression on her innocent young face. She had something to say.

'Mum, I want to join a dance group. Freya and Maisie both go. It's only next door in the Church Hall and classes after the summer start on Tuesday. Can I? Please Mum? Dad said I had to ask you first and I've been waiting all weekend to ask you Mum. Mum, you smell of smoke.'

'I don't see why not. We'll check if there's a spare place. It's very popular I know and if not then we can always put your name down on the reserve list.'

'Why do you smell of smoke?' Olivia asked, nuzzling into her top to smell it. 'And it's mixed with bitter smoke. You smell like you've been by a bonfire but you also smell like… the incense in Raj's shop. What is it Mummy?'

'Oh, it's fire and smoke and incense – you're right on every count, all in a vicar's working day!' she said, trying to make light of all that was whirring through her mind. 'Sometimes I make a home visit and they are burning joss sticks and you're right you can smell that. But today, just now, there was a vehicle fire in Henley Road and the fire brigade had to come and put it out. I was there. I saw it burn. There was lots of smoke and steam. I couldn't avoid it and you can smell that too.'

'You need to change, have a bath, wash away the nasty smells Mummy and be fresh again.'

'You're right. I'll certainly do that later. I'll just look in on Paul and see what he's been up to. Goodnight dear.'

Olivia had a troubled look on her face. She had something else on her mind and Ruth paused.

'Will you say a prayer with me tonight, Mummy, before you go?'

'Sure. What is it?' she asked sensing something was bothering her.

'I'm frightened Mummy.'

Ruth waited, then Olivia added pensively, 'you're not the Mummy you were.'

'And why's that do you think,' asked Ruth gently, rather taken aback by the profundity of the observation.

'You're worried and sad and forget things and you're too busy. Even Daddy says so. We don't have any fun any more. And yesterday there was a man with a knife outside. He might have hurt you. He came to the door. Our front door is broken. He might have hurt us and I've been frightened for you and for us this weekend Mummy. I don't like this house anymore.'

'The police have got the man in custody so we're all safe now, really we are. It's been one of those weekends. Tomorrow's bank holiday Monday, another day. I'm sure we can find some time to go out, have some fun – it's due to rain, so how about Brent Cross Shopping Centre? We can call in on your Aunt Sue and Uncle Jim in Muswell Hill on the way back.'

'Yes, yes.'

'It's a deal then,' Ruth concluded, as the two hit a high five. 'Let's say that prayer.' They settled quietly side by side. Ruth offered a familiar short prayer, some words from her own childhood coming to mind.

> *Now I lay me down to sleep;*
> *I pray the Lord my soul to keep.*
> *May God guard me through the night,*
> *And wake me with the morning light. Amen.*

The words of the prayer comforted and reassured them both. Ruth hugged and then kissed Olivia on her forehead, got up and headed off to see Paul.

'You've left this room smelling of smoke, Mummy, and I don't like it!' Olivia shouted after her.

Paul was also lying on his bed. He had headphones on and was staring with concentration at his electronic game device. It emitted tones of ever increasing frequency and persistent urgency. Ruth didn't want to interrupt him if it was going to upset him and she waited patiently for her moment.

Reflecting on her time with Olivia, she was troubled by Olivia's observation of her state and wondered how Paul was faring at the end of a difficult weekend. She watched his eyes darting and fingers twitching manically as he sought to master his game. She'd noticed he had been spending ever increasing amounts of time playing like this and wondered how good it was for him, especially so near to bed time. Suddenly, with a sour raspberry sound, the game ended and Paul threw off his head phones and slung the game down on his bed in evident disappointment and frustration, looking up as he did so.

'I lost,' he said angrily, 'eight short of my record and some more money.'

'Never mind,' she said not really understanding the technicalities of the game, as she sought to console him, stretching out an arm to hug him.

But Paul pulled away from her. He didn't want her cuddles. Reaching once again for his head phones the addictive device was summonsed back into life and the game was on once more.

As Ruth watched him, she felt a distance had opened up between them and it hurt her like the stab from a knife. What could she say? He'd walled himself off from her tonight and she needed to find a way to break through.

A couple of minutes later, with Paul still fully absorbed in his game, she heard the front door bell ring, the door open and Phil's voice as he spoke to someone. It was a woman speaking in measured tones. She couldn't make it out. The door closed. Her curiosity getting the better of her she got up and went downstairs to see who it was.

A smiling Julie was standing in the hallway facing her as she came down the stairs. Phil, standing behind her, shrugged his shoulders in an act of forlorn resignation at this latest intrusion.

'Julie wanted a quick word. Says it won't take long. I'm just making supper,' he announced flatly as if to ensure that the visit would be brief, before he disappeared into the kitchen pulling the door firmly closed behind him.

'Do come in,' said Ruth taking Julie into the lounge, wondering what it was this time.

They both sat down, Julie evidently so eager to share her thoughts she could barely contain herself.

'It's time we made life more secure round here. We've been so upset at what you had to deal with yesterday and everyone thinks we should do all we can to make the church and you, you our vicar, feel safe.'

'That's very considerate of you and I do appreciate the thought. I fully agree, it has been, well... a rather demanding weekend. What had you in mind?'

'The railings, wall and gate by the church door.'

'Yes?' Ruth questioned, not yet seeing where the conversation was going.

'They need to be made more secure. If we replace the rusty railings on top of the low wall with a new wall, high enough to stop people climbing over and replace the present old gate with a locking one the same height as the new wall, that would be a start.'

'A wall?'

'Absolutely! It would keep trouble makers out, keep you and us safe the other side. It makes sense, in tune with the times.

And so that you wouldn't be inconvenienced, we could leave the fence and gate between the church and vicarage as it is. Then you could move freely between the two without any fear of others attacking you. Both the churchwardens think we ought to discuss it in church, at the next Parochial Church Council. What do you think? Do you like the idea?'

'A high wall, a locking gate, to keep bad people away you say.'

'Exactly. The weekend's events have proved to us it's no longer safe in our neighbourhood, with all the knife crime and the new migrants. We all have to be so much more careful these days. As a church we have a duty of care. No-one is fully secure in the face of risk. Drugs are a big part of it you know. Drugs lie behind most of the crime in the parish. We must keep the church shielded and we must safeguard and protect you, keep you safe from harm.'

'But... but I don't feel unsafe,' Ruth protested, watching helplessly as her remonstration fell on deaf ears. There was nothing so immutable as someone's cherished idea.

'That's because you have a strong faith vicar, but the rest of us see things as they really are. We can see the tensions and the dangers. We're more practical than you are. In matters like looking after yourself, we know what we are talking about. We know our community. There are more Tony's out there with knives, dozens, scores of Tony Morrises, believe you me. With the way things are going you can't keep taking the risks you do. I've just been looking at your front door. It needs repairing properly with some metal reinforcement. That was such a near thing when he came to the door. You could have... you could have died, like poor Mr Chauhan. It's only afterwards you realise how lucky you were.

Someone looking over you for sure,' she enthused, trying her best to win Ruth round, to get her on board

'You don't think you're being a bit melodramatic, over the top?' It was as if Julie hadn't heard her. She was on a roll as she looked set to continue to galvanise support for what she was certain needed to be done.

'As well as improving the perimeter security around the church we need to do a full review of vicarage security and make sure you and your family are always out of harm's way. To my knowledge we in the church have never done this before. You know the other faiths, the synagogues and the mosques, they do this routinely. They are aware of the risks today. I think we need to look at safety, carry out a risk assessment and come up with a plan, like they do and well, like we've recently been doing with safeguarding. In fact I don't see there's much difference there. If you, if we, are under attack, as we are, then we need to seriously start thinking about the safeguarding of the Christian community in this place. We're all vulnerable people now!'

'I understand where you're coming from but this has been an unusual weekend. It's no good making a knee-jerk response to something that has now been dealt with. Tony Morris is in police custody. The vehicle fire in Henley Road has been extinguished. It's over with – end of. I'll get the front door fixed tomorrow or the day after. The temporary boarding will keep us safe until then, you'll see.' But Julie wasn't listening, she had something more to say and was trying to butt in. Ruth was beginning to feel battered. Julie was like a dog with a bone, prepared to take everyone on, obsessed by an idea and determinedly hanging on to what she saw as a good thing.

'My husband Roy's a freemason and he says the Edmonton Lodge would be very happy, under the circumstances, to offer the necessary funds to do the security work. What do you say to that?' she said, beaming in triumph, as if she had played her trump card, sealing a winning hand.

Ruth's heart sank. She knew the offence she would cause if she refused this offer but also knew that it was an offer with strings attached. Right now, she really couldn't contemplate having to deal with Julie, her husband Roy and the local Freemasons' Lodge. She felt under attack. She needed some respite.

'I really am most grateful for the concern, all the thought you've put into this and the generous response. What can I say?' Indeed what could she say?

Then in a moment of inspiration she saw a path to get herself off the hook and see Julie on her way.

'Tell you what, I'm due to speak to Archdeacon Stephen tomorrow morning and I'll tell him of your proposal, if that's all right by you, and see what he has to say. It is, after all, the kind of thing that falls under his jurisdiction too – faculties, clergy buildings, that kind of thing. It isn't something we could attempt without higher authority if you know what I mean.'

'Yes... yes, so this will get picked up at a higher level. And, Stephen is chaplain to the Lodge. I can see where you're taking this. I won't detain you any longer this evening, I'll leave you to get your supper. Make sure you put the chain on the front door tonight won't you.'

Julie seemed satisfied with Ruth's response and got up to leave. Ruth breathed an audible sigh of relief which thankfully Julie didn't hear.

Ruth accompanied her visitor to the front door and as Julie stepped outside. Ruth spotted her husband Roy parked right outside waiting to pick her up in their silver grey Ford hatchback. He wasn't going to risk his Julie walking the few hundred yards home, now was he? Ruth could see they not only wholly supported the idea of walling the church but lived a lifestyle fully believing the streets were too unsafe to walk in.

After watching the two drive off engaged in earnest conversation she closed the front door, pausing only to look at the flimsy door chain. The idea of a steel sheet reminded her of a film on TV she once saw where some people in the United States had built inner safe rooms in their homes in case an armed intruder got inside. A secure bolt hole those in the house could escape to. Maybe, she wondered, Julie will have added a safe room to her plans by the time it came to the PCC meeting.

Until this weekend she'd never bothered with the door chain, but tonight she once again put it in place, even gave it a tug to be sure, before going to rejoin Phil in the kitchen. Walls, walls, she thought, is that what we've come to, building barriers against violent outsiders? Once upon a time, didn't Christians celebrate when in Jericho, walls came tumbling down? Wasn't she following a Prince of Peace who didn't place any priority on protecting himself? What's the answer here?

Sitting down at the kitchen table with Phil serving up she couldn't help herself and asked him, 'Phil, are we under attack?'

He simply shook his head from side to side.

'And how would we defend our family if you thought we were?'

'In the end walls are never the solution,' he said.

'But what would we do?' she repeated.

'We'd need to think of something, like we always do.'

With that brief calm spoken response Ruth knew in her heart he was right and why she loved him. It was now late on Sunday evening and time to eat. She couldn't quite believe it was only yesterday afternoon when she'd locked up the church after the wedding that her life had started spinning so out of control.

11

Ruth couldn't sleep and had to get up for a glass of water. It was becoming a pattern and she wondered whether she ought to book a doctor's appointment soon.

She picked up her mobile, opened her diary page, typed in '*make Dr appt*' then, having second thoughts she changed her mind and deleted it, dismissing the idea as it would be perceived as a sign of weakness. With the archdeacon breathing down her neck any sign of physical weakness would call her well-being and competence further into question; it was simply not the best move to make right now. It would have to wait.

As she lay on her bed tossing and turning, she decided self help was best. She'd cut her caffeine input to nil after lunchtimes instead and try and begin to cut back on calories to lose some weight.

She must have drifted off, but by 6am, she was sitting silently and still in her study, the rest of the house quiet, like everyone else on a Bank Holiday Monday, sleeping in.

She gazed out of the window over her desk, looking across to the church in a mood of reflective, if not anxious contemplation. The church was locked up except for services. She wanted it open but the PCC wouldn't hear of it. Too risky, they said, and voted her down. When they come to talk about Julie's wall, they might well go for it, she thought. She really didn't know how she was going to deal with the matter when it came up. A few minutes later and she'd decide she'd enlist Phil's help. He had a gift for marshalling the facts and she knew he'd help her. It was a conversation not to be left too long and she wrote herself a 'to do' note placing it centrally on her desk. With that, the matter was parked up, for now.

She gazed out of her window. Bank holiday Mondays in London always started like this, with the world lying in and the roads unnaturally empty of traffic. For the first time in weeks she saw rain was beginning to fall, darkening the surfaces it touched, a steady, soaking rain. Above, solid-grey, leaden skies had replaced the hottest summer she could recall and this rain looked set in. Today people would definitely stay in bed and then complain amongst themselves about the lousy bank holiday weather.

She went to the kitchen, made herself a coffee and clutching it in both hands, as she always did, returned to her desk. Her eyes were drawn to the low brick wall, the old railings above it and the open gate. She tried to imagine the kind of replacement wall Julie had in mind.

A whole theology rushed in to endorse that approach – the embattled faithful remnant set in a hostile world full of persecution. The church as a rock, an anchor, a bastion set against the gathered forces of evil outside. The powers that be – engaged in a spiritual battle in high places, their bigger conflict spilling over into Holy Trinity parish, people even dying gloriously as martyrs. The images didn't sit right and Ruth knew she had to come up with a convincing alternative. As Phil had rightly identified, walls were not her way, never the solution.

In her mind's eye she tried to visualise Julie's security measures once in place. In her imagination she saw a new concrete wall, firm and tall, over two metres high, possibly with dark anti-vandal paint or rolling spikes on top. The present free-swinging, open gate replaced by a new, double height, burnished metal gate with a code box on the wall to permit entry only to those vetted and approved by the relevant church sub-committee. No, definitely no!

Once built, she even imagined a yellow vested security person, with a deputy in the wings, standing there to screen and reassure everyone still coming to Sunday services. They'd have to be volunteers as no one on the Council would vote to pay someone. Then she realised that no one, once inside the wall, would be able to see out to the street and no one outside would be able to see what was happening inside. The proposal created two worlds, ours and the other's. It definitely wasn't a good idea she told herself for a third time. Then she hesitated, she'd seen just what she feared somewhere before, already in place. It came back to her. It was at the synagogue she had visited. Security there was such it had shocked her.

The project was doom laden, it was a recipe for building fear and reinforcing unhelpful myths. Safeguarding her and the congregation in this way came at too high a price. But how was she to tell Julie? A sinking dread overcame her as she realised she'd agreed to speak to Archdeacon Stephen about it. She knew he was already busy getting churches to address inadequate safety matters and she didn't envisage a helpful response to her call. First though there was, notwithstanding it being Bank Holiday Monday, the routine of daily Morning Prayer in Church to attend to.

She had always seen it as a matter of principle that even if she were the only one present, the church would be open every morning at 8.15am and prayers would be offered for the parish in the side chapel promptly at 8.30am.

The familiar routine of getting herself ready kicked in and coffee now finished, she cheerfully picked up her floral brolly and headed off on the short walk across to church. Indeed, she thought, there would be no shortage of things to pray for following all the events of the weekend. The changed weather snatched at her brolly, cool rain hitting her lower body despite her efforts to prevent it. The weather was so different today, there was something shocking about it. It was with some relief she made it into the sanctuary of the church.

Once in her prayer stall and about to start the prayers, which she always read out loud, she held her breath as, not a little alarmed, she heard the unmistakable sound of the church door click open. Footsteps slowly approached and she was both surprised and relieved to see the familiar person of Gladstone Harris, rain-soaked, but coming to join her. He smiled as he approached. Gladstone was a Sunday at 8am only person and to her knowledge had rarely if ever been to Morning Prayer, so his appearance today was something of a surprise.

'Hope you don't mind. I don't usually make this service, but after yesterday, I thought you could do with a little support,' he offered, clearing his throat as he explained his presence.

'Delighted to see you Gladstone, I was about to start. Would you be happy to do the readings when we get to them?' Gladstone nodded and she passed him the Bible, ribbon marker in place, a separate typed note giving the passages of scripture, Old and New Testament, that were set for the day.

"O Lord, open our lips," began Ruth, immediately feeling the familiar rhythm soothing and carrying her, lifting her mood.

She'd always found prayers at the start of each day such a solid framework upon which to build everything else.

The service was less than thirty minutes long and things were well under way when she read:

"As we rejoice in the gift of this new day, so may the light of your presence, O God, set our hearts on fire..."

Upon saying, she caught herself choking on her own words as images of Raj's van as a burnt out charnal house flashed before her eyes. As she spoke she realised the words *"set our hearts on fire"* had recalled images she'd rather have forgotten – the two distorted, burned bodies lying in the back of his van.

She paused as for the first time she asked herself, who were they? It concerned her that she hadn't thought about them since that moment. Two people had died, their bodies burned black, they must have been known to someone surely? They were someone's dear ones.

Swift as she could, she tried to regain her composure and continued with the words of the short prayer, ending:

"...with love for you; now and for ever. Amen."

After a slight pause she lifted her head to see Gladstone looking at her quizzically, his level gaze straight in her eye. He'd picked up on her falter and she knew it.

'Sorry Gladstone,' she said, before returning to the text.

Having collected herself, the service now over, she thanked Gladstone for coming and they exchanged further pleasantries before he set off with a final, 'I'm off to my daughter's in Palmers Green today.'

As he strode purposefully out of the church he pulled his coat collar up and bent his shoulder to the wind to fend off the near horizontal rain as he determinedly headed out of the door.

Making her own way home, Ruth found her brolly immediately flew inside out. It was as if the very elements of wind and rain were conspiring against her. As Ruth made for home, once again she found herself looking around, sensing dangers in every shadow, behind every corner, as she did so.

Having made it safely back to the vicarage, she could hear sounds of life coming from upstairs as Phil was trying to get unwilling children to shower, dress and come down for breakfast.

'I'm back,' she called upstairs, shaking off raindrops as she pulled her brolly back into shape. She went into the kitchen to begin setting the breakfast table in readiness realising it was the first time she had done something for her family for days. Successive waves of guilt and helplessness washed over her as she went through the motions.

Job done she dropped herself in her usual chair. She didn't have to wait long, hearing the children descend quickly and heavily down the stairs as if they were in a race. Phil followed clutching armfuls of washing to go into the machine.

Ruth could hear her phone in the study ringing and a click as it automatically switched over to the answerphone. Whoever it was could wait. Another coffee, then lively banter over who got the remaining much favoured Choco-Crispy cereal and who got the Wheat Bites which no one wanted, then all went quiet.

'Mummy, what time are we going to Brent Cross?' asked Olivia. 'Can Fleur come too? Paul doesn't want to go, do you Paul? Can he stay at Garfield's house? Mum, Mum…' she persisted, tugging at Ruth's arm.

'I think we'll leave about 12 and we'll get something at MacDonald's for lunch. I've got to see to my car, call someone about fixing the front door, make one or two calls first. How about it you two?'

'I'm not coming,' said Paul quietly.

'Why not, Paul?' asked Phil.

'It's boring, Dad. I want to play games.'

'Look you can bring your games with you. You like MacDonald's and you like to see Aunt Sue and Uncle Jim. Besides they're expecting to see you. Sorry, you don't have any choice. I've told them we're all coming. You have to come. We can't leave you here alone… end of…' said Phil in exasperation.

Paul looked darkly under his eyebrows at his Dad.

'Look, we'll have some fun. Maybe we'll get you both things ready for the start of the new term. You've both grown taller and you need new jackets, especially if it's going to rain like it is right now,' said Ruth trying, but failing to lighten the mood. 'And why don't you arrange to see Fleur this morning before we go, Olivia? It won't be possible to take her with us.' She watched Olivia's face drop. She was getting very moody these days, Ruth thought.

Ruth started looking anxiously at her watch conscious the time was marching on. Phil saw it and they exchanged looks.

'Ruth, go and do what you have to do and give me a shout when you're finished,' he said, trying to smooth things, knowing what had to be done.

She nodded appreciatively, got up from the table and took the few paces into her study taking a second cup of coffee with her. The last of the day she told herself, remembering her health resolution of earlier.

Back in her base station as she saw it, she first listened to the recorded phone message. Archdeacon Stephen had tried to reach her, wanting her to return his call as soon as she was free to do so. He'd left his mobile number. It was then she remembered he was off to Walsingham later.

Taking a deep breath, Ruth punched in the numbers and made the call.

'Father Stephen here, Archdeacon of Hampstead. How can I help?'

'Ruth Churchill, Stephen.'

'Ah! Excellent! I was wanting to have a quick word, if I may, before I drive off to Walsingham. A number of things on the horizon. First of all, how are you my dear?' he asked, his voice dropping as if they're in the hushed space of the confessional.

'Fine, yes, fine,' she said hesitatingly, defensively.

'Not what I've heard Ruthie,' he said with a touch of triumph, I've got you there, in his voice. 'Unintentionally dropped a section out of the liturgy yesterday morning didn't we? A bit off message at the main service too perhaps?' he added knowingly.

Ruth fell silent. What had he heard? How could she answer the charge?

'No worries. Don't let me add to the pressures you're under. I know you had that dreadful murder and then that lady to sort out with food, didn't you? On the go, lots of pressure all round. I understand... I really do... Did one of your parishioners, a man who goes by the wonderful name of Gladstone come along to Morning Prayer this morning?'

'Why, yes,' she said, rather surprised at this sudden change in conversational direction, before feeling like a soufflé that failed to rise as the truth dawned – it was, she knew in that moment the Archdeacon who'd put Gladstone up to being there.

'And how did Morning Prayer go? Any bits left out?'

Ruth felt there was cruelty in this.

'Fine, yes, absolutely fine... nothing left out' she stuttered, remembering her hiccup when the word '*fire*' had appeared in the prayers. But she wasn't going to tell him any more than necessary, not give him the satisfaction of finding further fault and then she clamped up.

'Goody, goody. But let's talk about how we make you feel secure, safe in the world. Just remember it's my job to look after you and ensure your working environment is every bit as safe and secure as it can be.'

'Ah, yes, that's something I wanted to ask you about, Stephen, if I may?'

'I'm all ears, Ruthie.'

'I had a visit yesterday evening from one of our most active church members who wished me to consider, after the events of the weekend, replacing the low wall and railings at the west end of the church with something rather more secure. She included a higher wall and a set of new security gates in her proposal and I agreed to talk the matter over with you.'

'I need to tell you I took a phone call from Julie myself yesterday afternoon. Her words were music to my ears. If only every church had a Julie! It would make my job so much easier.'

'Indeed,' said Ruth.

'I spend all my time trying to get clergy to consider basic personal safeguarding and security, but it falls on deaf ears, it really does. The times they are a changing and urban, even suburban parishes, are no longer the safe places to live and minister in they were in the past. I'd like you to seriously consider implementing Julie's proposal.'

'Really?'

'Why of course! Take it to your next Church Council. Tell them you have financial backing – well that's what Roy tells me. It's so generous of the Lodge. You are so fortunate to have such support, Ruthie. Leave the administrative hurdles of faculty permissions and committee approvals to me. Just let me have your request with plans and estimates asap. You can do that can't you? Not too much on top of everything else is it? I'm looking for some reassurance here, Ruthie.'

'No, I'm sure it won't be a problem,' she heard herself saying, without believing her own words.

'And don't forget the extra helper?'

'Helper?'

'The extra pair of hands, the ordinand you're going to chase up. Don't tell me you've forgotten that too? Now come on Ruthie, or I'll start thinking you're losing it. Bye-ee! Must dash.'

With that he'd gone. Ruth grabbed a pen and left another note on her desk covering the main points of the call. Now she needed to get a man in to repair the glazing to the front door. Several attempted calls later and she began to realise that she was going to get nowhere on a bank holiday Monday and gave up. She had half thought at the outset it would probably have to wait until Tuesday before she started making her calls and putting the receiver down in its cradle, the family waiting, she regretted wasting her time.

As she got up, her phone rang and her heart sank as she imagined it was Stephen with yet another discovered criticism or new bad idea, but it turned out to be a distressed Darshana.

'Ruth, I need to see you. I don't know who else to talk to. Can you come, please, please?'

'I'm tied up until this evening. Is 7pm OK? Will you be alright until then?'

'Yes, I'll see you then. Something strange is happening.' With that Darshana had gone.

Ruth remembered Raj's van, then her car, a few minutes walk away in Henley Road. She needed to arrange to retrieve it if she could. A look out through the window at the heavy rain did not endear the task to her and she feared she might end up having a fruitless journey only to walk there and back getting soaked in the process. Then on impulse she thought she'd look on social media to see if the events of the weekend had had any coverage. It might at the very least give her some clue as to those who had died and the latest traffic flow arrangements in Henley Road.

On opening the Edmonton Community Facebook page she was shocked at what she found. Dozens of comments had been posted lamenting the road closure and ongoing inconvenience it was causing. She was surprised that there was no mention of the bodies in Raj's van, or indeed that it was Raj's van. A photograph had been posted only an hour earlier showing a lot of police activity, people wondering what was so serious as to be given so much attention when bigger issues like knives, guns and drugs ought to command limited police time and resources.

Ruth pondered what she saw. How was it there was no mention of the burnt bodies in the van? Was she mistaken? Was she wrong to think it was Raj's van? She put it down to the nature of local Facebook, truth being the first casualty in any coverage. She tried to see if any of the major news feeds were covering local events but there was nothing. If she went to collect her car she might learn more. It was so very strange, as if something were being deliberately hidden. What could it mean?

Part of her thought she might enjoy the isolation and escape that came with walking in the rain, so she grabbed her dog collar, put on her anorak and picked up her wet brolly. She told Phil, still busy in the kitchen, she was off to try and get her car and wouldn't be long and set off at as brisk a pace she could manage.

Even as she turned into Henley Road with its policeman standing at the end she could see things had escalated from where she'd left them yesterday. Well before she got anywhere near her car she could see the street was obviously still in lockdown.

She got polite nods from policemen as she continued to get nearer. The familiar person of PC Alice Such was spotted, standing on duty outside Angela Morris' front door. Taking deliberate confident strides in her direction, Ruth called her name and bemused police let her pass unhindered thinking she had cause to be there. Alice smiled in recognition.

'I've come for my car,' she explained.

'Afraid nothing can be moved from this end of the street whilst forensics are here. And I can't tell you how long they'll be.'

'So I wasn't mistaken when I saw bodies in the back of Raj's van,' Ruth said quietly.

'No comment, ma'am,' Alice replied, Ruth immediately understanding she was under orders.

'Oh, I see. But tell me, yesterday I was told I would need to give a statement, yet no one has been in touch with me yet. Can you give me any idea when someone will be talking to me?'

'It's not just being handled by local police, so I'm afraid I can't say. But I'm sure someone will want to speak to you soon.'

'Not local police you say, then who?'

'Counter Terrorism.'

12

Ruth arrived back at the vicarage wet, frustrated at not getting her car and puzzled at what the police were investigating. Not knowing what exactly was going on in her parish took some getting used to of itself. There was clearly a bigger picture to consider than a youth with a knife, a corner shop robbery gone wrong, the murder of Indian shopkeeper Raj, the burning of his van and the mystery around two burned bodies inside. What could it all mean, she wondered, why the hush-hush secrecy?

Usually police silence meant one of two things. Either there were more crimes or criminals the police wanted to get to grips with and to do so without unduly alerting their targets they were coming for them and, or, there were wider criminal circles involved than these local events in the London backwater of Edmonton. No doubt urgent enquiries elsewhere were being expedited before the criminal world caught up with what the police knew.

Moving into the kitchen, she explained to Phil what had happened, shedding her wet anorak and putting it in the drying cupboard above the central heating boiler as she did so. She decided to do nothing about the trail of wet she'd left across the kitchen floor.

'All very strange,' admitted Phil, 'the more so as I haven't seen or heard anything much on the news beyond the knife attack at Raj's shop. As with all these things, I expect more will come to light soon. Did you manage to get someone to come to see to the front door?'

'No joy there either, everyone's off work today. I'll try and get on to someone first thing tomorrow. We'll have to go in your car to Brent Cross. I'll call the kids. Leave it any later and the traffic will make it tedious. Did you ring Jim and Sue?'

'Yep, they'll expect to see us as and when. They said the weather forecast's so bad they'd planned to stay in anyhow.'

Ten minutes later they were all in Phil's Citroen Picasso creeping forward in the traffic toward Palmers Green on the North Circular Road. By now everyone had got up, taken one look at the weather and decided Brent Cross was also their destination of choice! However, once the single lane traffic bottleneck was behind them, they made good progress all the way to Brent Cross.

Brent Cross Shopping Centre lay on the north side of the North Circular Road, a 1970s concrete icon to consumerism, the big brands all staking their claims to the best retail positions. In recent years expansion plans had breathed new life into what was becoming tired and today the crowds were flocking there. The journey time began to increase the nearer they got to finding somewhere to park and as they queued to find a space they were all wondering if this had been such good idea.

'It isn't usually like this,' said Ruth, venting her frustration.

'It's a bank holiday and there's nothing else to do when it's raining. The world and his dog are here,' said Phil glancing this way and that to locate somewhere to park. He got lucky after several minutes when an elderly man in an old BMW suddenly pulled out as if he had had enough and Phil darted in, the covetous eyes of other waiting drivers looking on resentfully.

Once they were all out of the car and heading for cover, it was then Ruth noticed it wasn't just busy because of the extra bank holiday shoppers. There was some kind of demonstration at the entrance they were heading for and significant numbers of security personnel and police were milling around.

'Something's up Phil, keep close to us Olivia and Paul. I mean it,' she said anxiously, as the two looked non-plussed at her motherly concern.

They weren't to get much closer. They could see the entrance just a short distance ahead, but by then banners were raised and more people could be seen sitting on the ground blocking the entrance to everyone trying to get inside.

'It's Extinction Rebellion,' said Phil, as if the phrase explained things, 'it'll be a peaceful demo against climate change. Let's see if we can find another way in. Over there,' he instructed, pointing an arm to his right.

'Mum, look, those people have glued themselves to the doors. No-one can get in or out.' Olivia began to laugh, 'That's so cool. We had some girls in our school take time off last term to save the planet. They went down to Parliament and stopped the traffic. Can we go and see?'

Ruth was feeling anxious. She didn't want to go and see. The security men didn't look pleased and the police were busy talking into radios, no doubt calling to get extra help. There was a definite tension in the air and it was making her feel anxious. She perspired when anxious and she feared her heart might start palpitating. Now Phil too was looking concerned. Olivia was not going to be allowed nearer, no way!

'There's an issue. That policeman on his radio is telling someone they can't get people in or out of the centre because protesters have glued themselves across all the entrances and exits, not just this one. They are worried there is a serious safety issue. I'm not sure we should hang around. Oh no, look, the car park exits are now blocked by protesters. This is getting serious,' said Phil.

'Dad, is that lady hurting?' asked Paul, looking across and pointing out a protester being pulled by a burly security man. Phil could see that a woman who had glued her hands across two doors was in much pain, but the man wasn't showing any sympathy.

'Oi, you,' yelled Phil, 'yes you, lay off the heavy stuff, you're hurting her. Can't you see she can't move?' he yelled. Ruth was alarmed and tried to restrain his natural chivalry by pulling him back.

The security man, barely raised an eye in Phil's direction and continued to tug at the young woman's arm. There was a shuffling sound of shoes on ground and a groan as Phil was pushed hard from behind by two policeman in riot gear who were clearing themselves a path to make their way hurriedly forward to the trouble spot.

'You OK, Phil?' asked Ruth, her voice trembling.

'Daddy, Daddy,' yelled Olivia and Paul simultaneously.

'Yes, fine,' he said, brushing himself down, 'but I think we should try to move back with the kids, maybe wait in the car until all this is over,' he said with a surprising calmness.

'This is exciting Mum, can't we watch,' asked Olivia. 'The climate matters more than anything, can't we join in?'

'Olivia, no! There are other ways of protesting, your Dad's right, we should get back to the car.'

'Oh, Mum...' was all she could say as Ruth firmly grabbed her hand.

The numbers in the crowd around them were continuing to build and alarmingly they found themselves unable to move forward or backward. It was more like being in the jostling crowds at a football match than going shopping, but this was no friendly football crowd, people were getting very edgy, still more policeman in riot gear were appearing by the minute. They were pressing through the trapped shoppers, pushing them aside as they made their way, heading directly for the protesters.

More cries filled the air. The police began working with the security men to aggressively remove protesters, battering and dragging them none too carefully along the ground to a row of white police vans waiting to receive them, now parked along the inside lane of the North Circular Road.

A loud hailer crackled and boomed. 'This is Deputy Police Commissioner Stuart Thackeray speaking. All protesters are to remove themselves from this private site forthwith or face arrest. The safety of shoppers inside and outside this Centre will not be compromised. Please keep well clear of the entrances and exits as officers go about their duties.'

'Come on Phil, Olivia, Paul, hold hands and don't let go. Let's try and get further back from here,' urged Ruth.

It was impossible to move. As more police and people pressed into the ever more constricted space it was all they could do to protect the two children in the crush and stay upright. Ruth began to think of Hillsborough but dared not voice her fears. She looked across at Phil who was, despite what he'd said, nursing an injury, rubbing his painful shoulder as he looked this way and that. The noises in the air changed from the chatty buzz of shopper conversation to yells and shouts punctuated by screams as people became ever more aggressive, unpredictable and panicky in the developing melee.

Because of the pressing crowd Ruth couldn't any longer see what was going on which made her feel the more trapped. Phil, being taller, could better observe what was happening up ahead where most of the noise was coming from.

'What can you see, Phil?' cried Ruth.

'They're pulling the people who've glued themselves to the doors away. It's horrible... it's tearing their skin off, there's blood all over. Why? Why? I'm so angry... They don't do this normally, they use solvents. The police normally go in peacefully and accept Extinction Rebellion is non-violent. So why are they doing this today?'

'Because they've trapped people inside maybe?' voiced Ruth, unable to think of any better reason.

Olivia's mood had changed and she began to cry. Paul was silent and staring. Together the four formed an inward facing huddle, like wagons in an old western, a defensive circle against the surrounding hostile forces. The screams and shoves seemed to go on for ever, but after nearly an hour a sudden calm descended, the noise died apart from the occasional sobs, the policemen thinned out, the security men were nowhere to be seen and the last of the handcuffed protesters were en route to being placed in a white police van. Then it was over and an uneasy quiet descended, like a lull on a battlefield after the fighting and it was time to search the bodies.

Ruth and Phil, protective arms over their now very distressed and crying children made their way back to the sanctuary of their car and locked themselves inside. The car served as a familiar safe cocoon and the crying subsided, though no one said anything for several minutes as each tried to regain composure.

'Ruth, would you mind driving?' asked Phil.

'OK, I feel up to it, what's up?'

'It's my shoulder, the policeman struck me from behind as he came through and it hurts, nothing broken I don't think, bruised, but I'd be happier if you drove. Forget the shopping trip idea. Let's get to Jim and Sue's. It'll be just what we all need. Come on kids, it's all over, we're safe, enough excitement for one day, eh? Any Paracetamol in your bag, Ruth?'

Once under way, Ruth coaxed the car through the queues of exiting traffic and finally they re-entered the North Circular Road, this time heading east. Ominously, a line of ambulances, blue lights flashing and with sirens wailing were heading in the direction they had just come from, pulling up by the rows of white police vans. Then they were moving at a reasonable speed again, yard by yard, block by block, away from all the trouble. In a matter of minutes north London looked its usual self, lots of traffic, small groups of relaxed pedestrians under umbrellas walking purposefully in the rain.

Phil leant forward and put on the radio, tuning into a local station to hear live reports coming in from Brent Cross. It sounded like they had got off lightly as there had been many casualties amongst panicking shoppers. It was being described as the day when Extinction Rebellion got it all wrong! Out of sight from the Churchills, some shoppers, fearing they were trapped inside had formed crowds pressing against locked doors and there had been many crush injuries as a result.

In what was being called a misguided protest when police had used uncharacteristic brutality, many had suffered serious hand, arm and leg injuries as glued skin had remained stuck fast to objects when force had been used to gain open access. The argument the mayor of London used was that there had been an urgent health and safety issue and he fully supported the judgement of his Commissioner of Police to act with resolution to avoid further injuries. In conclusion the news reporter commented that the incident now looked as if it were over and appealed for calm as the remaining shoppers left Brent Cross. The Centre would remain closed for the rest of the day.

As she drove, Ruth was conscious of an uncontrollable tremor in her stomach and thirst in her mouth. They were nearly at Muswell Hill and she had to concentrate hard to maintain control of herself and the car. They finally pulled up and made their way the short distance to the front door and safety inside.

Ruth was white, in shock and feeling lightheaded; Phil, not much better, was asking Sue for more painkillers. The incident behind them, the children seemed to be none the worse and had gone into the kitchen to find drinks and snacks, following a familiar routine.

Then, with the children settled in front of the TV in the front room watching a film, Jim, Sue, Phil and Ruth stood in a huddle in the kitchen to talk through what the Churchills had just been through.

'It had to go wrong sometime,' said Jim, 'non-violent protests eventually become violent ones whether the protesters are peaceful or not,' he said in resignation.

'You should have seen the cruelty of the authorities in ripping glued protesters from doors,' said Phil, 'And there was no need for the police to thump me in the back the way they did.'

'But you did yell at that security man to stop hurting that young woman,' added Ruth.

'Didn't do any good,' said Phil despondently.

'And as for Olivia, I thought she wanted to join them. What are they learning in school today?' asked Ruth deliberately, both Jim and Sue being teachers.

'Kids are pretty aware of climate issues, more than most adults, I'm ashamed to say...' replied Jim.

'But the crowds were no better. It's as if everyone is against everyone else these days. People are so... bitter, unhappy, feeling angry and helpless all at once, looking for someone else to blame for how they are feeling,' said Ruth. 'Do you mind if I grab that stool, I feel a bit light headed.'

Ruth sat herself down and was handed a mug of tea by Sue, followed up by a chocolate biscuit. 'It'll do you good,' she said.

'You sure you're alright, Ruth?' asked Sue. 'I don't think I've seen you looking so peaky for ages.'

'Well to tell you the truth, it has been an awful weekend…' and she went through the events one by one, realising as she spoke how utterly exhausted just reliving those moments was making her feel.

Jim and Phil wandered off into the hallway their heads in quiet but deep conversation leaving Sue and Ruth in the kitchen. It was an accustomed routine. Sue had every bit the look of an over-concerned sister as she realised what a torrid time Ruth had been having. She recast recent events in the wider context of the past year whereby Ruth had been made the scapegoat for the Ali Muhammed affair and consequently been placed under the close scrutiny of that obnoxious Archdeacon Stephen Nicholls.

'How do you tolerate that patronising git?' asked Sue, not being one to hold a lot of sympathy for the Church hierarchy. 'He came to my school once and I could have punched him. He just loves to be the centre of attention, dressing up in fine high church clothes and wanting everyone to bow down to him. He just wound up the class and bounded out. They were as high as kites when he left, leaving me to fetch them down from the ceiling and calm them down again.'

'That's pushing it a bit far,' said Ruth, but laughed all the same.

'It's good to hear you laugh Ruth, I'm so worried it has all got too much. Do you think you'll continue at Holy Trinity. Can you have a break? Move to somewhere less demanding?'

'People, yes including Stephen Nicholls have been pestering me about taking a sabbatical, but the time's not right and I won't be levered out, which is what it feels like.'

'You'll need to do something. Can't you get extra help from somewhere?'

'Maybe, there's talk of an ordinand to help, we'll see. Tell me, I've been meaning to ask. How's your Adam doing? We're both not very good at keeping in touch with each other.'

'He's still in Dubai since his escape from Oman, churning out the news articles. Jim's opened a file on his laptop and keeps copies of them all. He's become quite the foreign correspondent and he's got a permanent position now with Central News Publishing International – a mouthful isn't it? CNPI he calls them. His reports from Oman last year gave him a flying start into his career. He was in the right place at the right time, he says. I say he was so lucky to have got out of there alive!'

'And does he plan staying on in Dubai?'

'Yes, it's safe, but he travels a fair bit around the Middle East. We worry when we hear where he gets to, but he's a grown man and responsible for himself. You never stop being a parent though.'

'And Raqiyah? How's she?'

'They share Adam's flat in Dubai. They kind of make out they're married and it saves a lot of hassles there. She's doing a Masters in Diplomacy and International Affairs at Zayed University. In the circumstances we're helping her with her fees.'

'Does she hear from her family in Oman? Can she visit them?'

'That's difficult. I'm sure you understand why… Look they are both visiting for a long weekend soon. We'll have to get you over and you can ask them all your questions yourself.'

'We'd like that, let me know when, I'm sure we'll fit it in.'

'Look, give me a hand with getting some late lunch together, I'm sure, despite the snacks, your two will be hungry!'

The two began pulling things out of the fridge and cupboards, lining up six plates and putting an array of items on the kitchen worktop so that people could help themselves.

'Grub up,' yelled Sue, the call being responded to quickly as everyone returned to the kitchen and dived in.

Sue went back to the fridge and pulled out a bottle of New Zealand Sauvignon Blanc. 'Guess we all need a drink,' she added smiling.

Ruth reached for four wine glasses.

Late afternoon and Ruth was beginning to worry that there were things back in Edmonton that she need to get back to. She remembered Darshana's phone call. She also wondered whether the police had been trying to contact her for a statement only to find her away from home.

An hour later, a final round of sobering, strong, Ethiopian filter coffee consumed, they said their good byes and headed for home.

Ruth couldn't help it, but with each passing mile in the short distance from Muswell Hill to Edmonton she felt her mood sink and an atmosphere of pervading gloom fill the car. Maybe the others were thinking of what faced them. Maybe Phil was mindful he was returning to his accountancy work first thing in the morning. The children's new school term was about to commence. She herself remembered the long list of unattended and unopened emails still awaiting her attention. Her mood sank further.

'Penny for your thoughts,' asked Phil as they turned the final corner, the vicarage coming into sight.

'Just thinking,' she said vaguely as the Citroen pulled to a halt, pondering where to begin, gazing at the damaged front door awaiting repair.

No sooner had they pushed the front door shut behind them than the doorbell rang and Ruth went to answer it as everyone else disappeared upstairs. Two steps towards her study had been as far she got. She felt her own faltering gathering of thoughts in a futile attempt to seize the initiative just a minute ago slip away from her as she turned with trepidation to see who was there. Her energy levels were so low she didn't know how she would respond. She dug deep to find her smiley face. Who was it this time?

13

A smartly dressed female with a familiar, smiling face, which Ruth couldn't for a second place, though she knew she should, was standing there, ready to announce her presence.

'PC April Cooper, come to see you,' she said.

'Of course! It was the lack of police uniform, it threw me for an instant. And how are you? Still following in your Dad's footsteps? I thought you'd moved to the West Country, Exeter wasn't it?'

'My Dad, yes, trying to. I was in Exeter and the South West of England, but now I'm back in north London where my roots are. We never seem to stay in one place very long. I'm still with the police, but they've moved me from Prevent and attached me to Counter Terrorism.'

Ruth quickly began to join the dots. Counter Terrorism were handling the local incident and she surmised April had come round to interview her.

'Ah, yes... Are you working on the, err... local incident?' asked Ruth.

'Spot on. And that's why I popped round. Do you think I might come inside and grab a few minutes of your time?' she asked, pulling a notebook from her jacket pocket. There was no mistaking her role now, thought Ruth.

They walked through to the lounge and April closed the door on them.

'We need to treat what we are talking about with a degree of sensitivity,' she began.

'OK,' said Ruth wondering where the conversation was going.

'There would be no point in letting local imagination get hold of what has happened. Think of the damage that might be done when local fears get stirred.'

Ruth was still puzzled where this was leading, but April was soon to get to the point.

'Let's begin with what happened in the churchyard on Saturday, shall we. Talk me through what took place outside your church after your wedding had finished.'

Ruth described Tony Morris's actions, his subsequent threats at the vicarage front door and the sequence of events later in the evening when he'd called back, which finally led to the front door being damaged and his eventual arrest late at night after his futile search for his knife.

April listened and made one or two scribbles. She seemed quite satisfied by all she heard, had no follow up questions and then went straight on to ask about the request the police had made that she go and visit Tony Morris's mother, Angela Morris.

'How did the police ask you to visit Angela Morris and why?' she asked.

It seemed a strange question to ask, phrased like that and Ruth took her time to ponder upon it. Surely April already knew from her colleagues why she'd gone round, what was

April looking for in getting Ruth to repeat what had happened? Was the police account suspect or needing to be verified, corroborated for some reason? Why did she want to hear all this background detail unless something very serious lay behind all this? She took a deep breath. She had to tell her how it was.

'Two police officers, Alice Such and Adam Dallow, both from Edmonton, saw me here after Morning Service yesterday, around midday, I suppose. They described their earlier visit to see Angela Morris as revealing someone in a rather unusual situation and in need of my help. So, after lunch, following their request, I walked round there, to Henley Road and I found it to be just such a situation as they had described. Angela really is a very strange lady... She appears to be more or less bed-bound upstairs and Tony her son, who is being held in police custody, was her main, indeed as far as I can tell, her only carer. So we, myself and a parishioner worked together to get her some essential grocery supplies and I took them round and gave them to Angela yesterday evening.'

'Yes, and...'

'On my second visit, to take her her things, I went by car... bit of a mistake that... that's when the van fire on the road directly outside her house took place. I could smell the smoke, then I heard noises outside and went downstairs to see what was happening. My Fiat Punto was parked right next to the burning van and the paintwork got blistered. I tried to get it back earlier to day but that end of the road is as closed up as Fort Knox. What I did learn was my car wasn't to be moved just yet, more forensics I suppose. Do you know when I can retrieve it?'

'If you leave me the car keys I'll see an officer brings it round later this evening. You told an officer you thought you knew whose van it was.'

Ruth unclipped her car key and passed it over to April. 'Yes, I'm certain, I know it was Raj Chauhan's van.'

'Let's go over the van fire again, if we may. Where were you when you first became aware of the fire?'

'I was upstairs with Angela trying to sort out some future care for her... it's going to be difficult. She can't possibly manage on her own and she's got no one I've yet managed to find who can help her.'

'Describe for me, if you will, how you became aware of the fire. I'm told she always has her curtains drawn.'

'As I said, I think it was a combination of the smell and the noise. Angela burns religious incense sticks and I became aware I was also smelling a different, additional, acrid smell. Then there was a rushing noise, fire bursting out I guess and that was soon followed by cries and shouts of people out on the street.'

'What did you do next?'

'I went downstairs to the street to see what was happening. Someone must have called the Fire Service as a tender was on site in minutes. Well, it's hardly any distance to come from Church Street. In fact the fire was soon extinguished, the van burnt out.'

'And what did you see?'

Ruth couldn't help but feel that they had reached a critical moment in April's line of questioning, so she fired back a question of her own.

'In what direction, in what respect, see...?'

'Well anything out of the ordinary?'

'Like what?' asked Ruth defensively.

'Well, anything in the van, for example?' asked April persisting with her line of questioning, Ruth knowing exactly where she was going with the 'in the van' prompt.

'There was a lot of smoke and steam coming out of the back of the van when the firemen forced open the rear doors. It was very difficult to see and I was almost immediately ushered away. But, I did see something and now I think of it there was a different smell of burning again, like we get at the crematoria sometimes, when the wind is blowing in the wrong direction. Inside I saw two contorted body shapes.'

'Are you quite sure that's what you saw?'

Once again Ruth didn't quite know what to make of April's comment. It didn't make complete sense. Was she doubting there were two bodies? Was there something else going on? Was Ruth being asked to forget what she saw? Why was there nothing in the news? She hesitated and April spoke again.

'You see it might have been something quite different, perhaps? Might that have been possible?'

Ruth's mind was racing. No way was it anything other than how she'd told it, or was it? April had sown a seed of doubt in her mind and she became uncertain as to her memory.

'You could be right April. I couldn't see very well.'

'Well, we'll leave it there and I'll see your car is back where it belongs in less than an hour. Henley Road should be open and back to normal by the morning. No-one will know anything ever happened. They've taken away the white van for further tests and everything is being scaled back right now. I really must be going and thank you for your help. It's good to have a reliable witness as to what occurred. I may need to talk to you again, but I know where to find you. Oh, and as I said at the outset, this is all sensitive stuff, we don't think it would be helpful to cause undue alarm by talking about what you might or might not have seen in the van,' she jibed in a clear and deliberative voice. 'Please don't get up, I'll see myself out... Bye.'

With that April had gone leaving a puzzled Ruth on the settee trying to gather her thoughts. It didn't add up. Something was going on, something was being hidden from public gaze. She'd just been shut up.

The April she knew was straight down the line, she wasn't normally like this, yet she'd deliberately planted a seed of doubt with the intention of keeping things quiet for investigative purposes that were quite beyond Ruth's comprehension. Either something was up or she was imagining things. Was all the pressure getting to her? Was she still a reliable witness? What was the truth behind what she'd seen? She'd been told more or less to forget what she'd witnessed, so what choice did she have and did it really matter?

Looking at the clock she remembered in a panic that she had promised to call on Darshana. It was still raining hard outside and she decided to brave the elements and though she could take Phil's car she decided to make the short journey on foot.

Stepping outside Ruth saw April opposite the vicarage sitting in her unmarked car and engaged in an earnest conversation on her phone. Instinctively she felt April was talking about her, about what she'd said and what she'd seen or hadn't seen. A sense of dread numbed her senses as she held her brolly close and hurriedly walked on by. Then she told herself not to be so paranoid. April was probably, even now, simply arranging for her car to be returned, like she said she would. Even so she told herself she must talk to Phil when she got back home.

Walking down Silver Street, the rain signalling a prelude to autumn, having eased to a light drizzle, left a reflective wet glaze on the pavement, dark puddles at the roadside and a hiss from the tyres of passing vehicles. Yet above the traffic noise she felt she wasn't walking alone and twice, for some unknown reason, she found herself compelled to check behind her to see if anyone was there. There was no one. She put it down to her tiredness or even paranoia. Nonetheless it was with a sense of relief when Darshana opened her door and she was able to go inside.

What she noticed immediately was the sight and smell of the incense sticks burning on the family shrine in the corner, so very resonant of those at Angela's house. Was this merely a coincidence? So much didn't make sense. To think there was some link between Raj and Angela Morris seemed unlikely, but the thought wouldn't go away. After all his van was outside her house, less then half a mile away and how was that to be explained? Her thoughts were interrupted.

'Would like tea, please?' asked Darshana.

'Thank you,' Ruth answered as Darshana disappeared into her tiny kitchen.

There was Raj's death and now two more probable deaths if those were indeed bodies she saw – was there some kind of link between the three deaths? Maybe Darshana could throw further light on these things? But this wasn't really something she could just come straight out with and ask her – it would be the height of insensitivity. First, she needed to show some empathy for her in her recent loss and then hear why she so much wanted to see her. Her own agendas would have to wait. Pushing the door with her foot, Darshana reappeared, two mugs in her hands.

'How are you doing, Darshana?'

Darshana looked this way and that as if uncomfortable and her eyes had the puffed look of someone who'd been recently crying. She held a tissue clenched in her hand and even under her white lace veil her culture required her to wear whilst mourning, Ruth could see her hair was uncombed and untidy. She looked at Ruth, then looked away as if she wanted to say something but wasn't certain.

'It's alright... I know it's a difficult time,' offered Ruth.

Ruth felt a natural warmth for Darshana. She liked her and the two got on and she felt quite at home with her. Darshana nodded as if to indicate she indeed wanted to say more.

'Raj's death has left me feeling very unsure of things,' she said barely above a whisper.

'How do you mean?' asked Ruth

'Strange things keep happening. I know it's stupid and I've seen nothing and I feel foolish telling you, but I think I'm being followed, watched. Even my phone sounds different, as if someone's listening in. Can't say why. Can't sleep at night. My brother, Ravi, been such a help, but then he keeps receiving and making calls I don't know what about. Then I had the police call this afternoon, only it wasn't normal police, a woman on her own, not in uniform, to ask me about Raj. I already tell them once…'

Ruth thought for a moment, then asked, 'Was her name April Cooper by any chance, smartly dressed?'

'Yes, that was it, April.'

'She came to see me too.'

'She said how sorry she was to hear about Raj, but then asked me whether he'd been to India recently, whether he'd had any visitors, that kind of thing. It felt like she was making him out to be linked with something illegal. Raj would never do anything like that. She asked me to tell, describe for her, as I had earlier for the local police, how Raj had died. I don't understand it. Why didn't she ask her colleagues? What was she after?'

'I don't know Darshana, I really don't know.' Sipping their hot sweet tea, both settled back into the leather sofas.

'But when you called me early this morning, was there something in particular on your mind, even before April called?'

'Yes, yes. A friend called me first thing to say Raj's burnt out van was found outside the house of that man who killed Raj, over in Henley Road. Why was his van there? Why did it catch fire? When I telephoned Edmonton Police Station after my friend tell me this, I couldn't get hold of anyone who would speak to me. That's not right is it? When I persisted they said someone would call. Did they mean that April policewoman? If so, she never explained nothing. I don't know what to make of it all, I really don't.'

Ruth for her part was equally confused and could only offer supportive comfort and the bland assurance that no doubt all would become clear in due course.

'I've asked Ravi, my brother, to come over and stay for a few days.'

'That sounds like a good idea at a time like this.'

'It's just that, well I think someone's been in here when I was out yesterday. But no one else has a key, so how can that be? I couldn't see any sign of a break-in.'

'What makes you think so?'

'I'm very precise where I leave things. Look around, you can see how it is. I can't help it. Everything has to be exactly in its place. Well when I went out to the temple yesterday I came back to find Raj's papers on that table had been moved, only about half an inch, but they definitely had. Also, the store at the back of the shop had been disturbed. When Raj brings in the stuff from the wholesalers we both stack it up. It is carefully done. We've always been very careful, labels to the front, that kind of thing. But it wasn't like that, the tinned foods had all been gone through, I'm certain of it, as if someone had been looking for something.'

'What did you do?'

'I rang the police just before I rang you. They said, they'd send someone round later, but no one's come, except that April woman and she wasn't interested in whether I'd had an intruder or not. It wasn't important to her. I don't feel I've been listened to.'

'I hear what you're saying. The police are probably busy investigating Raj's death and have had to prioritise what they're dealing with. They'll get round to your questions in due course, you'll see. They tend to prioritise things. Murders first, less serious crimes later…'

It seemed to Ruth that the two policing arms, local and Counter Terrorism were not communicating and that there was a possibility police were conducting covert enquiries to see whether Raj was connected to something linked with terrorism, even with people overseas and then she wondered whether his death was not a straight forward robbery gone wrong knife crime, but part of a somewhat different, bigger picture. All this was speculation and not something she felt able to share with Darshana right now. However, she couldn't help herself from asking a question that had been on her mind.

'What did Raj like doing in his spare time, not that I imagine he had a lot running a corner shop?'

'He was really good with social media, it was his hobby, he'd lots of Facebook friends in India. They sent him lots of messages and he them. He was aways very sociable. At the local temple he was keen to play his part and some evenings he'd go down there and meet with the other men. Being sociable was his thing. Everybody liked him. We never had any children… but he loved me, he loved me…' and at that, her words failed her and Darshana began to cry.

Ruth put her mug down and placed a comforting arm over Darshana's shoulder. She didn't need to say anything, just let her caring presence be enough, and after a few minutes, the tears and sobs eased and Darshana raised her head.

A few moments later, Ruth made her excuses and headed out into the evening's grey light, back into Silver Street and the short walk home. Once more she caught herself checking behind her. This time she was certain someone was loitering opposite the Chauhan's shop as if keeping it under surveillance. The man turned away from her as he spotted her gaze in his direction. She knew what she had seen. There was more to Raj's death than the police were admitting to of that she was now certain. This was more than an ordinary enquiry.

She was feeling unsettled and insecure. Her foot hurt as she tried to force her walking pace. She desperately wanted to get off the street and back within the walls of her own home.

14

As an unsettled Ruth walked the short distance home from Darshana's flat above the shop, the leaden, dull grey sky was giving the August evening an autumnal feel. But Ruth's mind didn't dwell on the weather, indeed she didn't even notice it, for her mind was in a flat spin.

What Darshana had told her of her uneasiness resonated with her own unsettled state. Her story made sense, it was her own story too and she was convinced there had to be more going on in Raj's death than one more London knife crime. But for now, whatever it might be, she just couldn't fathom. It just left her feeling uncomfortably bewildered and insecure.

She was so absorbed in her private reflections she found she'd suddenly arrived back at her own front door with little remembrance of the journey. As she put her key in the lock the sight of the crude temporary boarding over the window made her jolt at the recent altercation with Tony. Then she wondered just how such an aggressive young man one minute could be the caring, doting son in the next. Human nature was a constant source of puzzlement, she mused, yet she was supposed to be some kind of expert in it.

Phil had heard her come in and called her from the kitchen, 'In hee…re!'

She found him making up a salad at the table. 'Kids go back tomorrow so they've had an early night, all tucked up, school stuff's laid out ready for the morning. They're a bit anxious about new teachers and new classes, you know, first day back in a new academic year. And, today at Brent Cross, maybe coupled with the events of the weekend, it's left them, well, especially Olivia, a bit out of sorts. It took her a while to settle.'

'What? Olivia? Out of sorts?'

'She cried for a bit actually. I rather wish you'd been here. I've got a big day in the city tomorrow, southern accountancy team meeting, starts with a breakfast pre-meeting, 8.30am, down at Blackfriars. Early start for me I'm afraid.'

'Err… think I'll need to drop kids at breakfast club. No problem. Thanks. Was she alright, Olivia?'

'Think so. She keeps saying she's frightened of knives and that she didn't like being with all those people today. It was fine to start with, a laugh, but she was frightened at the turn in events Ruth – in fact she's adamant she never wants to go to Brent Cross again. She's always been such a self-confident girl.'

'And Paul?'

'He's harder to fathom out. He seems to find his electronic games a therapy. It's his bolt hole, his world. He retreats there and feels safe there. Can't say I'm entirely happy with that.'

'Shall we eat?'

'Sit yourself down, it's all ready. We need to talk, seriously Ruth, we nee-eed to talk. I said so on Saturday night and we didn't, two days on and we haven't found a minute. Can't say I've seen much of you for you and me time. I know it's been tough, incredibly pressured, but we mustn't avoid this. As far as I'm concerned this bank holiday weekend has been a disaster. It… I can't go on like this.'

Ruth was shocked. She hadn't seen this coming. Phil, the rock and support she totally relied on was wavering, shattering before her. She saw the seriousness in his expression and the determined gaze in his brown eyes. She sensed things had reached a new low between them. Things were desperate and she knew it.

'Phil, I'm sorry. Events have spiralled out of control and it's not entirely my fault. This has been an exceptionally challenging weekend as you know; more pressure has been put on us as a family than some families have put on them in a life time.'

'True, but we can make choices about it. We don't have to take it, do we?' he retorted.

'What are you suggesting. That I quit? That I take the sabbatical they're all pushing me to have? That we move parish? That I give up even? I leave?'

'No, no. Don't go over the top. We're talking about managing things better,' he said more calmly. 'I've been thinking. There are three things we need to do. First, put time out in your diary this week – time that is sacrosanct, time no one else but you and me have. Second, that you start taking some decisions about how much time you give to the kids. They need your time Ruth, you know I'm right; and third, you need to manage your work load or you will fall apart. I'm seeing the warning signs before my eyes and you know I'm telling the truth. You've stopped looking after yourself and how's that any Christian witness? I hate it! As for the two of us, our marriage has taken a nose dive and if we want to save… improve it, we need to do something – suppose that's number four.'

Ruth had been shifting her salad round her plate. Neither were eating, only talking. She didn't know what to say. She felt vulnerable, insecure and frightened for herself, her marriage and her family and didn't know which way to turn. More to the point she didn't know what to say and so no words came out.

'Ruth, can't you say something? I've tried to say it how it is. Do you agree it's like this? How I say?' he said quietly.

'Yes, but I don't know what to say and I don't know what to do,' and she began to cry softly at first and then in welling sobs. Phil simply came round the table and folded her in his arms and she clung on to him, shaking and crying her heart out like never before. Holding him she could feel his emotions grabbing his insides as he struggled to keep control too.

Gradually it subsided. She could tell Phil was shocked.

'What shall we do?' he asked gently. 'Do we get help?'

'Everything has got to be too much. It's been a terrible weekend and what bothers me a lot is that I don't think we're near the end of things quite just yet.'

Neither of them ate much. They followed the salad with a pot of tea which they took into the lounge. The TV went on and it being bank holiday they sat silently next to one another watching a film about a fairground showman, a man who'd come from nothing to greatness and then lost his way. Almost everything he treasured in his life disappeared, including the person he loved most, his life looked set for ruin. But they were both glad it didn't end that way. Ruth commented that being a vicar was sometimes like being a showman, keeping a team performing with her holding it all together.

Later, when Phil was asleep snoring gently, Ruth got up. She went downstairs to her space, her study. Sitting in her dressing gown with the lights off she rested her elbows on her desk and they in turn supported her hands under her chin as she stared out into the blackness outside. The angular dark forms of buildings and the street lights framed her view. The world looked empty. How, she wondered had her life come to this, blackness outside, blackness inside? Where were friends when you needed them? Where was God?

She wasn't sure if she'd nodded off, she could have been dreaming, but she heard a woman's soft voice speaking, maybe her inner self or maybe someone she thought she knew.

'There are two types of women who serve God, those who are determined, omni-competent, compulsive managers who push on like a snow-plough in winter, erasing every drift and obstacle in front of them as they are driven ever higher in the air in their progress onward and upward. The Church loves to see success like that.'

'And the second type,' Ruth found herself asking.

'They are the ones who are not up to it. They are the ones standing in the rain getting wetter and wetter until they are soaked to the skin, overwhelmed by the pressures assailing them from every side, the ones who eventually drown in the sea of demands placed upon them.'

'And what happens to them?'

'They fall away, forgotten. The Church is pleased when the problem they've become by being there has gone.'

'And who am I?'

'That's for you to find out.'

'And what did you find out in your time?' asked Ruth, feeling she knew this woman from somewhere in her past, 'And tell me, what do I call you?'

'Gladys – and I didn't fit in any of their neat little boxes. I was a reject, unwanted, unloved, facing threats and dangers you can only imagine. No fancy schooling, no money, no fine name. Rejection and the word "No" thrown at me at every turn.'

'So did you become one of those who fell away and were forgotten?'

'Ruth, when I was desperate I cried to God and I said, *"Here's my Bible, Here's my money. Use me, God."* and that's what happened. I discovered I was worrying about my call, yet God was helping me all the way. I felt weak, without courage, torn apart, thwarted by borders and powerful men.'

'How?'

'I said, *"I'm willing"*, even willing to go to China on my own.'

'And when you said you were willing and you turned and faced your demons and dragons, how did it all turn out?'

'I saw life at its most pitiful, death stalking people without mercy. Suffering and pain were so common, even for the children. Yet I wished to be nowhere else. I said to God, "*Do not wish me out of this or in any way seek to get me out while this trial is on.*" I knew in my heart these were my people. I dug deeper, I resolved to stand, to stay, to fight to the end. I had nothing, but had everything.'

'You were very brave and faithful Gladys, you became famous, I'm really not like you.'

And then there was silence, or rather she was disturbed as the night bus speeding along Silver St cast a brief white glow, enough to rouse her and make her wonder what had been happening. She pushed herself up from her desk, her mind full of a strange, dream-like, half forgotten conversation. Glancing at her collected books on Gladys Aylward, she realised she needed to get back to bed. When she did so, for the first time in days, she slept deeply.

When Phil woke her soon after 6am with a coffee she was in the middle of another dream. She was dancing in a circle with two other women. They were happy and singing. One was definitely Gladys. The other had blood on her hands, but was happy nonetheless. It was very weird, very surreal and was in a moment forgotten.

'You look better,' said Phil, standing before her smartly dressed in a suit and wearing a sharply ironed blue shirt. 'I'm off, but I thought I'd better wake you before I leave. Love you,' he declared, as he bent to kiss her on her lips. 'We'll work it out, always have, always will.'

Ruth drank her coffee in a warm fug of emerging wakefulness and unexplained contentment. Whatever the day ahead would bring, she hoped the feeling would last.

15

With Phil gone, a hectic round of showering, dressing, rousing grumpy children, cajoling and then taking them to breakfast club at school would follow, her aim to get herself back to church in time for Morning Prayer for 8.30am.

To her relief her returned fire blistered car had started first time and the traffic had been light. There was still a disconcerting hint of smoke and acridity in the car's interior which despite having had the screen fan blowing on full power never seemed quite to disappear. The children made lots of disapproving noises.

On her return, once she'd parked up, she saw she had two parishioners waiting at the locked church door, probably to join her for prayers. It was Julie and Stephanie deep in conversation.

'We both thought we'd come here for prayers and then stay on to support you at the meeting,' said Stephanie as Ruth approached them.

Meeting? What meeting? thought Ruth, finding her church key whilst suppressing the impulse to voice her ignorance and further evidence her incompetence, kicking herself for not having checked her diary earlier. Adrenaline fed panic seeped into her veins as she had the feeling that they were indeed right, she had slipped up again and there was an important meeting for which she had done absolutely nothing, just waiting for her after prayers. She'd almost recalled what it was when Julie interrupted her efforts at memory retrieval.

'Don't tell me you've forgotten? The area Housing Associations asked you to chair their community meeting this morning in the church hall. Starts at 9am. Roy's in there putting out the chairs, he's not one for prayers. Flo's in the kitchen on teas and coffees, heading up the hospitality front. Best we put on a good show, eh?' said Julie.

At this Ruth felt a sense of relief. She should be able to just turn up and wing it. It would be alright.

'We'd better get going with Morning Prayer hadn't we,' she said, trying to seize back the initiative, adding, 'time's tight,' as she led the way down to the side chapel at a brisk pace, before determinedly passing round the red prayer books as they sat down.

In spite of being wrong footed, somehow Ruth felt her spirits had been lifted since the previous day and this morning felt more manageable. She was starting a new week. The weekend had been full on, as demanding as ever, but the unexpected good night's sleep appeared to have recharged her drained batteries. Yes, she had temporarily forgotten she had a meeting to chair, but she told herself that was hardly surprising the pressures she'd been under, and in any case, no harm done, she was back on track now.

In fact the prayers themselves lifted her further. In the short time of open prayer when any one of the three had the opportunity to offer their petitions to God out loud, she was moved to find both Julie and Stephanie voiced a prayer for her, openly recognising the 'very great demands she faced.'

Buoyed up by their support, the three left church for the hall just adjacent to the vicarage with five minutes to spare. In fact the hall was a suite of four halls of various sizes, built in different eras and for different purposes. In part the remnants of an old National School and in part a former war time WRVS soup kitchen, the contemporary building as a whole looked in need of more than a lick of fresh paint to modernise it but it was a vital, much valued and unique community resource.

Roy had done a good job in setting the chairs out in a semicircular double row and they were already filling up. It was very obvious who were the local residents and who were housing association staff. They'd put themselves into two separate groups, younger housing staff in modern attire, older local residents comprising the usual mixture of the elderly infirm and those unable to work. Ruth was glad that the diverse ethnicities in the parish were well represented, something she herself had found difficult to achieve in other gatherings.

Ruth went up to the Chair of the North London United Housing Association whom she knew from a past joint summer project to improve community life for new residents by laying on a local summer holiday club and it was she who, some time back, had emailed Ruth to ask her to chair this morning's proceedings.

'Hello Pat, how lovely to see you, so glad we've a reasonable turn out from the community. Do you have an agenda? What's the format?'

She knew Pat O'Driscoll to be an omni-competent professional and true to form she produced briefing notes for Ruth and indicated that agenda papers had already been placed on all the chairs.

'The key thing is this Ruth,' she said under her breath in a confidential whisper, 'there's been precious little-to-no coordination between the various Housing Associations locally and the result has been, predictably – utter chaos. We've got asylum seekers from opposite sides of conflict zones abroad now living side by side in the same street in Edmonton, having been placed here by separate housing agencies who just don't talk to one another.'

'Yes, I've heard of the police having to sort out a couple of ugly street scenes,' said Ruth.

'Unintentionally, we've also recently discovered we've got one street with dozens of migrants filling up the road, mainly single men in multiple occupancy houses and flats and unsurprisingly this has caused a rise in resentment with locals.'

'I've picked up on that too.'

'Little to no work has been done with the local community, so people are feeling out of the loop, forgotten and overlooked and I'm so grateful to you for facilitating this meeting and lending your hall to try and redress this. I'm relying on you to be honest broker here Ruth, to pour oil on troubled waters, otherwise the growing momentum behind an 'us' and 'them', fed of course by the wider context we're living in these days, will keep growing and we'll have a massive community problem on our hands before we know it. Need to try and nip things in the bud, seize the day.'

'OK, I get the picture. Let's get started shall we. I'd like you to sit next to me and I'm going to ask Julie as a local resident to sit the other side of me. I've asked Roy to move that table between us and the audience. Is that alright?'

'You're the chair,' Pat said, smiling as she took her place. As Ruth moved to sit down and waved over Julie, she noticed Pat had a rather attractive multi-coloured but predominantly blue, striped jumper, neither too officious, nor one of the power-dressing outfits she'd so often seen women in Pat's executive position wearing. Ruth looked around, the seats were now all taken, maybe forty people, pretty good, she thought, for early on a Tuesday morning. As people chatted amongst themselves, she sensed an air of expectation rather than outright tension in the room as she moved to call everyone to order.

'Good morning everyone and welcome to Holy Trinity Church Hall. I trust everyone had a good bank holiday. True to form the rain came on cue! All I can say is, I hope you didn't do what I did yesterday, try shopping at Brent Cross!' People were listening. She paused as the last few people settled to give her their attention.

'I'm sure many of you will have already heard that our dear friend Raj Chauhan, who ran the corner shop in Silver Street was killed on Saturday. I'd like us to begin our meeting with a minute in respectful silence and quiet reflection before we get down to business.'

In the quiet that followed, she was in charge, in control, doing her thing, and today she knew she was doing it well.

The meeting was scheduled for an hour. With agreement it ended up running for an hour and a half. Ruth had been fully stretched to enable all the different voices and grievances to be heard in a respectful manner. Just occasionally things had completely boiled over and she had to exert her authority and skills as chair to regain control of the meeting.

One very elderly man, Alf, supported by his walking stick which he tapped harshly on the floor as he spoke, made his point about 'not fighting the war for things to come to this,' before leaving the meeting early, declaring it, 'a waste of time.'

After the meeting had formally ended most people drifted away by eleven. Pat and Ruth had stayed on to reflect over another coffee how each felt it had gone. Though the meeting had been better than either might have hoped and Pat expressed her gratitude for the way in which Ruth had steered them through, the feeling was that although grievances had been aired and they now had a better awareness of the real situation, they were both rather alarmed at how fragile and ill-prepared the community seemed in order to cope with the scale and speed of the changes they had recently begun to face.

Pat told Ruth of a meeting she had had at Edmonton Police HQ only the previous week when the highest ever level of race hate crime figures for the area had been discussed, figures which mirrored the picture across Greater London and indeed England and Wales. 'I had to tell them that the number of difficult resident incidents we were having to deal with in-house had also escalated. What's your take on it?'

'Sadly, I have to agree. I've had more street death funerals here for young people this past year than ever before. We've also more mentally ill calling at the vicarage because of austerity cutbacks in public services. Then there are more knives on the street too.'

'I was sorry to hear you had to close the Drop In as it used to be. It provided an invaluable service to so many of our Asylum Seeker residents and their friends.'

'There was no choice there – after the Ali Muhammed terrorist used it as a base, Church management said, "no",' she said, managing a weak smile.

'No one likes head office reports written by men in suits trying to cover their own backs!' Pat fired back in her typical no nonsense manner.

Ruth warmed to the empathy shown. 'But what's to be done when resettling asylum seekers through the dispersal programme is so randomly haphazard. There's just no forward preparation and without planning what happens is what we have here, in the poorer areas of the city where the housing, like ours locally, lends itself to getting used by the stretched housing associations to locate people. The result is that they all end up in the same place with a dearth of provision to support them. Chaotic under-resourced communities are a recipe for all kinds of trouble.'

'Exactly, and there's no quick fix. But, today was a first! I do think when we get people together to talk it helps, it's a start. There are definitely things I can take back to my own management but I think we really need to lobby for some political change. My only regret is that we didn't get local council and local politicians along this morning to hear what was said.'

'Tell you what, Pat. I'll get Julie to draft some notes. I'll write a covering letter and we can circulate it to the powers that be.'

'That'll be great. Thank you. Perhaps we can repeat the exercise again, does three or even six month's time sound good to you?'

'Sure. Just drop me a line.'

And with that it was over. A quick word to thank Julie, Roy and Stephanie, and Ruth was heading back to the vicarage. As she stepped out onto the street, she realised that it was already nearly midday and she hadn't yet checked her mail, her emails or her phone messages.

Ruth turned as she heard footsteps running up behind her, a woman's lightly clicking shoes on the paving. She swung round, it was Pat.

'Oh thank goodness I caught you before I went. There was one other thing. Just for your ears of course. One of our tenants is known to you – Angela Morris.'

'You'd better come inside a minute,' said Ruth, guiding Pat toward her front door, 'I saw her over the weekend.'

Once in the lounge, Pat sat down.

'I've got a problem I don't know how to deal with, so this is in confidence, between ourselves. Angela Morris is one of the longest standing tenants we have. Her tenancy found its way into our portfolio when one of the smaller Edmonton Housing Trusts folded and handed their properties and tenants over to us lock stock and barrel. The thing is, Angela Morris and her son enjoy a lifetime guaranteed, very low fixed rent which was part of the terms of the take over. Her son Tony lives with her, he's been looking after her. Things have, however, now reached a crisis point.'

'You know he's in custody and charged with Raj's murder, don't you?' said Ruth.

'Oh, I didn't know. Honestly. Oh my goodness! No, no, my concern was for Angela and her future. I see the house as unsuitable for her needs given her lack of physical mobility, though without a Needs Assessment, which we don't have because she won't play ball, we can't take things forward. With Tony in custody that might change things, mightn't it? She can't continue to look after herself alone can she?'

'I think you're right. I went round and Julie, sitting next to me just now, we both got her sorted with immediate grocery supplies. But it's an unsustainable scenario. I can't be her carer nor can Julie and we don't have a team to do it for her.'

'You know Raj Chauhan used to visit her, take her groceries round, help Tony and her out. He and a couple of friends of his from the Temple used to help Angela out quite a bit.'

Seeing the look of surprise on Ruth's face, she added, 'Now it's your turn to say, I didn't know!'

'No, no, I had no idea and...'

'And that was something else I was going to mention to you when you asked us to observe a minutes silence earlier. It reminded me that it was Raj who used to attend one of our other tenant's flats in Haselbury Road for Hindu meetings. Just so you know, we had to intervene and tell him that that kind of thing was not allowed in our properties.'

'What kind of thing?'

'Between ourselves Ruth, for this is sensitive stuff, they weren't simply like Christian Bible Study home groups quietly reading and praying, that kind of thing, these were political meetings, that's why other tenants complained to us. In my experience people tell us things either because they have a grudge or they are seriously worried. This was definitely the latter.'

'What kind of political meetings?'

'I don't know whether you follow politics in India much, but Raj had a bee in his bonnet about Hindus being in the ascendant in India but over here being sidelined, not heard. He felt the UK government were only ever interested in allocating resources to other faiths like Muslims, not helping good people, only trouble-making religions, as he put it. To be honest I don't know what his politics were, I'm only passing on what was told me third hand, but we had to tell them to stop meeting or lose the tenancy. That was it. The meetings stopped and we've heard nothing further.'

'This is all news to me. How was Raj about it?'

'I'm afraid Raj took it badly and saw our action as more anti-Hindu sentiment. On the face of it he was very mild-mannered and agreeable, but his politics, well that was quite another matter. Tell me Ruth, can a person have two sides to them, a caring side and an aggressive one?'

'I was only thinking that myself when I heard about Tony Morris.'

'Anyway, the complaints all stopped a month or two ago when our Haselbury Road tenant assured us the meetings were no longer being held at his flat.'

'But it sounds as if Raj was being kindly toward Angela at least,' offered Ruth. 'Personally, I never saw him fired up or politicised in the way you describe. He was always ever the smiling shop keeper to me.'

'Quite so, but we still have the problem of how Angela's future care and residential needs are to be met with no Raj or Tony on hand. And to my mind, speaking frankly, it's not the church's role to provide yet another societal emergency service in Angela's case, that's for the authorities, surely…'

Silence fell between them.

'Don't you think, given the present situation, Tony having just been arrested for Raj's murder, right now it isn't a good time for the Housing Association to start immediate proceedings to recover the tenancy? It could be seen as a reaction and upping the ante, just so you get the flat.'

'Well, I'll bow to your experience, I'll think further on that, but housing-wise we can't neglect managing this for much longer. Would you mind contacting me in a few days with your updated take on the situation. I'll keep you fully advised what we aim to do, send you a confidential email. I think it would be good to work together on this. There's too much that could go badly wrong. I'll ring the London Borough of Enfield, get them on board with future care.'

And with that and the exchange of a few more pleasantries, the conversation drew to a close and Ruth showed Pat out of the front door.

Finally, Ruth found she had a chance to dive in to her study, to check what new demands had come in and try and manage her life. However, even as she stepped in to her study, the phone rang. She reached for the landline handset and picked up. Who could it be this time?

16

Funerals! It was, recalled Ruth, the American, William Franklin who more than two centuries ago rightly observed that nothing was more certain that death and taxes. All morning, the local undertakers had been trying to reach her, unsuccessfully until now, with two funerals from the bank holiday weekend. She heard evident relief in Mr. Bernard, the undertaker's voice, as she picked up his call.

He explained that two families were anxious to discuss possible dates for Ruth to officiate at the services for their loved ones. The date was the easy bit and she duly obliged. The fitting in of the visits to see the family at different times over the coming days, a more demanding one, given the limited diary space. Over several minutes, Ruth took all the details from Mr Bernard, whose serious demeanour and dour voice perfectly matched his sombre occupation. They had a good, if perfunctory working relationship, which served them both. He politely thanked her, as he alway did, before signing off.

Ruth returned to other unanswered phone messages, playing each in turn, deleting all but two. Turning to her laptop she scrolled down the latest arrivals in the email inbox; deciding not to open them, she flipped the lid closed and strolled over to the kitchen. She wasn't quite ready to manage such a long list, not just yet any rate.

Her mind kept returning to Angela Morris. For some reason she felt an obligation to make a further call to see her. She wondered how she was coping in Tony's absence and thought she might discover more about her links with Raj, links which Pat had brought to her attention and had come as such a surprise.

After making a quick sandwich and filling it with the soft cheese spread left over from the children's packed lunches she sat at the kitchen table to take a break. After washing down the sandwich with cold water from the tap she was ready to go and decided it would do her good, provide a healthy option and give her some head space if she walked the short distance round the corner to Henley Road.

As she approached the house she noticed the black stains on the road where Raj's van had burned out, but there were no other signs that anything untoward had ever happened over the weekend. As usual the front door was on the catch and she walked inside calling out loudly as she did so.

'Hi Angela, it's Ruth. Just popped round to see how you are doing. I'm on my way up.'

She gave herself a moment to let her eyes adjust to the gloom before turning right and heading carefully up the narrow staircase.

'Angela, it's Ruth. OK if I come in,' she asked, pausing for a moment on the landing to regain her breath and wanting to make quite sure Angela had heard she was coming.

The bedroom door was slightly ajar and Ruth leaned slowly across to see if she could glimpse anything in the greyness of the room. Ah, she thought, she looks like she's dozing, so she called again to gently wake her. She didn't want to cause Angela undue alarm.

'Angela, Angel…aaa. It's Ruth, sorry to disturb you, just wanted to see how you were doing.'

Ruth edged further into the room, slowly and cautiously, her hands reaching for things to support her. She was aware something was different, something felt wrong and cold, even colder than when she had last visited. Then she realised what was at variance with her earlier visits, the incense sticks weren't throwing off their dense clouds of scented smoke. The air was cleaner, if still slightly musty. She felt relief and had got her breath back.

'Angela, your incense sticks aren't burning. Do you…'

Ruth's words were left hanging in the air unanswered. The bedroom now exuded an air of emptiness as if it wasn't just the smoke that had left, yet there was Angela, sleeping, oblivious and looking every bit as grey and pale and as dead as… as a corpse, she thought.

Ruth began to take her breaths more shallowly as the thought entered her mind that Angela might actually be dead. She dismissed the idea as fanciful, that her own fears were taking hold again, overriding her perception of reality. She'd need to check. She'd have to touch her.

She'd reached the end of her bed and gently touched Angela's right foot, mindful as she did so of the pain she had caused in touching her foot the last time. But Angela still didn't move. Ruth called out more loudly one more time, 'Angela…' and pushed her foot harder and more persistently, again without any response. This could be a medical matter, she thought, and made a mental check to be certain she had her mobile with her if needed.

Another touch, her hand lingering longer this time. The foot felt cold. This was serious and Ruth felt herself getting frightened. Perhaps Angela was unconscious, had passed out, or... worse. Moving more closely toward Angela's head, her one hand reaching to touch her brow, the other hand reaching across to the curtain to try and throw more light onto the prone figure covered in the great bedspread, in order to see what she was doing. Now she was horrified at how cold Angela's forehead felt to her touch. Still no response, so turning to the curtain, Ruth tugged it fiercely back to let in a shaft of bright light.

When she looked back at Angela, she knew in that instant Angela was dead. It was her still eyes, peering through a fixed, yet troubled gaze of milky greyness through almost closed lids. Her pallor was that of the dead. The light from the window revealed something else, red holes entering the eiderdown bed cover around the area of her torso – Ruth let out a gasp, the realisation of what was signified dawning upon her as her hand fumbled in her bag for her phone. This was a murder! The holes were those of a knife, the red... blood!

She stepped back from the bed and made a call in as measured and calm a voice as she could asking for the police, then in her confusion, not knowing what to do for the best asked for an ambulance too. After taking details the operator wanted to keep her on the line and was asking more questions, but Ruth became frightened and said, 'what if her attacker is still here in the house or comes back, I need to get out of here, I must get out, I'm going downstairs to the street.'

Holding her phone in one hand she made for the landing and hurrying into the dark stairwell began her descent, desperately wanting to get out into the relative safety of the street. Her foot slipped and she fell ungraciously, not forward which might have been catastrophic, but on to her backside and then began a bumpy sliding which ended up with her sprawled out in an unladylike heap across the foot of the stairs and hallway. She felt herself a frightened, vulnerable fool.

Looking into the darkness of the back of the house, she heard a noise, maybe the cat, maybe not, could be someone in there, but it was very hard to pull herself up and she wasn't sure whether she had done herself any serious harm.

She felt, rather than saw, what happened next as a dark figure, ran at her from the direction of the kitchen, stepping directly and purposefully on her hip causing her to wince in pain before springing out beyond her and through the front door. The sound of his running feet became ever quieter as he disappeared up the street.

Ruth couldn't move. Whether she was paralysed by fear or physically injured she didn't know. There was relief too as she pondered what might have happened to her. Held fast by the awkward weight of her own curled body, her next thought was whether there might yet be another intruder, and she tried to pull herself upright by her hands, her aim just to get out through the door and into the open street.

Before she was able to do so she heard the emergency services siren approaching and at that she flopped down, let go, in the relief giving up any further attempt to move herself. Instinctively, she simply pulled her dress down nearer her knees to give herself a modicum of decency.

It sounded like a car, doors slammed, footsteps ran and the front door flew wide open wide as the silhouette of a burly policeman filled the entrance.

'Ma'am, did you make the call?'

She nodded, 'Then I fell down the stairs.'

'Ambulance coming, they'll check you over. Alright?'

'I'm sure if you give me a hand I'll be OK. Can you just help me to get upright, then I'll sit on the stairs.'

'You're sure? You look a bit worse for wear. Are you sure you wouldn't rather wait?'

'No, honestly. Please, take my arm.'

The policeman was strong and effortlessly raised her up enough to enable her to sit on the second stair. She felt her shoulder which ached and her arm which she'd bumped and grazed, presumably on the bannister, her right hip and the base of her spine which had hit the stairs. She felt like she'd had a huge kick up the backside, but all in all she summed up her position as fortunate – a lucky escape with only grazes and bruising.

'She's upstairs, in the front room, Angela Morris. I think she's dead. I think she's been stabbed. A man's just ran off, came from the back of the house, stamped on me as he went out of the front door, ran that way so far as I could tell,' she said, raising an arm to indicate toward Haselbury Road.

She heard another emergency vehicle approach, the wailing siren going silent as an ambulance pulled to a halt in the middle of the road. A second police car arrived hard on its heels. She could hear hurried verbal exchanges being made between the officers. This tiny terraced house is going to get crowded, she thought.

'Would you mind helping me outside. I'll sit on the wall. I'm in the way here,' she said.

The officer checked again to see if she was sure, and then obligingly, helped her up on her feet and walked her very slowly to the low wall outside. As she sat herself carefully down, her head dropped low on her shoulders. The other officer who stood outside their car looked across and beckoned his colleague with a hand gesture to leave Ruth and come over. His face carried a look of serious intent,

Whilst the emergency services did their thing, Ruth, sitting alone on the wall, was left to her own thoughts. She thought of Julie wanting to build a wall round the church. This wall was Angela's wall. It was too small to save her. Her killer had walked straight in. If the door had been locked, would she have been safe? No one was 100 per cent safe. Life was risky. The only protection lay in coming up with something else, life beyond big walls. Being on a wall, like she was right now, she was both sides of what was Angela's and what was not. Learning to live seeing both sides of a boundary line, real or imagined, had to be a solution worth exploring. The building of walls to be safe behind was pure folly. What kind of a world would that lead to?

After a further brief conversation by the car, the two officers disturbed her reverie as they passed by her and went inside. the house. She heard their footsteps ascend the stairs, moving more slowly than she thought they would, slowly upward toward the front bedroom.

Almost immediately the burly police officer reappeared, went over to his waiting colleagues in the other car telling them to secure the scene. Shortly, once again, Henley Road was closed to traffic, initially with blue and white strands of 'Do Not Cross' police tape, this soon to be supported by two lines of orange traffic cones. The ambulance personnel briefly checked Ruth over and concurred with her own assessment – grazes and bruises. They left her alone and returned to sit inside their ambulance awaiting police instructions.

'I need you to come with us to the police station,' said the burly policeman. Would you mind sitting in the back of the car? I'm sure you'll find it more comfortable than the wall. Here, take my arm,' he offered kindly, this time more as a command not to be refused than a polite request. Ruth had no choice. This, she thought, could all take some time.

She watched as yet more police arrived in an array of vehicles. The police tape was lifted to let the no longer needed ambulance move away. Forensics in their anonymous white plastic, shroud-like garments moved in to begin their work. Extra lights, and a roll of transparent plastic sheeting were carried inside, for the stairs and floor, she assumed.

After about forty minutes the first two officers reappeared on the pavement and leaving their colleagues to it, got back into the car and they sped off with Ruth in the back heading toward Edmonton Police HQ, no sirens this time.

Once at the police station, after more enquiries as to her well being and the offer of and provision of a welcome mug of tea, she was then taken from one empty reception room to a formal interview room complete with recording devices and one way viewing window. Only then did she realise the seriousness of her situation. However nice the police had been to her, she was a murder suspect.

Then a wave of panic swept over her as she saw the time on the circular wall clock. Olivia and Paul would be coming out of school in fifteen minutes. First day back at school and she wouldn't be there for them. Taking out her mobile she pondered as to whom she should call and what she should say. Then glancing at the signal indicator she panicked. It simply said, 'No Service.'

She needed to get someone's attention, but was powerless in police custody, detained in an empty room miles away from their school. She looked up at the clock and could hear it ticking.

17

PC Alice Such put her head round the interview room door.

'I've had word with the school and they'll hold on to Olivia and Paul until I get there to pick them up. I've phoned your husband who is coming back to your house by taxi and I'll drop them off with him. You know how things are, we have to follow due process with our enquiries,' she said with a smile.

Ruth muttered some words of thanks and tried to collect her thoughts and composure. The bruising from the fall was beginning to make her feel uncomfortable sitting down and there was a patch of blood on her sleeve from the graze. It didn't look very professional. She felt dishevelled and untidy and now she needed the loo. She seemed to need the loo more these days and wondered whether that and the thirst indicated diabetes. She must get herself checked out. A trip to the washroom would give her the chance to tidy herself up before the questioning began, she thought. It was hard to accept that, time she didn't have to spare, was hanging suspended in the air and she could do nothing about it.

She was escorted to the toilet and sat herself down in a precious moment to herself. She decided, remembering who she was and the predicament she was in, this was just the time to pray. After, she spent time in front of the mirror.

Re-emerging five minutes later feeling more refreshed and altogether in a better place, she was led back to the interview room, to find she was facing two new police officers, a woman and a man of more senior rank.

Once settled, they introduced themselves and read off the time for the benefit of the machine by the wall rather than her and began taking her through earlier events. Half way through she wondered whether she should have asked for a solicitor, but deciding she had nothing to hide and it would only delay matters further, dismissed the thought. It was frustrating her that telling her story was taking such a long time.

In the end things became a polite exchange of thank you for your assistance with our inquiries and, if we need to speak to you further, we'll be in touch… Their more relaxed approach concluded with the much appreciated offer of a lift home which she accepted gratefully.

On leaving the interview suite it took a full thirty minutes before she was dropped off at her front door, the police car disappearing round the corner by the time she got to open it. She stepped inside to find Phil, Olivia and Paul together in the kitchen snacking on biscuits and sucking on fruit drink cartons.

'More everyday adventures in the life of an Edmonton vicar, eh?' quizzed Phil. 'Like to tell me why the police pick up our kids from school and call me at work to tell me to come straight home? What have you been up to today then?' He looked puzzled and worried, his usual calm composure clearly ruffled.

Ruth for her part didn't like the tone in his voice. It wasn't just jokey-friendly, it was more jokey and you've pissed me off. She deflected the comment.

'Hi kids. PC April picked you up, yeh?'

'Yes, came home in a police car. Pretty cool,' said Paul whose eyes lit up.

'She was nice,' said Olivia. 'She let me play with her make up bag.'

'Oh, good. And was Daddy here when you got back?'

'Yes Daddy was!' said Phil. 'We all arrived at exactly the same time, actually… OK kids, upstairs to the TV room or your own rooms until tea. Mummy and I need to talk.'

The kids obediently headed off taking their unfinished snacks and drinks with them.

'You don't know, do you?' countered Ruth taking the initiative.

'What?'

'That I found Angela dead in bed, stabbed to death.'

'No. No… Sorry, how was I to know? They didn't tell me that.'

'You blamed me when I came in, I didn't expect that, didn't need that…'

'Now whose making judgements?' said Phil. 'We can't carry on like this Ruth. Admit it, your life's out of control and it's affecting everyone else's. I'll ask you again, what are you going to do about it?'

'I don't know Phil, I really don't know. Now's hardly the time. Perhaps we can see that couple again, the ones who retired from that retreat house. You remember, Ed and Carol, we haven't seen them in years, but we're in touch. They're only in Islington and we need someone to talk to. The archdeacon can roast in hell for all the help he gives me,' said Ruth with feeling.

'He's not there to help, he's there to manage you!' added Phil. 'He won't like it one iota that you're creating for yourself some kind of notorious turbulent priestly troublemaker role again.'

'That's going too far. Anyway, forget him, he's gone off to Norfolk, to Walsingham for a few days, he said.'

'Well, come on then, tell me what's happened. If it's beyond us to sort it, then we'll decide whether to see Ed and Carol for some outside mindfulness support. I can't trust any of your clergy hierarchy anymore.'

Ruth suggested tea and they sat down at the kitchen table facing one another, mirror images, each cupping their mug in both hands. They'd decided to switch off their phones for the duration. Ruth began telling her story. Phil heard it out with barely a word of interruption, asking only how she was feeling now when she described her fall.

'I'm really sorry,' said Phil. 'How could I have imagined it? That's four deaths in as many days. Oh, and that reminds me, no sooner back than someone came to the door to drop off some paperwork for a couple of funerals you're doing. I've put it on your desk. What worries me is why they took you back to the police station to interview you as if you were a suspect. That can't be right. It makes me angry the way you've been treated. Does it ever stop?'

'Phil, can I just say this. By the end of the bank holiday weekend, by last night, I was all in, done in, broken, losing my mind I think. But today, even after what has happened this afternoon I think I've turned a corner. I feel OK inside, a quiet centre still, in spite of the raging storm going on around me. I can weather the storms, I've done it before, but that's not to say what's happening doesn't need to be managed, that it's not taking an unreasonable toll on me, on us, on us all. I do need to change a few things. I don't know what as yet and I don't know how, but I promise I will. I love you Phil and I hate what all this is doing to us. We're in the midst of a crisis and it will pass, I'm sure of it.'

'OK, OK. I had a hard day at the office too. There's something for me to tell you. I knew there had to be a reason to get us all in early on the first day back. The lack of business confidence across the country is hitting us accountants and my firm are going to be making redeployments or more like redundancies soon – none of us know where the axe will fall, the bottom line is, no one's post is safe, mine included. The thing is, I was feeling relaxed about it, that was until the police call came to tell me to get home. Then it felt like my world fell in.'

'Join the club.' A gloomy silence settled between them.

'Oh no,' exclaimed Ruth looking at her watch and jumping up from the table, 'I'm supposed to be at Sea Cadets soon, chaplain duties. They wanted me there because they have an idea how to address knife crime. I promised them weeks ago, before all this blew up. I have to be there.'

'You'll be back in an hour, promise me.'

She nodded. Phil got up and they kissed each other affectionately on the lips.

'Got any Paracetamol downstairs?' she asked him. 'Need to knock the pain levels on the head before I go out.'

Phil went to the kitchen cupboard and handed her the packet with a glass of cold water.

'See you later. Its fish fingers tonight,' she said. Tuesdays were always fish fingers nights, life felt easier having familiar routines.

Ruth drove slowly, negotiating the busy traffic round the North Circular Road to arrive at the Sea Cadets HQ as they were finishing their assembly parade.

As always, she was greeted enthusiastically, and realised that there had always been a warm welcome for her as chaplain from the uniformed groups she attended. Here they sometimes affectionately called her, "Padre". She was included as one of the group, as if they automatically accepted her role in uniform as of equal validity to their own. In the Sea Cadets' world, all had their given place, a clear role to play. She was valued and accepted. Even her inability to march to time when invited to join them on parade had merely resulted in good humoured giggles. "Look at the Padre," they'd say, whilst tittering behind their hands.

On her last visit she'd been told that a week previous, two of the younger cadets, two brothers, Greg and Archie, had been walking home after the regular Tuesday evening meeting when they'd been stopped in their tracks by three older boys as they were passing the secondary school in Windmill Road.

Fun was poked at their Cadet uniforms, which they absorbed and let ride, but it didn't stop there. One of the three boys produced a knife and briefly placed it against the chin of Greg, the older brother, asking if they'd like to contribute to the social charity they were running. 'This is a good time to do it, bro.' It was all said with a nudge and a grin before the small amount of cash they had between them was duly handed over. Pockets were frisked to ensure they'd, 'not been cheatin'.'

Robbery over, the knife reappeared and the older brother had the buttons cut off his uniform one by one before being sent on his way, the gang laughing off the whole affair as they ran off leaving the lad bent to the pavement scrambling to pick up his uniform buttons, each precious brass button stamped with an anchor.

Discussed at length in the following week's cadet meeting, the two had been commended for their courage and sensible response. It could have all turned out so much worse. The younger brother, Archie, told his fellow cadets he'd like them all to do something to protest against knife crime. So it was agreed and Ruth was invited along to help take the idea forward. Tonight Ruth briefly rehearsed with everyone the background incident before making a suggestion to the gathered company.

'Some of you will know that Jackie's Dad is a welder at the garage. He has offered to help us do something very special. Also, I've spoken to the Edmonton Police Station and they too would like to join us in making and supporting an appropriate response.'

'And what is it you have in mind, Padre?' asked Andy Winter, the Commanding Officer.

'There's too much knife crime. Too many people are carrying knives, too many using them. What I propose is that we use all the knives the police have collected off people and make a table.'

'I don't follow,' said Andy.

'We make a table of knives, the knives welded together, to make a table for all, one that people can choose to sit around and talk to each other across. It makes an alternative statement about knives. The Bible tells of a time of peace when swords are turned into ploughshares. I would love to see us make a bold statement about knives having no use but to be welded into something around which people start talking with each other instead of threatening and harming one another. What do you think?'

'I love it. You reckon the police will hand the knives over? Jackie's Dad, Bill, will weld them into a table, I'm certain of it. Three questions, How long will it take; can the cadets be involved in the project and what will we do with the table?' Andy chipped in crisply, his round boy-like face looking to her for answers. Ruth returned his gaze, thinking with his sharp focus, his positive can-do approach, he wasn't the unit CO without good reason.

'Well... Yes, the police will hand them over if we provide the necessary reassurances and meet their protocols – no problem. Bill is definitely up for the welding isn't he Jackie?'

She nodded with a smile, adding 'Yes, Padre. He likes doing that kind of thing.'

'It will take a few days to assemble and make, once the design work's done. I think we could take two or three names of volunteers to offer their thoughts and ideas on that one, don't you think?' She looked at Andy.

'Volunteers,' he echoed, 'that's be you, you and you,' he indicated, the matter swiftly settled. 'You three, see me after. We'll need paper, pens and a measure, a ruler.'

'Yes, Sir,' came back the reply in unison.

Ruth continued. 'I suggest the table is presented in church by the cadet corps and used as our temporary Holy Communion Table in our main Sunday morning service. It would make a powerful religious as well as public statement and we could invite along to the occasion as many people from… wherever… to take part and support our initiative, what we are doing together to end knife crime. People will be glad to know something's being done, a statement is being made. Alright?'

'Perfect,' said Andy. 'Thank you Padre. I can see you've put a smile on Greg and Archie's faces, brought good out of evil I'd say. You can provide us with a closing prayer and blessing if you wouldn't mind. Now is fine,' he said, moving to stand alongside her and call everyone to attention. Ruth duly obliged.

Feeling uplifted, she headed back for the vicarage, morale boosted by the way the table of knives idea had come together. The promise of doing something positive they could all do as a unit, make a stand, in the face of a frightening and paralysing knife endemic. Wow!

'At last, at long last we're doing something,' she voiced quietly to herself.

True to her word she arrived back at the vicarage within one minute of the hour promised. Phil met her at the front door, opening it, clearly in a move to intercept her. He wanted to talk, to brief her.

'The police are here,' he whispered. It's April Cooper. I've given her a coffee and put her in the lounge. She was very insistent.'

'That's fine. I'd better see what she wants.'

'Don't get up,' she said to April sipping from her mug. 'How's things?'

'Busy actually, so the coffee break is well timed,' she said smiling.

'What can I do for you?' asked Ruth, trying to get to the point and not erode more of the time Phil had tried to safeguard for themselves.

'I need you to come with me... to see Tony Morris down at the station, Ruth. He won't speak to us and he won't accept a solicitor. To be frank he doesn't trust the police, but he has said he would talk if he could have a word with you first and if you were with him during questioning. And that's it, he's spending his time either sitting or lying in his cell, totally silent and currently refusing to eat, drink or do anything helpful. To be honest you're our only card. I realise you've only just come in, but will you come with me? We can talk on the way.'

Ruth was both surprised and apprehensive at this. She shuddered inside at the thought of seeing the young man again. The fear he had inflicted in her was still raw and she wasn't certain she was ready to face him, even in police company. 'What does he know about his mother's death? He knows she's dead doesn't he? Has someone told him?' she quizzed.

'When he was told, it was like… like he'd been expecting it…'

'There's more going on than I know about isn't there?' There was a knowing expression on April's face. 'No don't answer that,' she said, April shuffling in her seat, clearly not ready to divulge more.

'Let me just have a minute with Phil and I'll be with you.'

'I've got a car here. I'll take you and run you back, least I can do and we can chat in the car,' added April as Ruth strode to the door.

'Have you any idea how long this will take?' asked Ruth.

'Shouldn't be too long. Can't say. I'll call the station to set things up, speed things along, tell them we're coming in. Get him into an interview room, nicer than a cell.'

Ruth knew she couldn't expect more than that and headed off to the kitchen. This wasn't going to be easy.

When she explained things, Phil could do no more than shrug, saying, 'See you when I see you, you really have no choice do you?' before he turned his attention back to the sink.

As Ruth stepped into the street and into April's unmarked car, a puzzle she hadn't yet resolved resurfaced in her mind.

Why were Counter Terrorism involved? And what was now being dealt with by local police and what by April and her Counter Terrorism colleagues?

'April, why are Counter Terrorism involved here? Have I missed something? Raj, Tony, Angela… into terrorism? It doesn't mean anything to me? I can't see a connection?'

'I can't enlighten you I'm afraid.'

'Because orders are orders?' pushed Ruth.

'Yes. There's a lot that goes on beneath the radar to try and keep our communities safe and you'll appreciate why it has to be this way.'

'I thought I'd ask anyway. And another question. Why do I see nothing in the media about the two bodies in Raj's van?'

'I'd be grateful if you kept that to yourself for a little longer. We're making enquiries and have felt it necessary to keep a lid on that bit of information until we can effect arrests. That's still just between us, Ruth, I have to trust you on that one.'

'Good. I knew I wasn't being told things! All I can imagine is that what I've been hearing is but the edge of something bigger and possibly with a terrorism connection?' she surmised.

'I couldn't possibly comment,' April replied with a wry smile. Ruth felt she was only now beginning to talk to the April she once knew, the honest and good, not subterfuge April, the girl who was her father's daughter, a straight police officer.

Parking up in the secure police station yard to the rear, they walked briskly inside the modern fortress that is Edmonton Police Station. April asked to be excused and disappeared whilst Ruth was led by a white shirted police woman straight into the familiar interview room she herself had been questioned in but a few hours earlier. In fact, the sense of deja vu was further added to when she saw the same two officers were sitting there as if they'd never left their chairs, with Tony sitting opposite them, in the very chair where she herself had sat. The officers smiled at her conspiratorially, knowingly, in acknowledgement.

She stole a glance at Tony. He seemed pale and sad, every bit a lost young man with the wind taken out of his sails, no longer the threatening terror at her door. He looked smaller than she remembered him.

'Hello Tony,' she offered as she reached across, took and shook his hand. He clearly hadn't expected that. He shook it limply.

'I was sorry to hear about your mother. It was me who found her actually...'

'Stop right there, if you don't mind. We are in the middle of enquiries and I wouldn't want you to be saying anything that could make things more difficult... for Tony or yourself,' said the officer.

'Or yourselves,' added Ruth quickly.

'Indeed, or in own enquiries.' The officer relaxed again.

'I understand.' She sat herself down, pulling her chair alongside Tony's. 'I'm here,' she said to him quietly, 'because I was told you and I might have a conversation.'

Tony nodded, which Ruth took to be a positive sign. She then turned to the two police and said, 'would you two mind leaving us for a few minutes. Two's company, four's too big a crowd.'

The two looked at each other and after a moments whispering behind hands, led by the more senior of the two, they left the room. 'Back in twenty minutes. Shout if you need someone,' he told her. 'There's an officer right outside, just call if you need help.'

Once the two had left the room, Ruth adjusted her chair to face Tony.

'Look, I think this is all very tough for you. You've been arrested on a very serious charge of murder and now your Mum is no longer with us. I just want to say, I've no idea what you've done or haven't done. Both as a minister and as Ruth Churchill, I'm here to help.'

Tony looked like he was going to speak. He shuffled and said, 'I know. You went to get Mum her food. Tha... Thanks,' he said hesitatingly.

'I was glad to do it. To be honest I was worried for her as she seemed to have been relying solely on you for everything she needed.'

'But it was getting better. Raj used to help as well. He brought her things round to the house... They got on. I thought it was weird. My Mum never saw anyone and then

Raj was like round every other day dropping things in for her.'

'How long had they been friends… how long had this been going on?'

'Only maybe a month or so. Mum had special powers and Raj called her his priestess, his yogi. It was like that.' He locked his thumbs together and pulled them tight to indicate a close bond. 'Don't get me wrong, but I'm not into religion, it's not me.'

'And did Raj bring round the the little shrine and incense sticks?'

'Yeh! He wanted her to pray, get him some protection, fix things for his family. There was things he needed her support for, something to do with India or Bangladesh or somewhere. He'd give her money, only cause he wanted to mind, Mum didn't ask for it. He'd always tell her she didn't have to pay for the things he brought round to her. He was very good to her, really.'

'So Raj wanted her help?'

'Yeh. She said if he was to bring her summit, any object that he felt would give her spiritual guidance, something that would help her "*sense*" him and his "*need*".'

'And that's why he took her the shrine and incense?'

'Yeh, yeh, that's exactly why he brought those things round. Mum was pleased. She's always been very spiritual my Mum, and at first she was happy to have what she called so "*deep a connection*". She's always liked to collect things with religious power. Guess you'd have picked that up. Some people thought she was a white witch, someone who could curse, bless, predict things, give wise words, cast spells, that kind of thing. Most of that was ages ago. She's hardly seen anyone for years. But when Raj turned up, it brought some life back into her. Well it did to start with.'

'So things turned out less well than she thought?'

'Yeh. Can I have some water please?'

Ruth called out loudly, 'Anyone there?' Almost immediately the young police woman who'd presumably been positioned just outside came in and asked, 'everything alright Ma'am?'

'Two glasses of water please, if that's OK.'

'Yes, yes, I'll see to it.' She disappeared, to reappear in moments with two paper cups of water which she placed on the table before disappearing again.

Tony gulped down his water, clearly thirsty.

'Do you want mine? Take it,' offered Ruth. He needed no second bidding and placed her cup in front of him.

'Something bothered your Mum, didn't it?' asked Ruth gently.

'Yeh. Yeh. She told me she kept getting dark thoughts about Raj and the future. She couldn't sleep any more. The shadows kept coming and she couldn't keep them at bay.'

'Things were very bad last Saturday. She'd seen Raj early on Friday when he was on his way back to the shop from temple prayers. I was in the kitchen downstairs but I could hear them talking. It was urgent, as if they were almost arguing about what to do. I think Mum was warning him, sharing her fears.'

'So she thought something bad was going to happen and she was warning him?'

'Yeh, and in the end, on Saturday afternoon she told me to go and see him at the shop, see he was alright, to tell him to be very careful.'

'And is that what you did?'

'Yeh. I went to his shop. He was there, but he wasn't alone. So I took myself off to the Red Brick estate opposite, saw some mates, then went back.'

'Then what?'

'I couldn't see him.'

'He'd gone out?'

'No. No. I heard him first... A groan, a moan, a sound like "*ahhhh*",' he said, mimicking softly. 'I found him on the floor behind the counter. He had... he had a knife in him.'

'Then...'

'He had both his hands on it. He was trying to push it out. He couldn't. His eyes told me to. I helped, I pulled it out. He didn't speak. Lay there. Then there was blood. Lots of blood. I... I ran. I think I ran on to the Red Brick estate first thinking I could ask a mate what to do, but I didn't see anyone. Then I ran down the street and round the corner into Windmill Road. That was when they nearly got me. But you saved me.'

'Saved you? Well you saw me hide behind your wall when the cops came lookin' and you didn't squeal.'

'That was because I was too slow knowing what was happening,' she countered, wondering if the police were listening in.

'Well, you know the rest,' he said quaffing in one gulp the remaining water. 'Now these dick heads think I did him in,' he muttered quietly.

'Unless you tell them otherwise and let them get on with doing their job.'

'They're idiots. I hear them squabbling among themselves as to who should deal with me – local plods or Counter Terrorism. Counter Terrorism or local plods. Both the same. Meanwhile, while they argue among themselves, as far as I'm concerned I might as well be in La La Land. Whenever they've come near me it's as if I'm another knife crime villain like all the others. So I decided to take control by non-cooperation. I'm not stupid.'

'Well if you're not guilty, I'll vouch for you, I'll stand by you,' said Ruth resolutely, feeling what she'd been told had some ring of authenticity, some truth about it.

'Mum thought you were a good sort, which is why I trust you.'

'So what happens next,' she asked?

'Dunno.' said Tony simply, 'except now you've heard my side.'

'Yes. Is there anything you want me to do for you Tony?'

'Yeah! I know I said I wasn't religious, but would you say a prayer for Mum and bury her for me when they let you.'

Somewhat surprised at this, she simply said, 'I will, I'll pray that she should rest in peace and when the time comes we can talk about a funeral, but the way things are, we may need to wait a while yet, till the police have finished their job.'

A short time later Tony was led off back to the cells, giving no indication his non-cooperation policy with the police had yet changed. April was as good as her word, thanked Ruth and took her straight home, albeit much later than Ruth had hoped.

On her return Ruth went into the vicarage kitchen, this time to see Phil's face glowering darkly at her.

'I'm off to read in bed,' he said, not wanting to engage in a conversation.

Alone, Ruth tried to eat her supper at the kitchen table, but no matter how much she chewed, food didn't want to go down. Things had, she realised, reached a new low between them.

Something else was nagging at her mind. Then she remembered. Tonight, Olivia was supposed to have begun the dance class with her friends Freya and Maisie. To her absolute horror, she realised she had done absolutely nothing about it. It was just as if she had committed a major crime herself and if there was any remedy for this misdemeanour open to her she couldn't for the life of her think at that moment what it might be.

18

They didn't speak and early in the morning Phil took himself off to work after expressing what he described as his forlorn wish there would be no more police interruptions today. Only after he'd gone and Ruth was getting up and showering did she recall he'd said that jobs were set to go in the firm and she wished she'd been able to say something. Though he must have been worried, he hadn't said anything about it to her. Once she'd got ready, the kids up and dressed and off to breakfast club, she thought she'd send him a text message.

It was whilst Olivia and Paul were arguing over cereals the front door bell rang. This was an early call, it was still before 8am.

Mary Olumbo was standing there with a smile on her face, her right arm lifted high and pointing in the direction of the church. Mary lived a few doors up the road. A nice, vivacious young woman with a smart dress sense, she was no doubt on her way to work. The two had always had time for a polite hello in the street whenever their paths had crossed. Ruth wondered what lay behind her unexpected visit.

'Mrs Churchill, I've seen the banners? I must say I like them and wanted to say congratulations on supporting the cause.'

Ruth must have looked mystified.

'You haven't have you? Come and see. They're superb!'

No sooner had Ruth taken three paces from her front door than she spotted two roof to ground banners suspended from the church's short tower. The left hand side read downwards 'CLIMATE', the right 'EXTINCTION', and across the top linking the two verticals was a horizontal 'ACT NOW'. It was all very professional looking, mounting hooks had been fastened on the brick work, no expense spared. It was so unmissable, every bus and car passenger going through north London must be able to see it, thought Ruth.

'Ah, those banners,' said Ruth trying to regain control. She gazed at them a second time.

'First time I've seen them actually. I must find out who put them up. Someone will know. First though, I need to get my children to school. You're right Mary, they make a bold statement! You have a good day, Mary. Thanks for calling.'

With that she closed the door to return to the kitchen. In her absence at the door the argument over cereals seemed to have resolved itself. The two children were happily finishing up. Now to make some early enquiries. She needed to try and find out who was responsible for the banner and this would need to be done before the undoubted flood of criticism would come in and overwhelm her.

A little later, school run done, Morning Prayer done, Ruth retreated quickly into her study to take control of her day. First she sent another peacemaking, holding text, to Phil, wishing him well and telling him she was thinking of him today.

This morning the postman knocked the door with a pile of mail to hand to her, one of which was too large an envelope to fit through the letterbox. It was from Julie and contained a detailed proposal and names of suggested contractors to approach for tenders for a new boundary wall and security gate to protect the west end of the church. Ruth threw it on to her desk, half minded instead to target the waste paper bin slightly to the right.

Time to play detective and find out about the banner, she thought, as she picked up the phone to call Stephanie. She was the PCC, the Parochial Church Council, Secretary. Waiting for Stephanie to pick up, Ruth looked out of her study window. To her surprise a crowd of around twenty people had gathered and photos were being taken with the banner as a backcloth.

It'll be all over social media, she thought panicking somewhat. Putting the phone down before making her call, she walked briskly outside to see what she might discover, only to be told where to stand as people wanted to have their pictures taken, with her in the centre. So this is what celebrity status feels like!

Children were arriving at the secondary school opposite the church and they too were stopping to see what the crowd was about. More pictures were being taken. Then a police car arrived, the officer jumping out to ask her if everything was alright, a call having been taken by the station saying that a large crowd had gathered outside the church and may lead to traffic problems. Suitably reassured the car continued on its way as Ruth sought to extricate herself from photo shots and get back into the sanctuary of the vicarage.

Once inside she thought to herself the banner was no bad thing. No publicity was bad publicity. This was an opportunity, but she still needed to know who had put it up and how on earth they had gained access to the tower. She imagined this would only lead to Julie's wall argument getting more backing.

Thankfully she didn't need to make a series of investigative calls, one call came in from Chris Darlington, her churchwarden. He said he could explain. Then in apologetic terms, he told his story. His son, Ed, a keen advocate of Eco-church, had been in touch with Climate Extinction friends and hit upon a direct action idea, the result of which was what was currently hanging from the west end outside wall of the church.

'But how did he do it?' asked Ruth.

'I'm afraid he took, err, borrowed my church keys and they let themselves up the spiral staircase and onto the roof from where they fastened their banner. I'm afraid they put in a couple of climbing bolts to ensure the thing doesn't blow away on the first breeze, but I'm assured everything is safe. I know they don't have permission, faculties, etc, but just view it as a temporary attachment to the fabric of the building, a bit of advertising if you like and then in due course it can be taken down. That shouldn't be a problem should it?'

'So you're happy with it?'

'Oh yes, hear the arguments Ruth, hear the arguments or have my resignation. I do feel strongly on the climate issue.'

'Well, put like that, it's a fait accompli. Let's try and take something positive from it. Thank you for letting me know Chris. I'd appreciate an earlier heads up next time something like this is on the cards, OK? I think I'll need to let the archdeacon know before he hears it from elsewhere, otherwise he'll roast me over the coals.'

'I thought the Inquisition was over?' he laughed.

Ruth did not laugh back. Sometimes she wished Chris was a better judge of inter-personal realities. Had he been, she would have had a better ally in her ongoing battle with her ever watchful inquisitor of an archdeacon.

19

By early Wednesday afternoon the media were outside too, photographers and cameramen with their interviewers, all after the story. The inevitable door bell rings followed as request after request were made that Ruth come and have her picture taken; be interviewed; express her views on climate change and finally be asked if she, representing the Church of England were a supporter of direct action on climate change.

Debbie Welch, the Deputy Head from the School opposite, also came across to ask her, rather officiously, two questions. Firstly, whether she thought her campaign would interfere with the pupils' safe departure from school later in the afternoon, there being so many people gathered on the street, to which the answer was 'no'; and secondly, whether Ruth was seeking to encourage pupils to take direct action of their own, something she was keen to see should not happen given recent pupil absenteeism in support of 'her campaign'. To which the answer was also – 'no'. Upon which Debbie, presumably satisfied with Ruth's assurances, strode off briskly to no doubt report back to the anxious Head who had sent her across in the first place.

For some while Ruth had personally thought that the lack of political will by government to address the need to check carbon emissions was something she too felt strongly about and as the afternoon wore on she increasingly warmed to the banner and its message, to the extent she even found herself proud of it and the fact her little corner of north London was on the map as a visible herald of the need to address the issue.

Her growing sympathy for the banner received its first set back when her mobile phone rang at 2pm. It was the Press and Communications Officer from Causton Street, the Diocese of London's HQ.

'Carlton Smyth here, picked up on the news feeds that you're in the headlines again. Got the right person, haven't I, Ruth Churchill?'

'That's me. How can I help, Carlton?'

'I'm getting Tweets and calls from Bishops as well as local churches asking after the Church's support for 'Extinction Rebellion'. Your name's coming up each time as a lead supporter. Can you fill me in on this?'

'Personally, when I first spotted the banner this morning I was shocked by it, the church, our church being used for a political stunt.'

'You mean you didn't organise it?'

'No, No! But don't you think its proving effective in the way its getting people to listen to the need; that its imperative we address our carbon footprint?'

'All well and good, but have you looked at how this sits with the Bishop of London's Eco-statement report? Didn't see you figuring in any communication forward plan. Caught us all out you did. Wrong footed us here. Don't you think you've stepped out of line with our response on this issue? Usually when something like this is on the cards, parishes ring us first to ask how we should handle it. Did I miss something? You didn't did you, call in earlier?'

'No…' Ruth felt caught off guard. She hadn't even heard of the Bishop of London's paper on the matter, but instantly recognised she was out on a limb. Even though the Bishop of London was known for wanting climate change addressed, even she knew the Bishop was no supporter of Extinction Rebellion, their actions seen as "troublesome", getting people arrested, putting people in prison and causing undue inconvenience to others trying to go about their hard-pressed lives.

Instantaneously, Ruth knew she was out of step and heading for another reprimand or worse, and she felt annoyed by Carlton who probably had no idea of what it was like to be in her situation, a situation not of her doing.

'So when are you coming here?' she asked him, 'to see for yourself and get the true story? Don't suppose you're interested in interviewing the young person whose idea it was, are you?' she said, trying to take some control. There was a distinct pause at the other end of the line before she got a reply.

'I'm always interested in a personal story, I find that's the best route to finding a way through the tricky political stuff,' he said, with a detectable spark of interest in his tone of voice. Rising to her challenge, he added, 'I can be at the vicarage in an hour.'

With that he had gone, leaving Ruth to wonder how the rest of the afternoon with an impending kids from school collection time coming up and more telephone calls to make concerning the couple of funerals from the weekend were to be fitted in.

She extricated herself from the milling crowd beneath the fluttering colourful banner and went back inside the sanctuary the vicarage provided.

Her first phone call was to churchwarden Chris to ask if his son Ed could get down to church within the hour to explain his actions as the Church Press Officer, Carlton Smyth, was wanting to hear the full story on the banner. Chris relayed the message on to Ed whilst she hung on. Much to her relief the reply came back, 'he'll be out of college pronto and he's very keen to be there. He didn't need a second invitation to skip his afternoon lectures.'

Ruth was concerned she might have caused some truancy, but bit her tongue, not giving a reply. She didn't know Ed well, but if he was anything like his Dad he should be able to give a good account of himself in front of Carlton.

More tricky was how to position herself. Her present situation in the church could at best be described as precarious, rather like that of a school under special measures. No doubt Archdeacon Stephen would be on the phone next demanding yet another explanation from her for this latest piece of deviancy and she could well do without that.

Feeling hungry and light headed she wandered into the kitchen and looked inside the fridge. There was precious little there and she knew she needed to find five minutes to place an on-line grocery order with the supermarket for an early delivery – they were running low on supplies. As a stop-gap, perhaps she could pop and see Darshana and pick up some items whilst she was there. Kill two birds with one stone. There were no biscuits in the house for when Carlton arrived, perhaps she could borrow some from the Mothers

Union cupboard, she thought and replace them later. An idea she rejected as unwise and too easily open to misinterpretation.

Like not getting Olivia to dance class, not being on top of the food shopping felt like another big oversight on her part, a sign that things were teetering on the edge of being out of control. She knew she needed to manage and gain some power over her life. The thought of not coping unnerved her much as if she were walking along a slippy cliff edge path and there was no fence between her and the waves dashing on the rocks far below. She was perilously close to falling.

She retreated again to her study with a coffee, definitely, she told herself, the last for the day. Funeral visits booked and necessary calls made she began looking at her email inbox.

Her unopened mail was an ocean of blue dots. They'd spread like duckweed across a pond, dominating everything. Overcome by the blue, she flipped her laptop lid down only to open it again and scan down to see if there was any reply from the theological college about an ordinand to help her. There wasn't. She concluded it was all too soon to expect any cavalry over the horizon and the college were probably still on summer vacation. The laptop was shut a second time and this time stayed shut. Emails would have to wait. She finished her coffee.

With Carlton Smyth on his way from Vauxhall she needed to arrange for someone to collect the children. A quick call to Freya's Mum and it was sorted, but not without pangs of guilt assailing her for not being there herself for her own children. Was every day this term going to be like this? All this wasn't going to help her relationship with Phil either and she wondered how he was, there being no reply to her texts.

The children would go to Freya's house in Palmers Green until Ruth picked them up 'whenever it was convenient'. In fact they'd be fed there Freya's Mum said – a welcome bonus, some extra space and time won.' There is a God!' she exclaimed under her breath as she felt a little extra diary room for manoeuvre open up.

Carlton arrived sooner than she'd expected. When she opened the front door his black cab was waiting outside, engine running, presumably ready to whisk him back to wherever as soon as he'd been fed his news piece. He suggested the interview should take place outside the church, in front of the banner with the still milling, if now even bigger crowd that had been reinforced by parents waiting to collect their school children at the end of the afternoon. It was a mixed bunch they had standing around them, many all the more excited upon noting the presence and interest of the press.

She'd seen Carlton before, once when he was busy taking pictures of her at the time of the Ali Muhammed report. He'd avoided talking to her more than he needed to back then, as if she were damaged goods, able to contaminate or infect anyone standing near enough to her for too long. He was still relatively new then. Who could blame him?

This afternoon he seemed much less guarded and more affable. Right on cue, a smiling Ed arrived, every bit the typical college student with a winsome smile. A much relieved Ruth made the introductions. Then, after checking Ruth and Ed were OK with the idea, Carlton placed a small voice recording device in his hand and switched it on.

'I am with Ed…' began Carlton looking at Ed.

'Darlington, Ed Darlington,' Ed added, right on cue.

'…and the Revd Ruth Churchill. We're standing outside the west wall of Holy Trinity Church, Edmonton, north London on a Wednesday afternoon where a crowd has gathered following the dramatic placing of a banner in support of "Extinction Rebellion". It has the words "Act Now" calling everyone who sees it to take immediate direct action on climate change. First of all, Ed, I believe this was your idea?'

'Yes, a group of college friends are fed up with the inertia around the most important issue of our time and I suggested it might be possible to put a banner up on this very public site.'

'And did you have any backing, any support from the local church congregation, before you did this?'

'No. That was our intention. Unless people are shocked out of their stupor, church authorities included, unless it surprises them, it won't result in any movement. Time is short, churches take years to agree to change their flower rosters or plan a jumble sale. This has been all done and dusted within five days, from idea to execution.'

'But how did you get access? How did you get on to the tower?'

'All it took was one willing key holder to turn a blind eye and the job was done.'

'OK Ed, like Martin Luther who made his argument for change by nailing it to a church door, you've gone one better and bolted your manifesto to cover the whole church wall! Are you pleased? Will people like what you say?'

Unexpectedly, there was a round of spontaneous applause from the people now listening in to what was being said with cries of, 'well done Ed!' and 'It's for all our future, you know!'

'And turning now to you Ruth, when did you, Ruth Churchill, as vicar, first discover your church was being used for a giant advert for climate politics?' asked Carlton pushing his recording device under her chin.

'Only when someone called at my door to tell me this morning as they were going to work.'

'And what are your thoughts on what it says? Do you think the church should stick to worshipping God or get itself involved in the contested world of eco politics?'

'The Bible and the church have always been involved in the world. Looking after the earth and everything created under heaven is part of what we do. The first book of the Bible tells us we are all children of Adam and all earth's stewards, that means carers responsible for our planet; the church has a voice it sometimes loses but needs to exercise. We speak because we care! Because... if we don't speak out... people will suffer and die.'

'So Ed's banner has your endorsement?'

'... Why yes, I believe it does.' This brought on another round of 'hear, hear!' and 'well said, Vicar!' followed by another outbreak of hand clapping.

This was evidently enough of a clip for Carlton. He had what he wanted and after quickly excusing himself, he dashed back to his waiting black cab. Half a minute later he'd gone, his cab struggling against the tide of traffic, eventually escaping the incoming flow of cars arriving at the end of afternoon school.

'Thanks Ed,' said Ruth pointing to the banner. 'Even though it rather wrong footed me, I'm glad for it. Well done.'

After talking to one or two of the familiar faces on the street, she once again headed back indoors. She needed to think about the next morning's mid-week communion. Though only a handful of faithful regulars came along it was important to prepare a few words for a short address and by late afternoon on a Wednesday she at least needed to have familiarised herself with the Bible readings set for tomorrow upon which her sermon would be based.

Outline sermon finished, she looked up from her desk. It was nearly 5pm. She felt prompted to make a call to Darshana.

She picked up, evidently much upset and immediately Ruth felt obligated and committed herself to going round to see her.

Reluctantly, she sent Phil another text message to say where the kids were, assuring him they'd have been fed and she would bring back some supper for the two of them to have later from Darshana's shop, all sent just in case he arrived home before she did.

She felt she was still hanging in there, but only by a thread. Deep inside herself, she wondered whether she was stretching Phil's patience to the limit, even beyond it and the thought terrified her. She needed to be with him.

20

It was just after 6pm by the time she'd walked the short distance down Silver Street to the Chauhan's corner shop with its small flat above. Lights were on, the shop open and Darshana and her brother Ravi visibly busy, now running things between them. On seeing Ruth enter, Darshana said something to him, presumably in Hindi, whereupon heads nodded in agreement and Ravi moved behind the till to occupy the place where Darshana had until then been standing.

The two women greeted one another warmly, walked between the cereals and jams aisles, then went out the back and upstairs.

This time the flat seemed more chaotic and untidy than before with papers strewn on every surface, brightly coloured clothes left airing across the window, nothing tidied or put away. Ruth saw in all this her own future – her slippery slope as she similarly struggled and failed to keep on top of things back at the vicarage.

'Don't let me leave without buying the things on my list,' began Ruth. 'I'll be in big trouble at home if I forget. We've nothing in the house for supper tonight!'

'A woman's work is never done,' replied Darshana clearing papers from a seat, placing them on the floor, so Ruth could sit down.

'Well, you're a working woman like me. How are you doing juggling everything at a time like this?'

'Not very well, but the shop must be open, 7-11 every day. Ravi has been such a help, though he won't be able to stay much longer. I'll have to manage on my own soon, best thing I try to take on a youngster – there's always someone wanting a job in retail.'

'Have you other family Darshana? I should have asked before.'

'My brother Hitesh, in Southall, but he's another single-handed shop proprietor. It's very difficult for him to get away. We speak on the phone and he'll be over at the weekend. Apart from him, my family, like Raj's, are all back in Gujarat. There are lots of Chauhans there, especially in Ahmedabad where we both grew up. The good thing is, with the internet, and FaceTime, we can talk to one another easily enough. India's changed such a lot.'

'I'm pleased to hear it. You need family at times like this,' said Ruth, thinking that there really was only Ravi nearby. Her breath caught on the strong scent of incense smoke burning in the near corner. It reminded her again of Angela Morris and prompted her to voice what was on her mind.

'The incense reminds me of Angela Morris' house. She had a shrine and incense just like that. She told me Raj used to help her by taking groceries and things she needed round to the house. That was very kind of him.'

'Yes... He was a kindhearted man like that,' she said, eyes cast down into her lap. 'It will help him in his reincarnation. I think Raj liked her because she was open to Hinduism. Raj was always very strong in his faith and he used to come back and tell me he thought Angela was a secret Hindu. She wanted him to say the prayers, to help her create a shrine for

204

worshipping the gods. Yes, he had soft spot for her. He'd usually call in on her on his way back from the temple. I was so sorry to hear she had died. But Raj say she very sick, in bed all time.'

'It's very strange to me that… that Angela's son Tony is the one the police have in custody for Raj's death. You wouldn't have thought it. He must have known your Raj was kind to his Mum. How does anyone explain that?'

'He never did it. Tony was always in the shop buying this and that for his Mum and himself. I don't believe he killed Raj no matter what they say. He looks a bit strange, wild even, but he's not the sort. The police weren't really interested in my theories on the matter. Their mind was made up.'

'Then who did kill Raj, Darshana, and are they still out there?'

Darshana went quiet, something clearly on her mind and she was reticent to say it. Her fingers were pulling at some loose threads in her white sari. Ruth sensed there was something there and gently prompted her to speak further.

'Do you know anything? Have you got some thoughts you'd like to share? I mean… if Tony is innocent… then we need to be making sure Raj's real murderer is apprehended before they do it again,' said Ruth, thinking that she had stumbled upon something significant and that Tony might be the victim of a grave injustice.

'I… I don't know. Things haven't been as they should be recently. Too many strange things have happened…' a comment that mystified Ruth further.

'I remember, when you came to see me on Monday, you said you thought you had been watched or followed and your phone sounded though... as though someone was listening in on your conversations. Do you still think that? Has it happened again? Is there something else?' Ruth pressed.

'One thing has been on my mind. It was what Raj said, about a month ago. He said he'd had a couple of customers in the shop who were from our part of India. He hadn't seen them before, they were strangers to him, but he said, they asked him a lot of questions and they certainly knew Gujarat, but they didn't speak Gujarati to him, nor did they speak Hindi, they spoke Urdu. They kept coming back to the shop and pestering him.' The significance of the different languages passed over Ruth's head, though she sensed what she was being told was important.

'What kind of questions?'

'When did he live there? Who were his family? That kind of thing.'

'Raj was very wary of them and gave them evasive answers. He was certain they were Muslims, because they stuck to Urdu. He never told me about when they came back to the shop again. But I knew they had, a customer told me. I also knew Raj and his moods... I had the impression Raj was really bothered by their visits, it was playing on his mind, I could tell. He became very short tempered with me for no reason. I did try asking him about it, but he simply said, "it's all in the past".'

'This could be important, don't you think? What do you think he meant by all in the past?'

'I didn't know and he didn't want me to talk about it, so we both put it behind us, forgot about it. It's hard work running a shop. We're always busy. But I remembered about it last night when I was sitting here on my own. Things come back when you're in the quiet on your own. Now I think about it, I agree, it might be important.'

'I think it could be. It sounds like it's something you should tell the police… and let's not forget about young Tony.'

Darshana looked confused, lost in her own thoughts. She seemed to be turning things over in her mind with a growing look of uncertainty and apprehension spreading across her face.

'Does something worry you, Darshana?'

'Yes. I can't think it's relevant. Just more customers Raj wasn't sure about I expect. We get so many difficult people in, minor pilferers almost every day. Mentally ill people can be the worst. Old people who are confused about paying too – but they're the easy ones, believe me. I think I'll ponder on things a bit before talking to any more police. It was all about what happened in India years ago, he said, I can't see how it can be relevant now.'

Though Ruth wanted her to, she didn't feel she could push Darshana to talk to the police if she didn't want to, but to her mind the two visitors to the shop seemed important. It felt like their past connection with Raj, even though Ruth hadn't any evidence to back up her hunch, had everything to do with unfinished business, whatever it might have been. It could have been a family matter, it could be something bigger, there was no way of her knowing. Yet she had a nagging suspicion it might even more likely, be linked directly with his murder.

'I definitely think you should do that, I mean ponder. It could be that Raj told you something important but you didn't realise its significance at the time. You didn't know it,' she added as a passing shot, expressing her firm instincts on the matter.

Ruth thought she saw a look in Darshana's eye which indicated, you know this is important and now I wish I hadn't told you. It was time for Ruth to think of going and not outstay her welcome. But as she stood up she had one other puzzle on her mind, something else she wanted to pass by Darshana before leaving.

'When I went to Angela's house late last Sunday afternoon, the van, Raj's van, caught fire right outside her house. Whilst I was in there, with her, it kind of exploded into flames and was very quickly, in spite of the efforts of the fire brigade, completely burned out. I've been thinking about that a lot since. Do you have any idea why the van was there, why it caught fire even? What are people saying?'

'That's easy. It wasn't always possible to park outside the shop. Silver Street is a nightmare for us. Raj would leave the van wherever he could in nearby streets. Guess he left it there because it was convenient. Maybe he left it there after he'd dropped in her groceries. I don't know. The police came and told me they'd found it. Asked me lots more questions. Don't understand…'

Ruth wasn't convinced. Darshana's reply seemed to be too glib, superficial, lacking in conviction. She couldn't put her finger on it but she felt Darshana was hiding something.

However, it was time to get her own shopping and return home, but she didn't want to leave on bad terms, and she saw buying her own groceries as a small reconciling act.

Leaving 'Sonny's' corner shop, Ruth was mindful of the banner still hanging on her church. She clutched her re-used plastic bag filled with items for supper and hurried home. It was a wet walk, the rain had returned with a vengeance, forcing everyone to bend their heads and anonymously dash to find shelter. As she made her own way, dodging the puddles in her unsuitable shoes, her mind was full of what she had just been told. She was back at her own door in minutes.

She asked herself, what did she do with this new information? A cynical voice inside said that it was all only conjecture, third-hand hearsay about two shop visitors from India, but a deeper inner instinct left her hanging on to the disquiet she felt.

Once inside she decided to sit on the information she'd been given for now, collect the kids from Freya's and get some food on the go for when Phil was back from work. It was good to think she had no evening meeting tonight, the two of them desperately needed to have some time together.

However, from inside the hallway, she heard the sound of the TV upstairs and called up. Phil was back and he came downstairs, taking his time. When she saw him he looked tired and crestfallen.

'Redundancy. Those are my things,' he said, pointing a finger toward a soggy wet cardboard box in the hallway.

The box contained all the personal effects he'd hastily cleared from his desk before leaving. Ruth felt the shock waves.

'I'm now on garden leave,' they call it. 'I'm not allowed back in. Standard practice.'

'Oh Phil,' she said, feeling insecure. 'I'm so sorry. What happened today?'

'We all got called to the main conference room this afternoon and were told the news. At the same time they sent a text message to each one of us personally. Whilst we were being told the score by Head of Branch, they were busy behind our backs. It was all orchestrated, cleverly executed, pre-planned for days. We were closed down, barred from accessing our computer accounts. Simply sent on our way. No thank you. No goodbyes.' Phil told his story without seeming to pause for breath. Ruth could see that he was deeply upset and trying his best not to show it.

'Some of the guys were livid, some were in shock, others had expected it and had kind of prepared themselves for the inevitable. My colleague Richard, has a desk beside mine, he never gets angry; this morning he threw his computer on the floor and then started to cry. It was awful. We were all told to wait until security took our key fobs and escorted us to the street. They processed us in groups of twos and threes, told us to get our things and leave. We were literally shown the door and locked out in the rain. That's it! The end!' Phil dropped his head, drew a breath and seemed to regain some composure before continuing.

'We were told we'd be getting official letters at our home addresses very shortly. Hadn't expected this. I'd thought my job would be safe, but they've done it to all the London staff as far as I can see, we've all gone; Head of Branch, he flew in from Hamburg. They're keeping all the company posts over in Europe. So much for independent Britain!'

'So sorry Phil.' Ruth said quietly and moved in to hold him. They hung on to each other in a mutually comforting overdue embrace. She whispered in his ear, 'What are we going to do now?'

'Well, you haven't got to collect the kids. Freya's Mum, Mol called me, she's dropping them round shortly.'

'She's been a star. She fed them too. I've got us some supper for us, Indian Jalfrezi chicken and rice, a ready meal. Been to see Darshana, picked it up there.'

'How's she doing? Your mention of her makes me realise my own troubles perhaps aren't so big in the greater scheme of things.'

'True. You'll find something else to do, you will, I know it.'

'On the plus side, it feels like good timing to be around home just now with all that you've got going on.'

Just then the front door bell rung.

'That'll be the kids,' said Ruth, making for the door first. However, one step in the porch, she instinctively knew it wasn't them. Opening the front door cautiously, she saw two men standing there. Small of stature and probably having Asian sub-continent roots. Her apprehension rose.

'Hello. How can I help?' she ventured, standing as far away from them as she could without appearing rude.

'We wanted to ask please, have meeting in hall next door? Man say first speak you,' he said in faltering English.

Ruth was curious. 'What kind of meeting?'

'Meeting for people from Myanmar, all people come, tell them about it. Speak what happen in my country.' The second man had yet to say anything and Ruth wondered whether he spoke any English at all, let alone the faltering patter of his companion.

Ruth felt a degree of sympathy for them. Interpreting between the lines she guessed the two were Rohingya Muslims who wanted to hold a meeting to canvas local awareness and support. It should be what the church was about. She had heard that things had been tough and certain men who'd been to the church Refugee Drop-In before it was closed had had to flee for their lives into neighbouring Bangladesh. Could this be some of them or London-based sympathisers?

She popped back inside to get her mobile. They exchanged contact details using their mobile phones, in the end agreeing the hall was free for them to use the following evening. Once they had clearly understood what she was telling them, they left smiling.

Ruth went to rejoin Phil believing herself to have done the right thing by them. Nowhere, she thought, not even her corner of north London was that far away from troubles in other parts of the world.

21

Next morning began like a day off, only it wasn't. It was an illusion framed by Phil getting up with Ruth and instead of heading off to the city, filling the too-long-vacant position of domestic engineer at the vicarage. Ruth watched him feeding, then taking the kids to school as he did his best to try and explain to them what had happened to him at work yesterday.

'No, I didn't get the sack... I haven't done anything wrong... It happens sometimes that people's jobs aren't needed any more in business' and 'of course I'll find another job...'

By the time the trio had reached the parked car from the front door, Ruth could still hear the incessant questioning from curious young minds who had no real grip of what Phil was going through. The final argument had been about pocket money and whether they would get any. Despite the questioning, she saw their children serving as a kind of therapy in the situation, giving Phil a role, some much needed self-motivation, a safe place for him to talk it all through and to be given purpose on a day he might otherwise have lacked any.

Thursdays always provided a kinder start for Ruth herself. There were no 8.30am early morning prayers to be said today. Instead, a so-called mid-week Communion Service in church replaced them at 10.30am and this was followed by coffee in the choir vestry for the handful of people who came along. There were usually, at most, ten people. In all it should be an easy morning procedure to follow, just what she needed.

Ruth took the time beforehand to make another attack on her email inbox. She always began this task in the same way, routinely striking out what she regarded as "the dross" as quickly as she could. Initially, the exercise always felt good as, at a single stroke, so many items were simply deleted. The next stage was to steel herself to look at the remaining 'total unopened' figure. She lifted her hands from the keyboard as she did so. Her heart sank, her hands dropped, as she registered it was, at 387 items of unopened mail, even higher than the previous day's stratospheric level.

There was nothing for it but to start ploughing through them. Whether it was really a good approach or not, she wasn't sure, but she always began with the more recent, "live ones". It always nagged at her that she had neither been given lessons in the administration of such things nor in the management of church projects. To have done so might have made such a difference. As she recalled, all such learning at theological college had to take second place to the study of the Bible and Mission. Once in parish life, the need for such further skills became all too apparent.

An hour quickly passed and before she had got nearly as far as she'd intended, she knew she had better stop and get over to church and begin setting up for the service. People would soon be arriving. The thought of the remaining emails in the inbox nagged at her as she walked over to church clutching her robes. She tried to cheer herself by thinking it was far better to be well-prepared for the service, ready to do what mattered most.

A quarter of an hour later, on the stroke of half-past ten, robed up, prayer offered, she strode the fews steps from the vicar's vestry to the little side chapel, pausing half way to bow in the chancel toward the high altar, before taking her place, standing, behind the chapel altar table, facing the congregation. She lifted her head.

No! It couldn't be. She looked twice. Much to her consternation, sitting behind the familiar regulars, several rows back next to the door, was none other than the archdeacon, Stephen Nicholls. His face was looking down, but it was unmistakably him.

Ruth's heart fluttered, missed a beat, as she asked herself in panic, what on earth he was doing there? A second or two later, having no time to guess the answer, she welcomed the congregation adding an appropriately polite special, 'warm welcome to our Archdeacon Stephen, who joins us this morning.'

As if permission had been given, all heads immediately swivelled round to eye-ball him. At this, head raised, Archdeacon Stephen smiled obsequiously. How she disliked the man. The congregation for their part didn't really know him, so they were probably either just puzzled, asking themselves, shouldn't he be up at the front or feeling simply flattered to have had him show interest in their church.

Whatever the reason behind his visit and there had to be one, Ruth felt his unexpected presence meant her ability as a minister was once again being tested and as the service moved forward, her heightened efforts at concentration as she checked and double-checked how well she was delivering the liturgy began to take its toll. Her confidence began to slide, her uncertainties grew, her focus wavered, until finally, halfway through the eucharistic prayer she stumbled through her words at the most critical moment, the point when this high churchman would expect the most profound attention must be given – the epiclesis, the blessing of the elements of bread and wine which happened at the central climax of the service.

In that instant she knew she had now confirmed his firmly held impression she was a failure, a liability to the church, and it took all her willpower to navigate her way to the final blessing, remembering just beforehand to remind her congregation that coffee would be served immediately afterwards in the vestry.

Ruth returned to her vicar's vestry with a dry mouth, her forehead covered with perspiration caused by her anxiety. She was keen to shed her warm robes and put on her navy jacket. That done and being the first back into the adjacent larger choir vestry she put the kettle on for the coffee and waited. After several minutes she realised something was very wrong. No-one had come in!

Water boiled, the kettle had clicked off. She was still on her own. Curiosity getting the better of her, she walked back into church to hear there was an animated discussion going on in the side chapel. The archdeacon was standing at the front engaged in conversation with her people. Curiosity roused, she hastily strode over to join them.

'Ah, glad you're here. We were just talking about things, how easy it is to let things slide,' he said, not really explaining what they had been talking about, but saying enough to leave her feeling under a critical gaze.

Where was this going, wondered Ruth, waiting to hear what he wanted to say? How the man loved the sound of his own voice, venting forth in front of a simpering audience.

'I've had a letter,' he said in a moment of drama. He pulled out an envelope from his inside pocket with a flourish and held it up for all to see. Ruth realised this was what he had been looking at earlier. It was this he had been holding and reading in his lap as as she had entered the chapel at the start of the service.

'A letter?' she quizzed.

'About your unauthorised banner on the outside of the church. We were talking about it. Don't you think it demeans what the church stands for?'

'The lack of authorisation or the message it carries? I'm not sure I'm with you?' she replied.

'Margaret here, was just saying, that she wasn't aware anyone had discussed taking such an action. The church council members she has spoken to are feeling totally ignored, even by-passed. She says, that banner,' his arm, extended by the white envelope in his hand, pointed toward the west end as if anyone had any doubt where it was, 'will have to come down until it has permission to be there. That's right isn't it, Margaret?'

'Yes, Archdeacon,' she replied meekly.

'And it didn't have my permission either,' added Ruth, giving rise to a look of utter surprise and disbelief on the archdeacon's face.

'I had a parishioner call at my door first thing yesterday morning to alert me of its presence. That was when I first knew, soon after first light, when someone came to my door. Yesterday turned out to be a very busy day, not least because of the crowds of people coming to the church because of it. Even our own Diocesan Media man, Carlton Smyth was in on the act to record a story and take pictures.'

'Ah, yes, I heard about that. Wasn't it your churchwarden who was behind it all? You said as much, you did! Isn't that right?'

'Yes, I soon got to the bottom of the mystery. Actually, it wasn't the churchwarden but his son, a student and climate activist who had been involved. I had no knowledge it was going to happen and to be frank, now it is there, the deed is done. What do you want me to do now, apply for retrospective approval?'

'As an act of vandalism, it needs to be removed and the church restored to how it was before.'

'And that was something I was going to discuss with the church council,' added Ruth, trying to keep the initiative with her. 'You see I need to work with people on this one. Clearly there are issues to be gone into here. We need to approach whoever it was who did this to see if they have the professionals able to remove this. After all it belongs to somebody, whether or not it was put up without permission.'

'Ah!,' he said. Ruth could almost hear him trying to give himself time to think at the other end and whilst she had the opportunity she pressed home her advantage.

'Also, there are health and safety issues as well as financial costs to be discussed. And what I've been hearing from people in the church is that there are mixed views on what to do now. Some people are very pleased to see the banner and want it to stay. Others, like yourself, want it removed. There are the local politics to be discussed. Be assured, Archdeacon, I will keep you fully advised as to how we are doing on this one, you will be the first to know how it's being managed... but I really only came across to let everyone know the kettle had boiled. We can continue our conversation over a hot drink if you'd all like to follow me.'

Not even an archdeacon can stand between Edmonton people and a cuppa. Feet shuffled and people followed Ruth into the vestry. With Margaret's assistance, she served everyone as they duly arrived. However, when she looked up, she could no longer see her adversary. The archdeacon had taken his leave.

Finding herself much relieved at Archdeacon Stephen's departure, like the pleasant freshness after a storm has blown through, Ruth much enjoyed her coffee, her regulars, now more relaxed, glad to chat about their own concerns for family and friends; the bigger issue of climate change was left to one side together with their earlier conversation with the archdeacon. There were one or two comments about the archdeacon being a bit edgy, but that was it.

Half an hour later, Ruth had cleared things away and went back inside the church to collect her prayer book and ensure all was left tidy, safe and secure.

Gazing around she saw, to her surprise, Archdeacon Stephen had not in fact left. He was sitting alone at the back of the church. Upon hearing her footsteps, he lifted his head, eyeing her from afar. She immediately headed over in his direction and he got up from his seat.

'I didn't read the letter out loud, it's for your ears only. Please sit down for a moment,' he insisted.

Ruth did as instructed, wondering what was coming next.

'This letter comes from the Bishop. He instructed me to come over here. He's most concerned. The dust has barely settled on the 'Lessons from a Day Centre' report. You really don't want me to go through that again do you?...'

Ruth shook her head.

'No, I didn't think so. This letter,' he said, waving it authoritatively under her nose, 'this letter, states that if there were to be a second occasion when adverse publicity becomes attached to you or your church, the Archdeacon is hereby authorised, and I quote, "to take such immediate peremptory actions as he deems necessary to safeguard our reputation". That bit, I assure you are his direct words. I'm sorry to have to put it like this, because I know you mean well, you do try so very, very hard, but I came here today having it in mind to serve you notice and to temporarily relocate worship at a neighbouring parish pending a full enquiry.'

'But... but there's been no adverse publicity... has there?' interrupted Ruth.

'Ah, you may possibly think not, but unlike you, I have been keeping my ear to the ground and my eye on the wider social media, seeing the bigger picture, Ruthie. The local Enfield Mayor is most concerned at what you and your church are up to and has tweeted as much. Some local children at the school opposite have kicked up a hoo-hah since yesterday, threatening to excuse themselves from lessons and the Head has also tweeted, concerned at the local church's support for disaffection, taking pupils away from studies at a critical time just as the new term is getting under way. Both the Mayor and the Head think you are meddling in matters that don't concern you and giving in to local anarchists. In fact I'm being asked by both for reassurances and this is a jointly signed letter from them to the Bishop.' He reached inside his blue jacket pocket and waved a second piece of paper in front of Ruth.

'I see... But as you've discovered, it really isn't anything to do with me or the church directly. The deed was done by others. We're victims here.'

At this, the archdeacon looked uncertain, wrong footed. His mouth dropped open but no words came out. He tried again, 'Mmm. You really do put me in a very difficult position. If it were up to me, I'd be the first to see you moved on, and give both you and this parish the fresh starts you both deserve. I need to go away and think on it further.' He made to leave.

'Whilst you're here, there was another matter, if you can spare the time,' Ruth ventured. He turned in surprise.

'I've been asked to consider the building of a new perimeter wall with the addition of a security gate. Some members of the congregation are concerned that we're not taking safeguarding and security sufficiently seriously given the recent spate of knife crime in the vicinity, even on church grounds. In response draft plans have already been prepared and shared around a few people here. It's to go to the next Church Council meeting. Already a financial offer has been received toward covering the cost, by the Edmonton Lodge, the local Freemasons, where I believe you are the chaplain.'

'Ah! Yes! Yes indeed! This parish is eating into my time rather more than others. I've been appraised on this one, the wall. I told them, it was a nice idea, but they need to find someone who can run such a project, as their present vicar certainly can't pass muster. They needed to remember what a mess you made of trying to run the church Drop In Centre which we were forced to close.'

Ruth's jaw dropped. 'So that's your assessment?' She knew it was pointless to try and argue.

'You know what Ruthie, we need to strike a deal. If I can find you a nice rural church somewhere outside London, better still a hospital chaplaincy without the responsibility of running a parish, a position where you don't have too much to do, would you be up for a quick no questions asked move?'

Ruth listened in silence.

'I've observed there's a good pastoral side to you, so let's build your future around your strong point.' He paused to let her think on the offer. He pressed on, 'I know I've fed in some ideas on you having a break or maybe getting extra help here in the parish, but to be frank I don't think that way any longer. Either wouldn't make the slightest bit of difference. You're what I consider to be incompetent. Let's make it clear, either you jump or I push... but for God's sake, let it happen soon!'

With that he turned and without so much as a 'goodbye' headed briskly out of the church door and he'd gone.

Ruth didn't follow after him, his final filibustering was only because both he and she knew she had escaped action this time. However, she now knew exactly where she stood with him and that meant that man would not be giving her another chance.

22

Once back in the safety of the vicarage Ruth was uncontrollably shaking. She felt she'd been on the receiving end of a calculated bullying attack. Thankful he'd gone, she was nonetheless fearful he might yet return. She'd thought he'd gone once earlier only to find him sitting at the back of the church, waiting to get her alone, ready to pounce on her like a wild cat.

Now it was all beginning to take its toll on her. He'd discredited her ministry to her face and described her as "incompetent". His outspoken criticism of her had been summed up in a forthright attempt to make her leave and do so immediately. Part of her wanted to give in, get away, but another part of her, her persistent, stubborn side, didn't want to give him the pleasure. She felt all the more insecure as she didn't know which side of her personality would win.

Hearing a sound in the direction of the kitchen she jumped in fright, only then recalling Phil had been made redundant. She called his name to hear his reassuringly warm voice in reply. He was sitting at the kitchen table cradling a mug of coffee, a half full cafetière in front of him. There were piles of groceries all over the kitchen table waiting to be put away. She remembered the on-line order, but through her earlier contretemps with the archdeacon had completely forgotten it had been scheduled to arrive at 11.30am. Thank God Phil had been there to receive it.

'Use some coffee?' he asked, deploying his foot to lever a chair out from under the table so she could sit down. He pushed cereal boxes back to create space. 'You look "*all shook up mm, mm, mm, mm, yay, yay, yay,"* as Elvis used to sing,' he intoned in a poor imitation.

'Oh, Phil,' she began, 'I've had that weasel man in church, that bishop's fixer, that poisonous toad, that…'

'You mean your friend the archdeacon paid you a visit?'

'Yes, him, wielding the invisible, metaphorical knife ready to cut me into little pieces. He wants rid of me Phil, like this minute if he could, or sooner would be better. He came to the service this morning. He was out to get me. That was all he came for.'

'That's a serious allegation to make of a man of the cloth,' he jested.

'No joke, Phil. "Jump or I push you… Jump or I push." They were his very words.'

'That makes the giving of my redundancy notice yesterday seem very civilised and at the time I thought the bosses in the city were the cruel ones. Both of us out of work in the space of 24 hours… mmm.'

'Well he hasn't made me redundant yet. I think he would have fired me there and then if he could pin the environment protest banners on the church as having been put there with my prior knowledge. Fortunately, he couldn't get that charge to stick, so he had to back off. He wants me gone, Phil. Even said he'd find me a quiet rural parish well away from London or better still a hospital chaplaincy where I wouldn't have any real responsibility, where I couldn't do any damage! Don't think my hospital chaplaincy friends would rate that particular comment!'

In a mood of increasing mutual gloom, Ruth and Phil drank coffee quietly for a moment, both lost in their own thoughts. Phil was the first to speak.

'I'm on gardening leave. I've had time to think. For the time being why don't I help you see off some of the pressures you're under? I don't want to spend all my time obsessing about finding another job. I've been thinking, I feel OK about letting this school term take its own course. If something comes up, something I really want to do, fine. If not, I'd quite enjoy spending more time at home, especially since we don't have help around any more.'

'How I miss Aneni's help. She was someone to talk to, company in the house and got so much done and the kids loved her too.'

'Look, if you're happy, that's what I'd like to do. Call it my sabbatical if you like. I've been thinking it would be good for me to take some time out from work and just now it could be useful. It's not about the money, we don't need it, we can manage. What do your think?'

'Well OK, if you're sure, but we've seen too many clergy spouses sucked into being unpaid lackeys for the church and I wouldn't want that to happen to you.'

'That's settled then… I've a suggestion to make.'

'You're full of surprises today.'

'It isn't for the first time you've found yourself buried by admin. I like it. Doing admin for me is like nectar to the bee.'

'You're odd, I've always known there to be a weird side to you,' she said, now smiling.

'Do you remember when they tried to close your Drop In Centre on financial grounds.'

'Yes, and you went through the accounts and found they hadn't claimed tax relief. If you hadn't scrutinised those figures I'd have been sunk. You have your uses Mr. Churchill!'

'Well, how about if I go through your email mountain for you. I won't just delete everything, I'll put things into manageable categories – then take you through what I find. I'd enjoy doing that this afternoon while you're at the crem.'

'The crematorium!...' Ruth started, her hand grappled urgently for her diary on her phone to see she was still in good time, then breathed a sigh of relief.

'I'd love you to do that. I need a few minutes in my study before I head up the Great Cambridge Road to the crem... Thirty minutes journey time to get there should do it. Feel free to attack my admin whilst I'm out. Sometimes I think I don't understand you,' she smiled.

Ruth quickly grabbed her paper work and funeral book, her robes and purple stole. Then she was out through the door heading north. Thankfully the traffic was light. A neighbouring vicar had once misplaced his diary with all his funeral dates in it and missed turning up on time at a funeral, the fear of doing the same was too awful for her to contemplate. If that ever happened on her watch, she thought, she'd leave the church even before the archdeacon got to hear about it.

The funeral was for retired nurse, Ada Shepherd, aged 84, who had lived alone for many years. As funerals go it was unremarkable. Her peaceful end after a short illness in hospital, following an earlier fall at her home, had been described to Ruth when her daughter from nearby Barnet had visited her last week. The daughter was there today in a navy outfit looking sombre but not overly mournful. There were just eight mourners. The familiar Psalm 23 – "The Lord's my Shepherd" was said by all, then the hymn – "Abide with me" and finally the innocently cheerful, "All things bright and beautiful" were sung, Ruth providing the vocal lead.

After little more than fifteen minutes it was over, the usher shepherding everyone outside to gaze upon the solitary floral tribute sitting on the gravel, fenced in by plastic chain link to separate it off from other tributes lined up in serried ranks at the back of the crematoria from earlier services.

The family were kindly and appreciative of the service. There was only a little crying, one dabbing of tears and then they politely excused themselves to head for a meal together, leaving Ruth to find her way back to the tiny vestry. She observed that already, the next funeral party was lining up on the driveway, a solitary hearse bearing its coffin waiting to be summoned forward when the coast was clear. One service following another throughout the day: there would never be a recession in this business, she thought.

Ruth gazed out through the vestry window as she began changing out of her robes. She was thinking it would be good to get back on top of things, win a bit of space. Thirsty, she looked around to see if she could find a drink. She was interrupted by a knock at the vestry door. She recognised the undertaker, it was dear Mr. Bernard.

'Hello, Reverend Ruth.' He was always politely formal.

'I want to ask you a favour.'

'How can I help?' She saw him hesitate.

'Will you take the next funeral?' he asked sheepishly.

'What?'

'This is a pauper's funeral. He's a homeless man. We only know his first and last name – Alan Thomas. Died in Brighton, on the street. Alcoholic, I think. He's been brought back here because his roots, so far as anyone knows them, were in north London. There's no family, no friends, no minister.'

'Oh.'

'It's just that the bearers,' he pointed toward the solitary hearse with the coffin and bearers still inside. 'We don't think its right we should just leave him here with the crematoria staff to deal with him. Would you mind saying a few words, for us, for him?'

Ruth felt strangely moved at this expression of dignified, respectful solidarity for a fellow human. What could she say but, 'Yes, give me a moment. I'll tell the usher. Alan Thomas, you say.'

Mr Bernard bowed toward her, in the way that he always did. She wondered if he bowed to his wife at home when he came in at the end of the day. People get so institutionalised in their jobs, she thought. She often wondered whether some clergy went to bed with a dog collar in their pyjama tops.

She quickly dismissed the irreverent thought to concentrate on matters in hand and began putting her robes back on. In the matter of death, she mused, all people were equal.

The impromptu service was strangely moving. The anonymity of Alan Thomas added to the special feel. Dignity was afforded because, as she told the bearers, he was "known only to God" and in that respect he was representative of all who live and die. 'In the end almost everyone is very soon forgotten and left in God's hands', she said. Prayers followed and the community of the homeless, the street people, were especially recalled.

Afterwards, Mr. Bernard was profuse in his gratitude and this in turn made her feel affirmed in what she was doing, even more so than Ada's funeral had earlier.

Gathering her things, she climbed back in her blue Fiat with the scorch marked bonnet to drive back to the vicarage. The recent rain was beginning to rust the damaged paintwork creating strange patterns. The car was another pending job yet to be attended to.

On arrival back home there was a note from Phil stating he had gone to collect the children from school and would take them to Pymms Park on the way back. It worried her to think once again she had not given them a thought and she realised that right now she needed Phil to be around for both her and the children's sake.

Throwing her robes down in the hallway, she saw her study door was open. She went in. Phil had been in there. She looked at her desk, the laptop had been left open.

Sitting, she pressed it into life to find he'd been busy already. Most of the unopened emails had been allocated new homes. As she gazed in wonder her spirits lifted as she realised her disorganised world was being tamed and managed for the first time in what seemed like ages. Before she could look further a noise outside caught her attention.

The front door bell then rang. It was PC April Cooper. Ruth's mind changed gears, tuning back into Tony, Raj, Angela and the two, as yet unidentified bodies, in the back of the burned out van. None of these deaths were ordered in her mind and she felt unsure of herself, worried she would be caught out by any questioning she might face. This time Ruth took April into the kitchen and made them both a mug of tea.

'What can I do for you, April?' asked Ruth.

'As you will appreciate we're mounting a complex and challenging multiple murder enquiry,' she began.

'And is it still in partnership with Counter Terrorism?' enquired Ruth.

'Correct.'

'But forgive me for interrupting, but I don't see why. This looks like the murder of a local shopkeeper and other as yet unexplained deaths, but I'm not aware of terrorism in our midst? Am I missing something?'

'I know I can speak frankly with you Ruth. We go back a long way, to the start of my police career here in Edmonton, so I don't want you not to be aware. However, you will know, as well as I do, just how sensitive talk about terrorism and terrorists is in the community and we definitely don't want to make things worse than they already are by frightening people.'

'But who are the terrorists? Religious or right wing extremists? Who? And what are they thought to be doing here? There's been no talk of terrorists in this parish since… since Ali Muhammed.'

Ruth had no personal wish to be unexpectedly caught out by terrorists at work in her parish. That would seal her fate in the archdeacon's eyes. She continued, 'We had some climate change people take direct action and put up a banner on the church, but I know about that. It really isn't anything serious. But I'm being silly, that can't possibly be linked with murder enquiries and real terrorism can it?'

'No, you're absolutely right. Presently, Extinction Rebellion's action is inconvenient, disruptive and some would argue extreme but not terrorist. What we're concerned about are events on the Indian sub-continent spilling over here.'

'India? Raj… surely not?'

'I want to begin by asking you about Raj. How long have you known him?'

'Since I arrived in the parish. He's always run the corner shop so far as I've known him. Must be five years. I'm always in there, Sonny's. I've always viewed him as an ally, a friend. Like hairdressers and newsagents, people chatted to him and Darshana.'

Ruth regretted her words immediately. If Raj was indeed a terrorist and she could be described as his friend… She could see the glee on the archdeacon's face, his row of white teeth as he sensed he'd got her cornered. She could imagine him telling her, "I've got you, supporting terrorists once wasn't enough for you Ruthie, was it?"

'So you've known him a long time. Do you recall over that time whether he has had different staff or visitors seeing or maybe even staying with him?'

Ruth thought back. 'Oh yes. He's known for giving local youngsters evening and weekend work. Believe me there was nothing suspicious about that.'

Then she recalled something else. Her buried memory had been re-awakened.

'Was there something else?' asked April.

'Yes. Earlier in the summer. I don't remember now when exactly, but I called in to the shop one weekday morning. I went in and there were loud voices, Asian voices. Darshana was at the till and she raised her eyes and then called out to Raj. It immediately quietened down, for my benefit I'm certain.'

'Yes…'

'Before I left I saw two men. When they saw me, they simply walked out of the shop. I remember the occasion because it was out of place. They hadn't been there to buy anything. It was something else and Raj looked, for the first time I'd ever seen him like that, well… distressed. I wasn't able to talk to Raj about it because he immediately excused himself and disappeared out at the back. It's the only time I can remember anything untoward happening there. Raj was always so good, a singular man of peace. Even though he was a Hindu he used to give a generous donation to every social event we put on at the church and always placed a full page advert for his shop in our parish magazine. Lovely man, a community builder.'

'And can you describe those two men for me?'

Ruth noticed April had pulled out her notebook and was scribbling away as she spoke. What Ruth said seemed significant.

'Yes, I have a good memory for such things. It was two men. I wouldn't know if they had friends waiting outside the shop. I'd say they were both around thirty years of age. I'd guess they had an Asian background like Raj. The three definitely had no problem understanding one another from the way they argued. In appearance they were much the same height as Raj but looked different from him somehow. I'm no expert on these things but Raj is as proudly Indian as they come and a devout Hindu and they weren't like that. No... they weren't Hindu or if they were, not specially so. But thinking about it they weren't overly western in dress, so not modern secular guys either. My hunch would be they were possibly Muslim. Yes, that would fit, two Muslim guys, probably arguing with Raj about religion, Raj would do that. That would fit. He used to go to the temple and meet with like-minded enthusiasts for India's main Hindu political party. I don't recall their name now. Raj told me enough times. The ones with the Saffron robes...'

'The BJP?'

'Why yes...'

'That's the Bharatiya Janata Party.'

'Yes. Raj had an orange and green flag with a lotus flower and the letters BJP on it. Those two guys took his flag with them when they left the shop. Come to think of it, it was a gesture of dislike for it.'

'How did Raj react to that?'

'He seemed to accept it. Couldn't do much else I suppose. He didn't want me to be involved. He shrugged in my direction and then excused himself, going into the back of the shop. I think he was both thankful I was there and simultaneously embarrassed by my presence. Definitely didn't want to talk about it that was for sure. That was all.'

'How would you describe the appearance, the faces of the two men?'

Ruth paused before answering. She was usually good at this.

'Both had beards, definitely, dark brown eyes, and come to think of it both were wearing head coverings, baseball caps, one red, the other green, yes red and green. They had T-shirts on, nondescript, the ubiquitous jeans and trainers but I can't say anything stood out, so maybe I'm guessing.'

April produced two small photos and passed them to Ruth without saying a word.

Ruth took a breath, 'I'm certain these are the two. Are they… are they terrorists?'

'They are the two found dead, burned in Raj's van.'

Ruth was silent. It all didn't make sense, didn't add up, but at least the police knew who the bodies were and were admitting they were there.

'I'm most grateful to you for the tea and your help. We needed to know there was a link with Raj. We've now established there was. I need to get back to the station. Thank you again, and if anything further comes to mind do call me,' she added, getting up, putting her notebook and photos away, whilst pulling out a personal business card to hand her.

Ruth didn't want her to go. She wanted her to explain more, but there was no stopping April.

No sooner had April gone, than Ruth recalled her recent visit and conversation with Darshana who had mentioned the two Urdu speaking visitors to the shop. Ruth wondered whether to try and contact April about that. Then she thought how that was really Darshana's call and that she'd left Darshana to ponder on it.

Maybe, wondered Ruth those two men she was talking about were one and the same. They'd been pestering Raj, they were Muslim, it felt too unlikely to be a coincidence. Darshana might be able to identify them to the police. But that was her call. Then the knowing look Darshana gave Ruth when she'd asked her about Raj's van being parked outside Angela's house came to mind.

Once again Ruth felt there had to be something linking all this but couldn't for the life of her see what it might be. She concluded the police were best left to conduct their own enquiries and if Darshana had something to say that it was up to her to tell them.

Ruth went into her study. She wanted to find something. By nature she was a hoarder, ever reluctant to throw things away. Somewhere, in her roll top desk she had kept a card from Raj and Darshana. It had to be there.

Working methodically, she picked up each stored bundle in turn, releasing its green ribbon bow. She flicked through several piles of old correspondence until she found what she was looking for. In triumph she held it up.

It was the small postcard Raj had sent her the previous summer when he had gone back to Gujarat to visit his family. She remembered his excitement at the prospect of a visit to India after so long in this country.

She looked at it carefully feeling a strange connection with him as she followed his handwriting. She turned it over in her hand again, not quite sure what she was looking for. In the end she left it on her desk to come back to later. Its significance would come to her, she knew it.

The front door opened, Phil, Olivia and Paul were back. It was time to feed hungry children.

23

As Ruth stood at the kitchen sink facing the road outside, she was struck how busy it was getting on the pavement, lots of people waiting around. This was not unusual at certain times, especially when there were events on in the church hall next door or parents evenings opposite at the school. Then she remembered her visitors of yesterday who had asked to use the hall for their Rohingyas of Myanmar awareness raising evening.

What she'd consented to, was to her mind, to be a low key gathering of a relatively small number of people. She had no idea it would be so big and a little wave of panic passed through her as she realised she might have seriously miscalculated.

'Phil, can you be a dear whilst I pop over to the church hall? I need to check on something.'

Phil nodded in a relaxed way as she slipped in her dog collar, grabbed her jacket and walked out onto the pavement. She glanced at her watch; it was only 7pm, early yet too. She tried to spot the two who had called in to see her the previous day, but it was like trying to spot a needle in a pile of needles.

Looking around, she noticed those gathering on the street were all male, for the most part youngish men. Car after car was turning off Silver Street and into Windmill Road, dropping off more and more attendees before disappearing. It was getting quite congested and she wondered why the hall hadn't been unlocked and pushed forward to see why, her own keys at the ready in her hand.

Pushing through, she found the two hall doors were in fact wide open and to her consternation it was equally crowded inside. She pushed her way in as bemused men gave way for this exotic amongst them.

Then she spotted them, her two visitors down at the front trying to line up chairs behind a table on a portable raised platform. They saw her and with a friendly wave beckoned her over to join them. Someone had placed a bunch of tired looking, artificial, red roses in a glass jam jar on the table in a vain gesture of offering aesthetic hospitality.

'Mrs Ruth. Please. Please sit,' said the one. 'Thank you… thank you.'

She did as she was instructed, knowing it was probably futile to try and hold a meaningful conversation. Given the numbers of people now in the hall her mind turned to health and safety and the need for a risk assessment, but she soon dismissed this bureaucratic default thought as totally impossible to attend to. How on earth could she, on her own, against all this noise, begin to limit the numbers in the hall? As so often before, she had to just bite her lip, say a prayer and hope for the best, trusting this event would not add further fuel to the archdeacon's fire.

After what seemed like an eternity, voices began to quieten. By then there must have been around 200 men standing in the hall, all eyes to the front. Still others were pressing to get inside. There was more shuffling at the back, then unmistakably and quite unexpectedly the Mayor of Enfield was standing in front of her. She stood up and welcomed him with a handshake.

'Though we might not agree entirely on matters of theology,' he said, 'I have always admired your commitment to practical Christianity. That is something we both understand,' he said, smiling and shaking her hand for all of a minute before sitting down next to her.

In an aside for her ears only, he added confidentially, 'I do think the church dealt with you rather harshly for the good work you were trying to do. It doesn't take an experienced politician like me to see when someone's been stitched up to be the fall guy.'

Ruth appreciated the supportive sentiment and nodded politely. Past events were one thing, but she was feeling increasingly concerned about events in the present. Tonight she had already been caught out twice, firstly by the large numbers and secondly by the arrival of the mayor. Now she was about to be caught out a third time.

From her lefthand side she saw the imam from the local mosque walk confidently in, chaperoned by an elderly man with a long white beard she know to be none other than the brother of a man called Aziz who used to frequent the Day Centre once held in these very halls. Alarm bells began to ring in her head. Where was this all going? What kind of meeting was this?

Once at the front, the imam nodded politely in her direction and sat on the seat furthest from her. It wouldn't do for him, a man to sit next to a woman, she thought. With the mayor immediately next to her sitting on the end, the two men organising the event finally took their seats between the mayor and the imam. She'd ended up on a platform party of five, before an audience of hundreds and as she was all too acutely aware, the only female in sight.

With a nod from the man at his side, the mayor stood up first and took out his tablet where he had his earlier-prepared speech all ready to deliver.

'Lady vicar, esteemed imam, gentlemen. Thank you for coming here this evening. Some of you have travelled across London to be here. Many of you are living in difficult circumstances and your families back home are in camps and have endured much. In my capacity as mayor it is my pleasure and duty to welcome you. I welcome you! Enfield welcomes you! Might I begin by asking that we observe a minutes silence remembering the more than 10,000 victims of the genocide and those people from over 350 burned villages who have had to flee for their lives.'

His words gained a murmur of approval. Ruth shuffled and joined everyone else in standing up. A respectful silence was observed around the room before the five resumed their seats. Only the mayor remained standing ready to continue.

'I want you to know brothers, that the all too slow media recognition and the failure of the political powers in this county to support you in your suffering must not continue. The actions of the Myanmar government, its political and military leaders, must be held to account. The suffering of all the exiled victims must be addressed, especially the needs of the 723,000 refugees who have fled to neighbouring Bangladesh. This evening I am announcing that this year I am dedicating my mayoral charity to the Rohingya cause.'

As the mayor sat down there was a round of spontaneous applause and cries of appreciation for the mayor's proposal, a noise so loud that Ruth was concerned that the neighbouring houses might well be disturbed. Complaints from the neighbours would be yet another problem she could well do without. Her life seemed to be governed by the fear of what might go wrong. She was living on the brink, on the very edge of disaster herself. One incident, one more black mark against her and that would be it. She felt increasingly vulnerable in the hall and questioned her wisdom in allowing the event to have taken place at all. So much for hindsight, like a raft on a strong tide, she had to resign herself to be allowed to go with the flow.

The imam spoke next, beginning with words from the Qur'an and a prayer. Ruth made her own prayer – that no one would get to hear of this. An imam praying on site. If the archdeacon knew about this, he would never believe her this time if she said she had no idea Muslim prayers would be offered.

Fortunately the prayer was brief and could be explained as merely an introduction to what he then went on to say. He mixed English with what she guessed was either Arabic or Urdu. He began by expressing gratitude to Ruth for her hospitality, then gave thanks to the mayor for his active support and his solidarity with his Muslim brothers from Myanmar who were living like wanderers in the desert. He then talked about, 'the Prophet Muhammed, Peace be upon Him, who had likewise found himself alone in the world and in exile. But,' said the imam, 'it would not always be so.' With that and after a long discourse Ruth lost track of, he encouraged those gathered to be endlessly patient and work tirelessly for justice and the return of the land stolen from the Rohingya.

After what seemed like an age, but in reality the hall clock told her was less than an hour and a half, one of the organisers asked that a collection be taken for those in need. That done, people started breaking up, some remaining to talk in small groups, others spilling outside onto the street. Ruth not wanting to be impolite, was nonetheless keen to leave and get back to her children.

Surrounded and pressed in on every side by so many men speaking in foreign voices she felt for a moment that the days of the Drop In Centre had returned. It felt just like a day from the past only more crowded. The feeling alarmed her as she had been so strongly censured for that and forbidden thereafter from running anything like it again.

Fears from the past became mixed with fears in the present as she spotted the mayor's driver busily taking mobile phone pictures of the meeting. How long had he been doing that she wondered and where were these images now going to go? It all felt like it could only turn out badly for her.

Downcast, she hurriedly retraced her steps back to the vicarage and pulled the door firmly shut behind her. If she thought she was finding sanctuary, she was soon to be disabused of this fanciful notion.

It was not unusual for an emergency service siren to be heard at the vicarage, even for the occasional police helicopter to circle overhead, but this time the siren went on longer than usual and she felt compelled to look outside and she stepped into her study to look through the window toward the street corner.

It was the fire brigade. A red tender straddling the road, already causing traffic chaos. A hose was being run out and

to her horror water was soon spraying in the direction of…
the church!

'Phil! Phil!' she shouted, 'a fire, the church…'

Phil who had simultaneously arrived at the landing window,
was able to see the same view unfolding. 'It's, it's the
banner,' he yelled down as both watched pieces of flaming
plastic circling and falling on to the church grass.

Ruth ran out into the street to get a better look but was
restrained by a fireman who instructed her to keep back.
Taking a different path, through her front garden, she could
then see what was happening. She gazed up, only to see a
huge piece of flaming plastic descending on the evening
breeze toward her. She dived to one side, as she did so
slipping on the wet ground and striking her head on the
railings between church and vicarage. In an instant she
found herself lying on the ground and being generously
sprayed with water by a fireman whose face said, 'idiot'.

Then Phil was at her side. He pulled her back toward the
house. Turning her head to look back in the direction of the
church, Ruth's first assessment was that thankfully any fire
damage was superficial. More worrying was the large
amount of water on the ground, undoubtedly seeping under
the west door and into the church.

'You were lucky,' Phil pronounced, once he'd guided her
inside. 'What the hell do you think you were doing?'

She didn't have an answer for him. Her head hurt, she
wanted to change out of her wet things; she pulled away and
slowly made her way upstairs.

24

It was Friday morning and it was Ruth's day off. An unexpected bonus was that Phil was with her. Surely they might do something together, escape the parish for the best part of the day, a trip out to St Albans, lunch at the abbey perhaps? First, preliminary arrangements to make it possible had to be attended to.

At 8am a prolonged ring on the front door bell announced the arrival of a workman from JB Builders in his clean white van, a rotund man in blue overalls and noisy steel-capped boots. He'd been engaged by Chris Darlington to repair the vicarage front door. There was a lively discussion as to how the job was to proceed – where he could plug in for his electric supply and the importance of the security of the vicarage whilst they were out, as well as the all important delivery of a mug of tea with four sugars before any work could begin. In fifteen minutes all matters concerning the front door repair were settled and Greg, the builder, was left to it, already chipping away with a hammer and chisel, a set of Ruth's spare keys in his pocket to post through the letter box when he'd done.

Back in the kitchen, Phil had the two children fed and ready to leave for school.

'We're both taking you today,' announced Ruth.

'Sure you can remember the way, Mum,' replied Olivia with unusual sarcasm.

'Won't be long before she's a teenager,' whispered Phil in Ruth's ear.

They all left in Phil's Citroen, leaving Ruth's tired looking Fiat sitting in the drive with additional bits of burnt debris from last night's fire lying on the roof and rusty bonnet. Ruth wondered whether the burnt plastic would be easy to remove. Like a can kicked on down the road, that was another task in her inbox that would have to join the long queue of other tasks waiting for her attention.

As they drove to the school, Ruth was busy making last minute calls on her mobile to get the two churchwardens to look at fire brigade water ingress and clean up the west end. In the event she could only reach Chris Darlington and thankfully he was keen to help all he could, a kind of wishing to make amends for his son's action probably explaining his response. He wanted to chat and Ruth to get away from the phone. She pointed out to him that after the fire the church were fortunate to still have a building.

'Someone's watching over you, vicar,' was the inevitable comment, followed by, 'of course I'll help. I'm on my way down there right now.' With relief in his voice, he admitted the church had had a lucky escape. No doubt some element of conscience or blame came into play, thought Ruth, as she closed the call.

Ruth admitted to herself she didn't feel very watched over, but more scrutinised and found wanting. She remembered how the Christmas tree and its lights placed outside the west end door of the church in her first Christmas in the parish had all been stolen. She should have seen that coming in Edmonton before it was agreed to put the tree up – similarly such an obvious flaming torch target as the climate change banner must have seemed like a red rag to any passing bullish Edmonton arsonist. She hoped no one would be trying to blame her for the fire too.

Children safely deposited inside the school gate, Ruth's eye caught sight of the new fortifications that had been erected over the summer. Having acquired a recent interest in such things, she asked Phil to hold on a minute whilst she took a closer look. It was remarkable. An impregnable wire-mesh fence now stood where previously a low wooden fence had sufficed and entry to the school grounds was now monitored by both a CCTV camera and an electronic gate, no doubt controlled from the school office. So this is how it is done, she thought. Perhaps Julie had been on to the head, she mused, playing her safeguarding card.

'Phil, why on earth do we need to fortify schools? Not only do children not walk to school anymore, they're even imprisoned behind fortifications when they get here. What's that, a video camera?' she asked pointing at the gate.

'Cool it, Ruth. It's the way of today's world, chill out...' replied Phil quietly. My late office in the city was no different, really.'

Her feelings vented and curiosity satisfied they headed north up the arterial A10 road, signposted Cambridge, but after a few minutes turned off well before then onto the M25 orbital motorway heading west. It was liberatingly pleasant, motoring along quickly out of London, unlike for everyone else sitting stationary in their vehicles going in the opposite direction with a day's work in mind.

'Missing the office, Phil?' she asked, with a head tilt in the direction of the waiting cars.

'I've been let out my cage,' he replied, smiling. It promised to be a good day. They had to be back at the school by 3-ish but that gave them a fabulous six hours all to themselves. By 10am they had parked up in historic Fishpool Street, just a short walk from St Alban's Abbey.

Leaving the car they walked down the Street admiring the variety of different houses and buildings, a hotel here, and modern courtyard fitted in tastefully there. At the end of the road they turned left, past the ford, which had been refreshed by recent rain into a lively flow, and then turned left again into Verulamium Park.

For the first time inside a week it felt dry and warm enough to be comfortable outside. Finding a seat looking out toward the duck covered lake, they flopped down. In minutes both realised how utterly exhausted they were. The two leant against each other silently, two pillars balanced against one another to prevent the other falling.

How long they rested neither were quite sure, but it was Phil who spoke first.

'Fancy a coffee? We can wander down to the Waffle House, it should be open.'

'Yes, I could do with one, otherwise I'll fall asleep.' Ruth grasped Phil's arm and held him close.

'Not the only one, guess the week's taken its toll on both of us.'

The short rest must have done Ruth some good, for she felt energised and she had an idea to share.

'Phil… You had any more thoughts on your future?'

'Give me a chance,' he said teasingly, 'it's only two days since I became a man of leisure. Why, had you something in mind?'

Ruth watched a pair of swans, white wings spread wide, swoop down to land with a double splash in the lake before them.

'Don't you think, when you step out of a situation, you can see it more clearly?'

'Mmm. That's true as far as how I see my recent job. When I was there, working for the Harrison Accounts Partnership, I was, well, like, fully on board, a city accountant through and through, loyal, professional, never missed a day, worked hard, wanted to achieve, wanted to earn good money and I did!'

'But now…'

'Now, in so short a space of time, I'm happy on a park bench, just being with you. I feel… released, free, for the first time in ages. My big worry isn't how to get another job, there'll be one out there with my name on it, of that I'm certain, I'm more concerned at what your job is doing to you.'

'It's different being in the church.'

'You mean the ground rules aren't clear. You are employed but none of the employment norms seem to apply, or the employees themselves don't see it that way… The management structure, isn't at one with its front line operatives. For a start there is no agreement as to what the corporate strategy is meant to be. Then when one considers the supervision and support systems that ought to be in place to ensure things are working at grassroots – well, it doesn't work, in fact it's entirely left with the employee's enthusiasms and personal resources as to what happens. If it goes wrong, they come down on you.'

'That's a bit harsh.'

'No it isn't. As I observe the extraordinary pressures you've been under, a lesser person would have either cracked or become a harshly managing autocrat. In fact I've been thinking you've been that near,' he said, pinching his thumb and forefinger so they were almost touching, 'that close, to falling apart. So, so close to tipping point, that I... I became afraid for you.'

'I know, I know. And I tell myself I'll manage, it'll get better if I do this or that, or simply hang on in there.'

'Tell me Ruth, what are your dreams for the future?'

With the late summer sun shimmering on the lake before them and the incessantly quacking flotilla of ducks idly swimming round in circles, periodically dipping their heads under the water here and there without an apparent care in the world, time seemed, for a rare moment, to stand still. Ruth gazed vacantly ahead, almost trance like, letting the end of August sun warm her face.

'It might be better if we have a fresh start somewhere different, another parish. And do it before the children are locked into secondary school; whilst you are between jobs we can look around. So that I can put some space between all the pressure I've lived under these past years and the ministry I still feel called to. I think I'm dreaming of a fresh start, Phil, a new beginning.'

'Are you sure?'

'Yes, well maybe…'

'Do you want to phone a friend? Is that your final answer?' he said smiling, sounding like Chris Tarrant hosting the TV show "*Who wants to be a millionaire?*"

'Final Answer.'

'Then you win!'

'Win what?'

'A new start and lunch with me at Carluccio's on my redundancy payout?' he said beaming, rising to his feet and pulling Ruth up.

'You haven't had it yet!'

'We can still do it though,' he added.

She took a deep breath. The air was good, she felt restored and was so enjoying the time with Phil.

'Let's go. Does the redundancy stretch to a glass of wine?'

They sat outside for lunch, enjoying time and space, chatting leisurely, people watching, laughing, making the final coffee last, until Phil suddenly interjected.

'It's after 2pm. We're responsible parents, two kids leaving school within the hour.' The bill was hurriedly called for and quickly settled. Then they walked briskly back down Fishpool Street and headed south back to Enfield and school, arriving in time to park up reasonably close and stand against the new metal fencing until the children were let out.

Rather than go straight back to the vicarage they took a detour to Pymms Park and treated the children to ice creams. By 5pm Ruth knew with a sense of growing dread inside her that inevitably reality was calling her back. She had a picture of a grey glove inside her squeezing her guts, turning them over and tying her inside into knots, so much so it was making it hard for her to breathe, a feeling she kept to herself.

Just before 6pm they pulled up in the vicarage driveway. Getting out of the car, it was a pleasant surprise to see the front door with its Edwardian coloured glass looking like new once again, the linseed smell of fresh putty lingering in the air as they went inside. Would it be enough to keep them safe, wondered Ruth, or should she ask the diocese for stronger defences, interior metal bars behind the pretty glass maybe?

It was equally good to find no parishioner waiting on the doorstep as they arrived and a relief to find only her spare keys from the builder and no urgent pastoral note pushed through the letter box requiring immediate attention.

The kids ran straight in and dashed upstairs, relaxed and playful, shouting and trying to trip each other up as they went. The weekend beckoned.

Phil went to put the kettle on. Ruth couldn't resist the enticing red flash LED of the recorded message button on her answerphone and pressed "Play". There was only one message. Pen poised, she leant over her desk to listen to it.

'Ward Sister Thomas here, A and E, North Middlesex Hospital. We have Darshana Chahaun with us and she's asking for you.'

Ruth went into the kitchen silently to have some tea with Phil. She knew the day off had just come to an abrupt end and sat herself down at the kitchen table as they waited for the kettle to boil.

'Phil, I'll have to go to the hospital later. Darshana's in the North Mid.'

'OK,' he said accepting the situation, 'we had a brilliant day. I'll see to the kids, catch up with you later.'

As Ruth went to change and slipped in her dog collar, she gazed at herself in the mirror and asked herself just how many times lately had they promised to catch up with each other later? Today had been a lifeline, but when next will we be able to again?

25

'I think I'll walk down to the hospital, the exercise will do me good,' said Ruth as she headed out of the front door, her badge of office dog collar once more back in place.

It took her maybe 20 minutes to get there. She made her way through the sanitised antiseptic corridors and passed the technologically crammed ITU unit where Raj had so recently died. She pushed on past the waiting queues by the door, the smokers in groups of twos and threes outside, then into the crowded foyer of A & E where she paused and looked around.

Then she saw her. A nurse in her smart blue nursing uniform was walking toward her with Darshana leaning on her arm. Ruth stepped forward to intercept them. Introductions were made, Darshana, head held low, was unusually quiet.

'We've told Darshana we don't recommend she leaves until tomorrow, but she's insistent and wants to return to her shop. I said if she had someone to take her home we'd let her go. So...'

'You were wondering if I would see her home?' said Ruth.

'Yes,' said nurse Thomas, smiling.

'But I walked. I could go back and fetch the car.'

'No need. I can walk,' said Darshana.

'Are you OK?' asked a puzzled Ruth.

Darshana looked down saying nothing.

'She took a few too many Paracetamol tablets. We had to make her sick, that's all. Someone needs to keep an eye on her at a time like this,' nurse Thomas added knowingly.

'Darshana, how are you feeling?'

'Still a bit nauseous, but fine and I can walk. I am walking now, aren't I?' she said, with a hint of resentment in her tone.

'Is there anything else to be done before we leave?' asked Ruth.

'No, she'll hear from her GP next.'

'If you've got everything? Then let's go then.'

With that they started walking or rather ambling very slowly toward the hospital exit and Silver Street. Ruth didn't really know where to begin. She knew a Paracetamol overdose could kill a person. Had it been intentional or a cry for help? What could she ask? She concluded the direct approach was the only option to take. It was life or death and she'd never forgive herself if she didn't try to understand what had happened. What she resolved however, was that the conversation would be at Darshana's pace and she'd let her talk when she was ready.

In fact, as they walked, hardly a word, apart from simple questions like, 'shall we cross here' and 'what time were you admitted to hospital?' were said. All Ruth learned was that Darshana had called for an ambulance of her own volition around 8am that morning, she didn't volunteer much else and seemed to have withdrawn into herself.

When they got to the shop Ravi looked up from behind the counter giving Darshana only a cursory glance. Strange, thought Ruth.

'Would you like to come in?' asked Darshana.

'Sure. Perhaps we ought to put the kettle on? Are you up for a cuppa?'

'I think so… I want to explain… You've been very kind to me and I don't know what you will think of me now…'

'Me… I've heard and seen many things and I'm rarely surprised by what people tell me. But yes, I'd like to hear what happened.'

Once in the flat, Darshana turned away to deal with the tea and beckoned Ruth to take a seat on the brown leather sofa. A couple of minutes later and the spiced scent of Indian tea was steaming from the pot. Together with a couple of mugs it was placed on the coffee table in front of them.

'I was very upset last night and couldn't sleep… I kept thinking of Raj… I kept thinking I would be attacked… our shop burned…'

Ruth was beginning to think that maybe Darshana was suffering from Reactive Depression and that she ought to take herself along to the GP, get some medication for a while to help her through, but she thought to keep this diagnosis to herself and listen attentively to her for the time being.

'Oh, I can see in your face you think I miss Raj so desperately I wanted to end everything… No, no… it isn't like that. Yes I miss Raj but you see he wasn't the man I thought he was.'

'How do you mean?'

'I had some more visitors to the shop.'

'Like the ones you said were arguing with Raj a while back?'

'Yes, I think they were different people this time. They were older people. They said Raj was a murderer. I told them I didn't believe them.'

'How do you mean Raj, a murderer?'

'It all goes back to 2002 when Raj was in Gujarat. That part is true. He was, he stayed a month. I had to remain here to run the shop. He'd gone home for his Father's funeral.'

'Did something happen in India?'

'That's what they're saying and yes those were difficult days in Gujarat, everyone knows. In Godhra, some pilgrims, Hindu pilgrims were coming home on the Sabarmati Express train when the train was set on fire by Muslims and a lot of our people died. What followed was that Hindus took revenge. It was terrible, Raj said he'd seen what had happened, so I know he was there, but until now I didn't know there was more to Raj's involvement.'

'So Raj was in the troubles?'

'These Muslims who came here say Raj was with those who murdered the men and raped the women from their district. He was recognised when he went there to visit family last summer. They traced him back…'

'I said I couldn't believe that it was true. Raj was such a gentle man. Ask anyone, I said. But they showed me photographs on their phone and jabbed their fingers. "That's him," they said, "That's him!" "That's him!" I think his face was one of them in the rioting crowd. He was holding a long stick, like a police baton.'

'Was it? Was it Raj in the pictures do you think?' asked Ruth gently.

'I think so…'

'And do you, did you believe these people, that Raj had done these things?'

'Yes…' she said barely audibly, 'and I can't live with it.'

Ruth paused to pass Darshana her tea, which she took with shaking hands. She was clearly in a very delicate state of mind.

'We don't know for certain though do we? You weren't there. You've been shown some pictures that may or may not be genuine. And Darshana, whether true or false, you yourself are in no way culpable, but I do understand how all this must leave you.'

'The visitors were angry, really angry, not only with Raj but because the believe they've been denied justice in India. The Chief Minister of Gujarat, they say, who was behind it all, he's used his high office to put himself above the law, and protect guilty people, hindus like Raj. The two say they're the only ones who can deal out justice and I had it coming to me too.'

'They threatened you?'

'Yes. I've not told Ravi everything, but said he was to be very careful because of what happened to Raj. He keeps something under the counter now.'

Ruth didn't want to know what kind of weapon Ravi kept under the counter. What she had heard made her wonder if Darshana herself were safe and whether the shop might be attacked next? Living in the flat directly above the shop, Darshana could be very vulnerable. What if they set the shop on fire... someone had set fire to the banner outside the church, hadn't they?

'This morning... I hadn't slept... I wasn't thinking straight... I went to the bathroom and took all the Paracetamol I had. I just stuffed them in and swallowed them. The hospital said I'd only had sixteen... When I realised what I'd done. I didn't want to die. I phoned the hospital. I was very scared Ruth, I thought if I didn't die I might be seriously unwell or the hospital might lock me up with the mad people. I was so pleased to see you. I am alright now. I am. I think you must be worried I will try and do it again. No, I made a mistake. I won't be doing it again.'

'I'm pleased to hear that. But I do think Ravi and yourself need to take great care if threats are being made against you. Don't you think you ought to tell the police?'

'OK. OK. Leave it with me. If you don't mind, I am very tired and I would like to have a lie down. Then I must help Ravi with the orders from the wholesalers.'

With that Ruth set off back home. It wasn't far to walk, just a few hundred yards along Silver Street and around the corner. She was feeling distinctly uncomfortable and looked around her on leaving the shop to see who was on the street. There was nothing suspicious. She settled into walking slowly back to allow herself time to reflect on at what she had been told. Walking was a surprisingly helpful way to collect one's thoughts.

Thinking about Darshana, it was all rather more than providing pastoral care for a bereaved woman, someone whose need of care had just increased one hundredfold following the taking of an overdose. It was more, Ruth had been told things of consequence about murders here and elsewhere and what did she do with that information. Further still, in her gut she feared that this wasn't the end of the matter. She shook at the thought of what terrible events might lie ahead. The worst of it was Ruth didn't know what the right thing was to do. How did she help? Who did she turn to?

Back home, she pushed the Linseed Oil putty scented, newly restored and repaired front door firmly closed behind her. She immediately sought out Phil for an urgent conversation. There were exceptional times when one didn't just keep things to oneself and this was one of them.

Though she didn't really want more tea, she took the one Phil offered her and the two sat facing one another across the wooden kitchen table.

'I'm all ears,' he said, 'It's got to be important.'

Ruth explained the unfolding situation, Raj and Darshana's story that had filled her past two hours. Phil listened intently, realising just how serious the emerging issues were. When she'd finished, he spoke.

260

'Firstly, this is potentially very serious and can't be left where it is, just with you; and secondly, I think you did all the right things in the situation. That's why you do the job you do and why you're so good at it.'

Ruth needed to hear that and it both reassured and lifted her spirits.

'Thanks, thanks... I've been thinking I should talk to April Cooper. I like her, I know she's holding back but nevertheless I trust her and she'll know what to do for the best.'

She reached in her pocket to pull out the Business Card April had left with her. It seemed to invite her to make the call. Phil agreed and left her to it.

'Hi April, Ruth Churchill, Holy Trinity Church here, is it a good time to call?'

'Yes, fine. What is it?'

'Can I see you? Not so easy to talk about what I have to say over the phone.'

'No problem. Can you give me an hour and I'll see you at yours. It can wait until then, yes?'

'Yes... I'll have the kettle on,' before realising as she ended the call, still more tea was the last thing she wanted. Her life in ministry seemed to rely on her ability to drink endless cups of warm brown liquid in all its rich variety.

Ruth spent the waiting hour with Olivia and Paul upstairs trying to play with them and make good for lost time. It was a welcome distraction from the dark and deep matters of earlier.

She realised how lucky Phil and herself were having two lovely children. Then she thought of Darshana and thought it sad, especially now that Raj had gone, that Darshana had no children herself, how alone she must feel. She was puzzled as to why they were childless. It wasn't something easily asked about. Her reverie was interrupted by the ring of the doorbell downstairs. She heard Phil making his way to take it as she set off downstairs herself, slotting back in place her handy collar.

'Hello April, thanks for coming over.' The two went into the lounge with purpose, Phil taking himself off to the kitchen to make them both tea.

'April, I need to talk about matters of a personal and sensitive nature and I feel I can trust you to hear me out and hopefully offer me some advice.'

'I think you may be asking too much of me.'

Ruth pressed on anyway explaining the call she had taken to go to the hospital, how she'd found Darshana and her earlier conversation with Darshana back at her flat.

'You see what I mean? There are so many things which are buzzing away, like loose electric connections when someone has spilled lots of petrol and everything could just explode.'

'That sounds like a good analogy. In the spirit of trust, I feel I should tell you something in return. My involvement in this case as part of Counter Terrorism is precisely because we have been concerned how rogue terrorist elements from the

Indian sub-continent might spark a conflagration locally or even more widely across London and beyond. Take it from me that it is not fanciful imagining on your part to think Raj Chauhan was engaged in the Gujarat riots on 2002. In part that is why the criminal investigation was taken over by our department.'

'I'm sorry to hear that. It is hard to think the Raj I knew could have been associated with such violence. So those images shown to Darshana were based on truth?'

'That would be a reasonable working assumption.'

'And is all this to do with Hindu-Muslim hostilities arising from way back in 2002?'

'Well, if it was just a revenge matter, one life for another and it ended there, Counter Terrorism wouldn't have had a look in. But, there have been other deaths, which though the media were not told about them, you were aware because you saw with your own eyes, the evidence in Raj's van.'

'Who were they?'

'Two Muslim males... These two men had called on Raj in his shop on a number of occasions in recent weeks to confront him with the evidence they had found for his active involvement in the death of Muslims in the Gujarat riots.'

'Do you know this?' asked Ruth.

'We have some CCTV footage and mobile phone evidence to confirm they were indeed there, in the shop. Maybe we should keep that under wraps, please.'

'Sure. But why and how did they die?'

'There are a number of active lines of enquiry being pursued.'

'Hmm. Thinking out loud. One might be that if Raj was as bad as you make him out, he killed them to silence what they knew. Another... another might be that other Hindus, Raj's accomplices in Hindu terrorism, killed them with or without Raj's connivance and then Raj was using his van to... to dispose of the bodies somewhere later. How am I doing?' asked Ruth.

'We're still in the early stages I'm afraid.'

Then Ruth remembered the postcard from Raj she had retrieved in her study earlier and its significance hit her. She went to retrieve it and showed it to April. 'Look here, Raj had said, "I'm desperate to get back home." It had struck her odd that Raj had said he was desperate to return when he'd been so excited at spending all the time could out there. Instinctively she knew the truth, he had indeed been identified whilst in India.

'But where does all this leave us with the death of Angela Morris and was Tony really involved in some way?' Ruth asked.

'As I say, enquiries still have a long way to go.'

'OK, back to the pressing situation of Darshana. Do you think she and her brother Ravi are in real danger?'

'We are closely monitoring that situation.'

'So I can rest easy in my bed tonight?' asked Ruth.

'I hope so. I really must be getting along, but I'm so glad you called me and we compared notes.'

'Yes, I feel reassured it's in your hands. Thank you for hearing me out.'

With that Ruth saw April out of the door. Watching April walk to her car she had the feeling that things were not as safe for Darshana and Ravi as April might have wished her to believe, but what could she do but leave their protection in the hands of the police?

She stopped in the hallway. April had done it again, she thought, held back on important details. It left her feeling uneasy and that matters were still out of her control. Their meeting hadn't achieved all she'd hoped for.

Shutting the repaired front door firmly behind her and carefully put the safety chain in place, not for the first time, she felt she was being drawn into things possibly dangerous to her and her family and even a newly repaired front door was an inadequate barrier in the face of determined violent men.

26

It was Saturday morning, just a week since Ruth had taken a wedding service which had so soon been followed by Tony Morris hiding in her church grounds after the death of Raj Chahaun. How time flew by!

She took herself off to take the 8.30am Morning Prayer service in church leaving the family in the kitchen finishing a leisurely breakfast. Today, not even Gladstone was there and she recited the liturgy, read the readings and offered the prayers out loud with only God for company.

Afterwards, as she put her books away on her prayer stall, with the page marking ribbons moved to their new places ready for 8.30 am Monday, her mind went back to the wedding she'd taken. A week on, she hoped the couple would be celebrating this minor one week anniversary as the first of many happy anniversaries to come.

With that thought, she headed back to the vicarage thinking it would good to have another coffee before working on Sunday's services in readiness for the morrow. Once she stepped inside the vicarage door, her plans had to be curtailed as Phil called out, 'visitors to see you, in the lounge.'

Ruth paused, she didn't share the jollity in Phil's tone. She needed the time in her study. She pushed open the lounge door wondering who it could be this time.

'Adam! Raqiyah! What a surprise and how well you both look,' she exclaimed in delight, hugging them both in turn.

'How's Dubai? How's the job and the studies?'

Adam, in smartly tailored navy trousers and open neck check shirt sat next to Raqiyah who looked a picture of health and elegant beauty. She wore a loose, multi-coloured headscarf and a pale pink two piece; a slim-fitting outfit, which seemed to combine the modern and traditional in Arabic dress. Ruth suddenly felt very proud of her nephew Adam, a working man with a good job. He sat there beaming, Raqiyah a smile to match.

'Hold on,' he said. 'That's too many questions at once.'

Co-conspirator Phil wandered back into the lounge to join them, wearing a smug smile, carrying a tray and four mugs of coffee.

'Bet you're surprised? I was,' he said, looking across at Ruth as he handed round the coffees.

'Dubai's fine for now. It's a good base for me really. Being a Middle East Correspondent, however junior, takes me off all over. Just back from Qatar, my first trip there. Wanted to find out why it's got a reputation as "*the Club Med for Terrorists*". Its only land border is with Saudi, but they don't get on. America likes wall building, Saudi's done the same, walled itself off and wants to isolate Qatar by building a canal. Fascinatingly resilient people the Qatari are – watch out for my next article!'

'You're obviously enjoying yourself, and Raqiyah, how are your studies?'

'Yes, good. I've made a few friends and we've seen my Uncle Abdul in Istanbul a couple of times. They all came to see us in the Spring. It meant such a lot to me.'

'And news from home, Oman?'

'Not much. Nothing really. Scraps, third hand… occasionally. I'm an embarrassment and its risky for them to contact me even if they wanted to and things are still pretty unsettled there.'

'It's so lovely to see you both and looking so well. How long are you over for?'

'Just the weekend. It was all the time we could take off,' said Adam, 'but we have a favour to ask. We want to get married and we'd love you to be involved.'

'Oh, wow, how lovely. Of course… of course,' replied Ruth, immediately thinking of all the administrative and other hoops lying ahead.

'We'll have a legal wedding in Dubai, where our home is and where our new friends are. Look, it might mean Uncle Phil, Olivia and Paul flying over and yourself taking some kind of service for us. Would that be OK? It's what we both want. You could do some kind off ceremony in Dubai, yes?'

'Yes, of course. I'll need to make a few enquiries about things and you'll need to keep me up to speed on the legal side and local practice. Then there's the question of when… when are you planning on it taking place?'

'Soon. Autumn half term, Mum and Dad both being teachers, it's a good time. Also Olivia and Paul can come too.

It'll only be small numbers. How does your diary look Aunt, you're the one I always think of as being so very busy?'

Ruth pulled her mobile out and scrolled through her diary to check.

'There's nothing in here that can't be moved. That's lovely, so exciting. How are your Mum and Dad? Pleased?'

'They're really pleased, and from the first, they've always made me feel part of the family,' said Raqiyah beaming.

'And what about the Christian-Muslim bit?' asked Ruth, who thought, as soon as she'd raised the matter that perhaps this question should be left until later. Had she opened her mouth too soon?

'We've talked a lot about that,' said Adam seriously.

'And argued about it,' added Raqiyah smiling.

'Islam is quite prescriptive about these things. Requires me to convert, requires any children to be brought up as Muslim, etc.' said Adam.

Raqiyah added, 'but neither of us feel comfortable with formal, prescriptive religion. Adam, so far as I can drag it out of him, thinks of himself as Christian by background and lifestyle. Being in the Middle East has been an eye opener Adam, you've said so many times yourself.' Adam nodded.

'He feels the Church of England is part of his spiritual identity, well, on a pick and mix basis. He likes the liberal openness, it's a, what do you say Adam? yes, a *"broad church"* with room for wayward people like him. Is that fair?'

'More or less,' said Adam beaming, 'but less about the wayward. I do think my background has been far more positively shaped than I realised by the effect of Christianity on my life and my culture. That's not the same as saying I've started going to church regularly or anything...'

'As for me, I'm enjoying some postgraduate studies in Dubai which are leading me to discover areas of Islam I'd never come across before, the sufi mystics for example and that there are other perspectives than the Ibadi Omani tradition I grew up in. The thing is I feel somewhat anaesthetised against grasping religion too readily with all that we went through when I was last in my country. We almost died because some people read Islam one way and others took another course. We were lucky to escape across the border out of Oman with our lives.'

I can understand that,' said Ruth.

'I share with Adam a sense that my identity is Muslim, but now... well... open Muslim. I believe that Christians and Muslims worship the same God, whom we call Allah. I can also appreciate how Christians see why Jesus is more important to them than Muhammed, the prophet of our tradition. The thing is this, Adam and I have looked at the Christian marriage service and come to the conclusion we want a Christian wedding blessing.'

'My, I'm impressed. You've clearly done a lot of thinking already!' said Ruth.

'I took the liberty, whilst you were at Morning Prayer, of phoning Sue and Jim to ask them over later,' said Phil, 'and they'd love to come. So we're all having a meal here this evening.'

'And we're going over to Muswell Hill to catch up with London friends and share our news. We want some of them to come to Dubai in October. We'll be back here again this evening,' said Adam.

And with that they were on their way. As they went out of the front door, Ruth was surprised to see Andy, the CO from Sea Cadets arriving, another unexpected visitor. Ruth invited him inside. Was it going too be another of those days when her own plans had to be placed on hold?

'I've a big favour to ask,' he began, a worried look on his face.

'It's been quite a day for favours already,' she replied, smiling.

'Bill's done it and its magnificent,' Andy said.

'What, done what? Oh, do you mean the table of knives?' she replied, suddenly recalling Tuesday evening's visit to the cadets.

'Yes. It stands about four feet high. I had no idea the police had picked up so many knives locally. Knife crime's endemic Ruth, it really is. Quite a few knives came in as a result of the recent knife amnesty apparently. The table, it's quite splendid. They've been so helpful too and backed the project all the way. The thing is, the favour…'

'How can I help?'

'Is there any chance we could present it in church at your morning service tomorrow morning. You see we were meant to have a training morning for the cadets and the Centre

271

we'd booked to take them called earlier to say they were terribly sorry but they can't accommodate us tomorrow. I just thought, as all the cadets are around anyway, we'd bring them into church for an impromptu Parade Service, you'd dedicate or is it bless the table, say some words about knives and the need for peace – well you know what's best said and done on these occasions. How about it?'

'Why yes. That would be lovely.' Ruth was thinking to herself that all of a sudden her unprepared service for tomorrow had just fallen into shape.

'I have sounded out one or two people in case you said "yes",' said Andy, every bit the organising Cadet leader. 'The mayor wants to come and two representatives from Edmonton Police Station. I thought after I'd spoken to you, I'd just send a quick message round to all our cadets to tell them of the proposed change of plan and that they can invite their parents along. OK?'

'Brilliant. Will the two boys who were threatened with a knife be present?'

'Yes, I think so.'

'And can you be sure to invite Jackie's Dad, the welder?'

'Will, he's on my to do list. He'll be along.'

'Well, I'd like them all to be there and I'd like to say something personally to them, if that's alright.'

And so it was done. Andy went on his way, another happy caller. Ruth left thinking that a significant statement was about to be made on knife crime. Whilst Andy was busy making all his calls, she'd also make one or two of her own. One would be to Carlton Smyth at Diocesan House, another to the Enfield Independent newspaper. It was time to test out whether good news stories and peacemaking initiatives carried any weight.

As she wandered into her study, she realised that despite an afternoon of good news, other darker events cast a shadow beneath which she seemed unable to entirely emerge.

27

There was a certain unrelenting routine to parish life and the fact that Ruth had three Sunday services to prepare for invariably focussed her mind on Saturday afternoons. She'd stolen glimpses of the set Bible readings in previous days, had a telephone call with Gill, the organist about music, but now she needed an hour to two in her study to think and pray about what was needed from the pulpit.

All had to be fitted in around talking to Phil about what to do for supper when everyone came in from Muswell Hill later. The latter was resolved by Phil coming into her study carrying the Kohinoor Indian Take Away menu card – offering the ideal solution. It was swiftly agreed. Ordering could wait until everyone arrived.

Left alone again, Ruth looked at Sunday's sermon, an as yet empty document file on her laptop. As she reflected, the letter to the Hebrews chapter 13 and verse 2 kept coming back into mind, "*Do not forget to entertain strangers, for by so doing some people have entertained angels without knowing it.*" She flipped open her Bible and read once again this verse in its broader context, the set reading, for tomorrow morning.

It took only a few minutes more for her to realise that "*entertaining strangers*" would be the theme for her sermon. It promised to be a lot more fun than the widespread practice of threatening 'others' with words, exclusion, or even worse, with knives. So often local knife crime was because someone trespassed on to another's home territory. "*Entertaining strangers*" was spot on. Her fingers began to type furiously some outline notes. After an hour she thought she had something useful to use.

She emerged from her study to wander into the kitchen with a feeling of relief. She'd been spared further interruptions, she even considered herself ahead of the game, she could enjoy the celebratory evening ahead.

Feeling thirsty again. Tea was poured and drunk. As Ruth stood to put her empty mug into the sink she looked up to see Darshana standing outside her window on the pavement waving to her, not in friendly happiness but with a look of panic on her face as she glanced warily first in one direction, then the other, before indicating she was heading for Ruth's front door. Ruth went to let her in.

'I can't stay at the shop, I can't,' she blurted out. She kept looking up and down the street, trying to make herself look inconspicuous in the small vicarage porch.

'You'd better come inside,' said Ruth, recalling what was now a sermon-to-self as the words, *"entertaining strangers"* came back to mind.

'What has happened? Are you all right?' Ruth knew something was up if Darshana would leave the shop late on a busy Saturday afternoon. Maybe she was distressed since it was a week since Raj had died.

'I'm frightened, I think they want to kill me too.'

'Why? What's happened?'

'A man called at the shop. I thought it was strange, I thought he might be a shoplifter as he just walked around, picking things up, putting them down, waiting until it was quiet. But no, he was just waiting until Ravi popped out the back, then he came right up to me and said, straight out, Raj needed to lose everything for what he'd done to his family.'

Ruth listened intently.

'I said I didn't know what he meant. I said to him, what had Raj done?'

'He said, I needed to know that Raj and his Hindutva mob had killed his brothers and burned his family house down in Gujarat. For that Raj had died but that still wasn't enough. I was terrified. I thought he meant I was next. I said I was sorry to hear that, even if it was true and I had no way of knowing, but for my part I was nothing to do with that. I wasn't even in India.'

'It sounds like he meant to intimidate or even threaten you. Do you want me to call the police, I think maybe we should?'

'No, no… I don't want to annoy these people.'

'He said Allah was merciful but his brothers were not. Have you friends in the Temple, he asked me. I told him I rarely go there but Raj did. Any friend of Raj is an enemy of God's true people, he said. He was so very frightening. He leaned right over the counter at me, called me a "*kuffar*", and unbeliever, he made me feel… feel like I was responsible fro killing his family, but it isn't true… He didn't want to hear my side of things. His mind was… all made up.'

'I think you did the right thing coming here,' offered Ruth.

'I think he was trying to warn me and when he'd gone I told Ravi to look after the shop whilst I came to see you. Ravi was quite happy that I should leave him there. He's got his mobile and something under the counter should he need it. I needed someone to talk to, to help me know what to do. So I came here.'

She began to cry, Ruth reached for a box of tissues from the window cill and placed them into her lap. Darshana looked a pathetic, frightened person, all hunched up as if she wished herself invisible. She pulled her dark red sari tightly around herself as if for comfort.

'Have you got somewhere you can go? Friends? Look, if you're stuck, you can stay here until you can arrange something… if you need to.'

'I don't want to be any trouble, but I'm frightened to go back to the shop this afternoon. Ravi says he'll close up early today, then he'll go to the Temple and warn them, tell them to be careful. In part, people will think, if we shut early today, it's out of respect for Raj as it's, it's a week, since…' she added, her words drifting into a drawn out silence.

'Just sit yourself there and take some time out. You're quite safe here. I'll see if we can rustle up some tea. No sooner had she said the words then, as if on cue, Phil appeared with a tray in the doorway.

'Phil, Darshana feels unsafe working in her shop this afternoon and I've told her she can stay here until it closes. She's left her brother Ravi in charge. He's OK about that.'

'Fine. I'm sure things will work out, Darshana. You're welcome here.' With that he left them to it.

'I'm going to leave you in here for now, in the lounge. You might want to ring the police. If you'd like to watch TV feel free. There are some magazines to look at over there. I'm going to see what our two kids are up to, but give me a call if you need me.'

'That's fine, I'm so grateful, I'm happy to sit quietly, maybe look out on to your lovely garden.'

First, Ruth went into the kitchen to explain things a little more to Phil. He was accepting of the situation and suggested if she was still here later, then she might like some Indian Take-Away too. Phil wanted Ruth's assessment as to what danger Darshana might actually be in. All Ruth could give were vague feelings based on third hand conversations Darshana had had with a mysterious caller.

She added quietly that she wasn't too sure how well Darshana was, how reliable she might be, given all that she had recently been through. Perhaps it was for the best to let her have a little space to recover herself. For the moment she seemed happy enough to be left to her own devices in the lounge. At the same time, the police needed to know, but Ruth didn't want to go behind Darshana's back to make the call. Then there was also family to think about and everyone descending on the vicarage so very soon. It all left her feeling so very uneasy, things left hanging so to speak. It didn't sit right with her.

At that, Darshana in the lounge and Phil in the kitchen, she went upstairs to find Olivia and Paul. Ruth felt as if she was waiting for a firework to ignite. A fuse had been lit but she was left expectantly waiting and watching, distracted by her children. What would happen? Would things settle like a damp squib or explode like a rocket?

28

Saturday evening, 6pm, the door bell rang and the four high spirited visitors from Muswell Hill arrived having travelled together in the one car. Ruth was conscious Darshana was still in the lounge and could see a problem looming. Darshana was bereaved and frightened; the family high spirited, joyful and excited. A titanic crash of emotions was pending.

Her home management strategy was to usher everyone to join Phil in the kitchen where she explained she had a visitor in the lounge before excusing herself saying she wouldn't be a minute.

Darshana had switched on the TV and was vacantly staring at the screen. She didn't turn her head when Ruth entered.

'Darshana, how are you feeling now?'

'I feel safe here,' she said quietly.

'I have family visitors, just arrived, you probably heard them. I'd like to bring them in here, in the lounge.'

Ruth hoped that this might be the prompt to get Darshana to think it was time to make a move. 'Do you think Ravi will be closing, locking up the shop by now and you might be able to return home?'

'Yes, I'm sorry. You come in the lounge. I'll give Ravi a call in the hallway, then see myself out.'

'Are you sure?' said Ruth looking at the forlorn, crumpled figure sitting in front of her. Then taking her by the arm, Ruth led her into the hall. High spirited conversational noises were inevitably escaping from the adjacent kitchen. Ruth felt the situation to be increasingly awkward, but she didn't want Darshana to feel she was being moved out of the way and said, 'you can use my study if you like.'

With Darshana in the study making her call to Ravi, Phil's head appeared through a partly open kitchen door. He nodded in the direction of the lounge in a move asking if the room was now free and Ruth nodded back. Then clutching their drinks, Olivia and Paul entering into the up-beat mood too, began leading a family procession across the hallway.

At that point Darshana reappeared. Standing framed in the study doorway she suddenly let out an outburst as she caught sight of Raqiyah and then stared at her. 'I never did anything to you,' she shouted, 'I never went to India, I never killed any Muslims. Leave me alone. Leave me alone!'

Ruth stepped forward, placing herself between them immediately and without a further word everyone else went into the lounge closing the door behind them leaving Ruth and Darshana in the hallway.

'What was she doing here? Why?' asked Darshana. 'I thought I was safe here and you bring a Muslim woman in, to... to torment me.'

'No, no, its nothing like that. Calm yourself. Did you get through to Ravi or the police?'

'No. I've left a message for him to call me. Sorry, sorry. Look, if I wait in here until he calls is that OK. I'd feel better if he came to pick me up, see me home.'

'That's fine. I think I'd better get back to my visitors.'

So Ruth, feeling torn between addressing the needs of Darshana on the one hand and missing out on the family celebrations on the other, slid out and back into the lounge. It wasn't easy being a go-between, yet so often that was a role she carried. She whispered placatory words of explanation for Dashana's unfriendly outburst, pouring oil on troubled waters, tending the emotional disequilibrium. Fortunately, things soon settled, the explanation was accepted and a measure of calm restored.

The hallway altercation with Raqiyah didn't seem to have dampened the family high spirits and Sue was the first to speak, wanting to re-tell the story of what had been a surprise visit by Adam and Raqiyah for them too.

'It was about 8-o-clock last night,' she began, 'there was this knock on the door, Jim went to get it, and it was them! Such a surprise! I hadn't any food in to give them, but it didn't matter. They just wanted to tell us what they'd decided, that they're going to get married at half-term. Look Ruth, you and I will have to fit in a shopping trip – we'll both need something to wear. Something cool and colourful! Oh, and I'm so pleased you said "Yes" to taking the wedding blessing, so very, very pleased.'

And so the hype and chat, the re-living of the moment of Adam's proposal on Jumeira Beach, the hearing of plans for their future home in Dubai, the roles they had in mind for Olivia as a bridesmaid and Paul as ring bearer, it all led to

Ruth feeling awash under a wave of contentment and deep happiness, all else subsumed under the family's all-pervading excited happiness. Everyone was in high spirits when the front door bell rang.

'That'll be the Indian take away delivery,' said Phil getting up.

Only it wasn't.

'Call for you,' Phil said looking toward Ruth with a look of seriousness on his face. 'Call for you...' Something wasn't right, and all but the children sensed it and their conversation momentarily hushed.

'Sorry, everyone,' said Ruth as she left the room, to see uniformed PC Alan Dallow with a serious face waiting to speak with her in the porch.

'I'm afraid we've a situation down at Sonny's Foods,' he began.

'Sonny's, you mean Raj's shop? Why, what's happened?'

'There's a fire, the Fire Service are there now. The shop's ablaze. Apparently customers say Ravi had an altercation with a couple of people. He saw them off, we're thinking that maybe they were responsible for the fire. We're making enquiries of course. We don't know where he is, but we were wondering if Darshana was with you? I was asked to pop round here to check if she's safe.'

'No, she was here, but left soon after my visitors arrived.'

'How long ago would that be?'

'Maybe twenty minutes ago, maybe thirty. About that.'

'And where did she say she was going?'

'I thought she was going back to the flat, above the shop, you know, where Raj, no… she lives.'

Without a further word Alan picked up his radio and made a call, obviously to the Fire Officer. 'Darshana Chahaun is not here, believe she headed to her home, the flat above the shop.'

There was the briefest verbal response which ended the call before Alan spoke to Ruth again. 'The Fire Service are making every effort to check the premises, but given the severity of the blaze I am not optimistic. I need to get back there. Thank you, ma'am… and let me know if you hear anything further as to the whereabouts of Ravi or Dashana.'

Ruth closed the door after him, wondering whether there was anything she could do. Apart from an arrow prayer, she felt herself to be utterly helpless. It hardly seemed possible she could enter back into the joyfulness of the lounge, so she paused to try and collect herself before rejoining them. So often in ministry she felt she was performing emotional acrobatics, flipping between joyful and mournful as the dice of life rolled passed her door.

She had hardly pushed the door shut when the door bell rang again.

She turned back to open it.

'Delivery for Churchill,' the young man said, smiling as he held out two large carrier bags of food.

After paying him, she carried the bags into the kitchen. It somehow seemed easier now having the food as a welcome social distraction. She called the others and the children came running, the adults following more slowly behind. Phil and Sue both looked at Ruth knowing that behind the smiles, she was wrestling with angst. As to what had happened to Darshana since she left, Ruth had no idea not knowing whether she was alive or dead.

Until news came in, Ruth decided now was the time to be with family. There was little else she could usefully do and she began to organise everyone, handing out plates and cutlery, pointing out the Chicken Vindaloo from the Lamb Passanda, the Chapatis from the Papadums and the dips to go with them. Food was therapy and the celebratory atmosphere soon returned as they all tucked in. Only Phil noticed Ruth herself wasn't eating, making several unsuccessful attempts to offer her something. Each time he looked at her, he had anxious, puzzled looks written across his face.

The children stayed up very late, in fact until the Muswell Hill party left just after 10.30pm. 'You're working in the morning, Ruth,' Jim had said, as he tried to persuade people it really was time to go. It had been a truly special family evening, the first time they'd all been together for very many months and with something happy to celebrate, though no one called it an engagement party, to Ruth's mind, that was exactly what it was.

Visitors waved off, Olivia and Paul, despite their protests, were put smartly to bed and went straight to sleep. Phil and Ruth were soon back downstairs and beginning to clear up, the pervasive smell of left over curry hanging in the air.

'I'll put all this straight outside in the bin,' said Phil, opening a window to freshen the kitchen. He disappeared with the two greasy carrier bags full of take-away detritus in his hands. When he returned they loaded the dishwasher and decided on a cup of tea together before hitting bed. Ruth asked Phil to ensure the kitchen window was shut and the window lock secure.

'You've not really said why the police called. It rather dampened things, must have been something serious?' said Phil.

'Sorry. It's still on my mind. There's been a fire at Raj's shop this evening. Sounded like arson. The police wanted to know whether Darshana was still here. Given the time she left us, she could have been there when the fire broke out, in her flat. I need to know she's OK. She's been on my mind all evening. If we hadn't had family round, I'd have gone down there. I couldn't sleep without knowing.'

'You could go now. Or maybe ring first? I know its late, but in the circumstances, I think a call is probably justified,' said Phil.

Ruth picked up her mobile, but even though she tried twice there was no reply.

'I'm going down there. Shouldn't be long.'

'I'll wait up. Don't forget to take your mobile, keep your eyes about you. You could take the car. Forget that, we've both been drinking, just take care,' he said, picking up her phone from the table and passing it to her.

Ruth found the fresh air, as fresh as London air got that is, a welcome contrast to the kitchen. There seemed to be few people about; it was quiet as she set off.

Walking briskly she turned the corner past the church and into Silver Street. Then she knew why it was quiet, a white police van with its blue lights flashing was parked at a slant across the road, traffic cones signalling the road was entirely closed to traffic. A lone officer stood facing her way as she approached. Ruth reached for her neck, double-checking she was wearing her dog collar. At times like this it could be useful, so often a key to locked doors. She didn't recognise the officer.

'Good evening. I'm the local vicar, Ruth Churchill. I had a visit earlier from PC Alan Dallow, is he here?'

'I'll make a call,' he said, walking a little way off out of earshot. She waited and looked over to see what she could of the shop. A large red Fire Tender blocked much of her view. Two others, hoses rolled out and lining the street were parked in a line nearby. On the skyline a tract of white smoke could be seen rising into the never dark urban sky. More police and emergency service vehicles were parked a little further off. The officer returned.

'I've been asked that you wait here with me, ma'am. Won't be long,' he said.

The officer was not forthcoming when Ruth tried asking him questions. His main attention was on traffic and sending any voyeurs off on their way. These amounted to small groups of bored teenagers seeing what the excitement was all about. Some anxious neighbours pressed pale faces at nearby windows to see what was happening from time to time. A few minutes later, Ruth turned to face the direction of Raj's shop as she heard footsteps approaching.

'Hello Ruth,' said the familiar voice of April Cooper. 'Would you please come with me,' she said, nodding to the policeman on traffic duty to indicate she'd taken charge.

They walked toward the scene, the gutter awash with blackened water. Then Ruth gasped as she caught a glimpse of what was left of the shop, a blackened wall facing the street and nothing left of Darshana's flat above.

'I expect you came down to find out what exactly's happened. Please, come this way but be careful where you tread. We need to keep well clear of the shop front.' She led her to April's unmarked police car where she was shown into the front passenger seat. April climbed into the driver's seat beside her.

'It's easier if we talk here. I understand Darshana Chauhan called to see you this afternoon?'

'Yes, and then left about twenty to thirty minutes before PC Alan Dallow came to see me to ascertain where she was. I told him she was going to her flat. Is she alright?'

'Can I first ask you what she came to see you about?'

'She was frightened. She didn't feel safe there,' she said, pointing to the burning building. 'I said she could stay at the vicarage. She did, that is until my visitors came, about the time she said Ravi was going to shut up the shop. He was going to do so earlier today, about 6pm because, because they'd had threats…'

'Did she say who made the threats?'

'I suggested she tell this to you. She had two visitors a while back, who showed her a picture of Raj when he was in India for his father's funeral back in 2002. Raj was part of a Hindu mob, carrying a baton in the photo. Then another man had come to the shop on his own today. I don't know any more about him. He told Darshana she had blood on her hands as well and Raj had paid for it. He thought she supported Raj and led her to believe the shop, even she herself was in danger as there was still a score to be settled. Sorry I don't recall the exact words. Darshana told Ravi to be careful... watch out for himself... but didn't tell him more. Well, that's what she told me.'

'At this early stage of our investigation, the fire service have identified what they believe was an accelerant, that is subject to testing of course, and have told us their preliminary assessment is that the fire here was started deliberately.'

'So Darshana was right. Is she, is Ravi safe?'

'The badly burned body of a male was pulled out from inside the shop by the firemen. I think that he remains subject to identification...'

'Ravi?'

'We can't confirm that at this stage,' April said, but leaving little room for any other interpretation in Ruth's eyes.

'And Darshana?'

'We still don't know. The site isn't safe, it isn't possible to search it. But… we've not heard anything and she hasn't responded to our calls.'

'That doesn't sound good,' said Ruth. 'And what about the two men and then the one who called?'

'We have two men helping us with our enquires. They are currently being held under the Terrorism Act. I cannot say anything further.'

'There's nothing else I can do by being here is there?' stated Ruth.

'I don't think so, can I drive you home?'

'Thank you, yes. Will you let me know April, about Darshana, as soon as you can that is. I'd been trying to help her… because she was so very low and vulnerable. She tried to take her own life…'

'I didn't know,' said April, before adding, quite unexpectedly, 'I take my hat off to you Ruth, in a world where there is so much bad stuff going on, you really care. It's late, I'll drop you back. Come on, you've a home to go to.'

April's car was waved on its way by the traffic duty cop. Parked up outside the vicarage, Ruth had one outstanding question come to mind. 'April, what happened to Angela Morris?'

'We are currently holding two detainees under the Terrorism Act… I can't say more.'

'She was a strange woman. I never felt comfortable in her presence. But she didn't deserve to die... Thank you for the lift.'

Phil, who had been waiting and was watching at the kitchen window opened the front door to let her inside. Linseed oil putty ranked as the stronger smell over stale curry, she thought. As the door closed behind her, she turned, remembering to slide the safety chain in place.

29

Early Sunday morning and the 8am church service passed without incident, except that Gladstone had the nerve to tell her that unlike the previous week, this time she had, 'got it right!'

Truth be told, Ruth's mind was mainly focussed on the bigger 9.30 am service. She was beginning to feel that maybe it wasn't such a good idea to hold the dedication of the table of knives with the Sea Cadets at such short notice. She just hadn't had sufficient time to mobilise her effort to pull it all together. Hastily she spoke to her churchwarden Chris Darlington to brief him on the forthcoming proceedings. She reckoned he owed her one after the climate change banner incident.

At 9.20am precisely, she was impressed to see a line of smartly dressed Sea Cadets following their CO Andy into church, the group filling the first three rows. Then, four more cadets came in through the wider double door entrance in Silver Street struggling between them to carry a weighty metal structure which turned out to be an impressively welded work of art in the form of a table of knives.

Without needing to be told what to do, they carried it solemnly down the central aisle and deposited it in front of the congregation on the flat dais by the chancel steps. The four bowed respectfully toward it and then went and sat down behind their comrades. Impressive, thought Ruth, their conduct and the table. The table itself had a magnetic presence about it, her own as well as everyone's eyes were upon it.

It was an immovable statement in welded metal – redundant knives rendered, disabled, sharpness bent, blunted and re-shaped, re-cast in creating a unique place to sit around or offer the sacrament from.

By the time the service was due to start the three rows of seats opposite the cadets were filled with invited dignitaries, representatives from the police, fire service personnel and the other local uniformed group leaders including the Scouts and Guides. In addition Julia was looking after the Mayor of Enfield who had appeared and to her surprise had the local imam sitting next to him.

To Ruth's delight, five minutes later, she observed a much bigger than usual congregation had turned out, numbers further strengthened by all the parents of the Cadets who had come along, many squeezing in at the last minute. Finally, just as she was about to welcome everyone, she saw to her horror the archdeacon slip quietly into the back of the church. There was something serpent like in the way he slid himself into the back row.

Momentarily his presence made her feel insecure, like prey, but then her self-confidence returned, boosted by what was happening before her very eyes. This morning felt good, very good and she told herself firmly that the presence of Archdeacon Stephen Nicholls was of absolutely no consequence. Lifting her head confidently she began giving her welcomes.

Although she explained the presence of the table of knives briefly at the outset of the service, her plan was to dedicate it and say more about it mid-service at the point when it was customary to share The Peace amongst the congregation – a period of visible bonhomie as everyone shook hands, embraced and even kissed one another, offering their friendship and goodwill. It was the obvious liturgical moment. How fitting, she thought, standing right behind the table, these reconstituted, rearranged knives no longer pointed outward in aggression, but provided a table around which all were gathered and at peace.

Twenty minutes later, the time had come. She stood in front of the throne and introduced the words of The Peace,

> *"We are the body of Christ.*
> *In the one Spirit we were all baptised into one body.*
> *Let us then pursue all that makes for peace*
> *and builds up our common life."*

She then invited everyone to greet and share peace with one another. As she moved amongst the congregation to shake hands with people she had a surprise. Sitting next to Andy, the Sea Cadet CO, was none other than Tony Morris. She had to look twice to be sure, then went straight across to see him.

'Hello,' he said simply, 'They let me go this morning. I wanted to be here to say thank you. Saw Andy. His son was in the same class as me at school, we were mates. He told me about the service, brought me in. I saw him as I was walking home. We got talking. Decided to come. Nice table vicar,' he added with a knowing smile and a nod in its direction.

'So pleased to see you. Peace to you Tony,' she said, offering her hand then shaking his. 'Would you mind if we have a chat in front of everyone? Would you be up for it? I'd like you to come and stand behind the table with me, OK?'

'I'd rather not, another time, but can I talk to you on your own, after, like? Need to explain a few things, say sorry, ask you a favour.'

'Sure, I'll see you afterwards.'

Ruth moved away to greet others, shaking hands all round, before moving back to her seat. It wasn't her best judgement call to try and get Tony up to the front, probably a good thing he himself said "No" she thought. There was still too much unexplained stuff to deal with first and she really wasn't sure in retrospect whether Tony was in a good frame of mind.

Standing, facing the congregation, Ruth gained everyone's attention as they shuffled back to their places.

'This morning is a special day. Our community has seen the savage brutality of knife attacks in recent days. Raj Chauhan at Sonny's Supermarket lost his life just last weekend. On another day, a little while ago, two of our own Sea Cadets were robbed at knife point as they made their way home. These are but the tip of a chilling knife crime iceberg. Local police have either removed from people or had handed in to them all these knives, knives which have gone into the making of this table. Knives have become a modern plague, a scourge on our streets, an evil that we must work together to bring to an end.'

Ruth went on to commend the Sea Cadets for their contribution to community life, for the vision they had in wanting to turn a nasty incident into a positive statement, and to praise Bill Harris for his skill as an artist and welder in creating the impressive table of knives. The Bible, said Ruth, speaks of seeing swords turned into ploughshares, and it is in this tradition of seeking a better future today we see knives being turned into a table, a place to gather round together. A table where we meet, discuss things, work things out. In a world of so much blatant hostility, the Bible calls us to show hospitality and when we see strangers not to fear them, but entertain them...'

Then in turn, the Mayor, followed by Andy, said a few words, each energised by the meaning and peaceful statement the table made for them. Then, after the speeches there was a round of spontaneous loud applause from the whole congregation who stood up in an act of solidarity and support for one another and for Ruth.

At the end of the service Ruth invited everyone into the Church Hall where coffee was, as ever, freely available and it was there she spotted Tony again, trying to hide himself away from people as one who was embarrassed. He was standing next to, or rather just behind Andy's shoulder and was clearly waiting to see her. Andy got to speak first.

'Hugely indebted to you for this morning, Padre. I've left the cadets having photos taken. A press photographer arrived as we came out of church. Don't think you saw her. One group photo and now they're all standing around the table in turn. It was a great message, knives made redundant and recycled like this. The two lads who started it all off are chuffed to bits. And as for fitting us in at short notice, I take my hat off to you – brilliant on your part Padre, just brilliant!'

'It's been a pleasure.'

'There's one further thing,' said Andy.

'Yes.'

'We'd like you to have this broach... A thank you from us.'

Andy opened his hand. Lying in his palm, the light catching it, was a delicate, shiny circle of metal, little bigger than a pound coin.

'Bill Harris took the tip of a long narrow butcher's knife and fashioned it into this cross. We hope you like it.'

Ruth was moved by the beauty of the object itself, but even more so to have been appreciated. The jewelled object appeared symbolic of some deep truth which profoundly touched her and she was momentarily lost for words. Finally she expressed her gratitude as Andy pinned it to her lapel.

Ruth turned to Tony. 'They released you then?'

'Yeh! Got two other guys. You see it were never me who killed Raj, I just found him, dying, a knife in his chest. Thing is, I'd gone to the shop for Mum. He was arguing with two guys. There was nothing Raj could do. He didn't like them one bit. He was shouting at them in a language I didn't understand. I've never seen him so... so angry. Then it was all over. I don't think they even noticed me there. One of them grabbed Raj around the head and the other pushed a knife into him. It was so quick. They were running off when they saw me. The one looked at me and put his finger to his lips meaning me to stay quiet and then he drew his hand across his neck to say, if I didn't, I'd have my throat cut.'

'How terrifying.'

'They disappeared, but Raj wasn't dead, he was leaning against the counter groaning. I knew he wanted to say something. I got close to him. He got my hand and put it on the knife and together we pulled it out, but the blood, the blood, it flowed and flowed – no stopping it. He fell down and said, "Muslims from Ahmedabad, Muslims from Ahmedabad"'.

'Oh my…'

'Then he couldn't talk and fell quiet and I was left there holding the knife by his body and I panicked. I ran. That's when you saw me hiding. I was so scared of being caught. If I was caught they'd blame me and who would look after Mum. I'm sorry for what I did. I just wanted you to keep quiet about it, I just didn't want to get caught. I know you are a good person, you were kind to me in the police station and you saw to my Mum. I want you to take her funeral, that's all I wanted to ask, a favour, you to take her funeral, that's all.'

'Tony. I'll help where I can. Everything will take time, so nothing will happen quickly, and yes, I'll take your Mum's funeral when the time comes.'

Ruth could see Tony was getting in a state, so she turned to Andy who had been listening. 'Andy, any chance you could see Tony home. He's got no one now his Mum's died'. Andy was happy to oblige. She asked Tony if he would like to drop by the vicarage later in the afternoon when they could talk further. He agreed.

As they parted Tony went over to avail himself of the biscuits on offer, in the other hand taking a coffee Andy handed him. Andy had the social sensitivity to use his big frame to shield Tony in a corner and protect him from the unwelcome attention of the curious. Where would we be without people like Andy? thought Ruth.

By the time Ruth had talked to everyone on what was one of the busiest Sundays since before the summer, she was exhausted, but it felt a qualitatively different tiredness, a contented and satisfied tiredness, rather than a stressed and anxious one. She believed something important had been achieved.

Back in the vicarage, her thoughts turned to the archdeacon. She'd forgotten about him altogether and she hadn't seen him afterwards. He'd simply disappeared. She hadn't noticed when he'd left and he'd definitely not come in for coffee. She wondered what on earth he'd made of it all. No doubt he'd be in touch soon.

Then she thought of Tony. It was so unexpected to see him in church, but then church life was full of the unexpected. The whole service had been unexpected, a table of knives from nowhere, the mayor and police, a church full of cadets and their parents as well as the regular worshippers. Recalling the experience felt affirming and positive, a time when the church felt like it was at the heart of the community. As for Tony, he'd be coming to see her again soon. He would need her time and she guessed some support.

Tony had probably been traumatised by what he'd seen, frightened at the threats made against him and in a state of bereavement and loss at the death of his mother... Then it struck her, Angela's death, who was responsible for it?

Could she be sure the people in custody were the same ones who had killed her had killed Raj? Had she been killed because they thought Tony had or might talk to the police? Was it a message to him by them or was someone else involved? Ruth began to feel uncertain, she needed some thinking time and what was going through her mind for some reason made her more than a little afraid. Things were resolved, she knew that to be so, and she thought she'd give April a ring to help her clarify her thoughts.

Picking up her mobile, she couldn't get through. In the end the best she could do was leave a message for her and hope it wouldn't be long before she called back.

Soon lunch was ready on the kitchen table and the four Churchills sat down together to eat the roast leg of lamb and two veg Phil had prepared for them. Sunday lunch had the effect of making Ruth forget her worries and she began to relax and smile. As Phil sat down with them he said, 'I see they've finally given you a medal Mrs Churchill,' his hand reaching across to touch her new broach.

'And long overdue,' he added.

'I like it. A cross with an Arts and Crafts style to it.'

'The Sea Cadets made it for me. Andy gave it me after the service… a knife transformed. I love it.'

30

As usual the children ate more quickly than the adults and had long absented themselves from the dinner table by the time coffee appeared. Ruth was pleased that they were generally easygoing kids and quite happy to amuse themselves for long periods in the private upstairs area of the vicarage. Whether being self-contained was something in their DNA or gained from force of habit through parental neglect she didn't care to decide upon. Their contentment was a convenient state when she was pre-occupied, as she was right now.

'Something on your mind?' asked Phil, accurately sensing her mood.

'Yes, Tony Morris. His situation. I don't feel at all at ease about it. I need some news, reassurance, that its been fully dealt with by the police. That he's safe.'

'You could call them?'

'I've tried, I left a message on April's phone to ring me, but she's not come back to me.'

'Come on! Penny for your thoughts. What's bothering you?'

'Tony's innocent of Raj's murder, I'm fine about that, oh, and he's coming to see me this afternoon. I'm fine about that too.'

'And…'

'One of the things he wants is for me to agree to take his mother's funeral. Of course I'm happy to do that, but it's early days yet and in my experience the police won't allow her body to be released for ages, what with an ongoing murder investigation in hand.'

'True, but a future funeral isn't the issue here, that's not what's really bugging you, is it?' Phil persisted.

'Hmm. Just think about it with me for a minute will you, Phil. Hear me out. A week ago, Tony saw Raj's murderers, two men in Sonny's Supermarket and now I'm assured they're in custody. Tony says they killed Raj and presumably the police agree, but did these men kill Angela too?'

'See what you mean…'

'And who killed the two in Raj's van? The police haven't told me that piece of the jigsaw.'

'More unfinished business… The two in custody perhaps?'

'No, most unlikely I'd have thought. My guess is the two in the back of Raj's van were Muslim. Now it's highly unlikely they'd kill their own side don't you think?'

'Agreed. So who did? Do you think it was Raj? It was his van! When did they die? Didn't Darshana say to you that Raj could well have parked it there? So however unlikely, it is at least conceivable that the guy you always considered your friendly corner shop Hindu friend, Raj, he could've killed them with or without help from other Hindus?'

'I don't know. I don't feel I know Raj anymore after what I've heard. If he was involved in those Hindutva riots and the

301

photos seemed to be pretty authentic evidence, then he could have done what they say he did in India and if he did that, then who's to say what he was capable of doing here?'

'That seems a reasonable assumption to make, even though you've always held Raj to be a friendly enough man until now. Just goes to show that when you think you know someone, something happens and then there's a darker, hidden side that reveals itself.'

'My instinct is this isn't over Phil. I'm worried for Tony. He's out there, a lad on his own and maybe he's still a target like his Mum was. He did, after all, split on the guys now in custody. What if there are others we don't know about? There was no obvious police officer keeping an eye on him earlier and Tony himself seemed totally oblivious to any sense of danger to himself. So I'm worried for him.'

'Best talk to the police then.'

'Which is why I'm waiting for April to call me... And Darshana, what's happened to her? Did the two in custody set the shop alight before they were arrested or were there indeed others involved? Whoever burned the shop almost certainly murdered innocent Ravi. I've got too many unanswered questions and the more I think about it, the less I like it.'

'Only ones who can help you are the police, like I say...'

Her mobile rang. She reached for her phone hoping it was April, only to see "Archdeacon SN" on her screen.

'This is all I need. The archdeacon!' she mouthed in a whisper to Phil.

Ruth quickly got up from the kitchen table and strode across the hallway to take the call in her study.

'Yes, Ruth Churchill here.'

'Ah, Ruthie dear. You may have spotted me in your flock this morning. Had a free morning, thought I'd drop by, swell the numbers. Looked like I didn't need to, had a struggle to find a seat at the back. Sorry I had to dash off without a goodbye, I had garden party event in Hampstead at lunchtime…'

'Yes, I did see you…'

'You know I'm not the one to listen to other people's story-telling. I like to see things for myself. Partly why I came I suppose. Much as I find it hard to imagine myself saying this, I have to say I was incredibly impressed at what I saw this morning. You did wonders… the table of knives thing, so very inspired. Couldn't you have got our Press and Comms guy Carlon Smyth in? He'd have liked that, liked it a lot. Great story, really great. Never miss out on telling a good story when you have one. Missed a trick there, Ruthie, next time call Calton, eh?…'

'I see what you mean.' She didn't like to point out the archdeacon was mistaken in that Carlton Smyth had in fact been briefed but had been unable to make it.

'But you got the crowds in didn't you? I just can't make you out. On the one hand all this negativity stuff and then this morning you pull a big one out of the bag. So well done, Ruthie, well done! Must go. Bye.'

Ruth returned to the kitchen holding the phone out at arms length before her in utter disbelief. 'That man! That man!'

she blurted out, 'Now he rings me to say, "well done" for this morning, the obnoxious fellow.'

'Appreciation late is better than never at all.'

'Even so he couldn't hold back on telling me off for missing a trick in not telling a good story to the diocesan press officer.'

'Well, I'm glad he appreciated you, and not before time. Sounds like he's off your back for now then!'

'Yes, who knows? But what about April? She's the one I really want to have a call from.'

Ruth picked up her phone to try April again and failing to get through then called Edmonton Police Station asking for either PCs Alan Dallow or Alice Such. The line went dead whilst enquiries were made.

'Alan Dallow here. Is that Ruth Churchill I'm speaking to?'

'Yes. I've been trying to get hold of April Cooper, Counter Terrorism, but haven't been able to reach her.'

'Is it about the Raj Chauhan, the Tony Morris case?'

'Yes.'

'I'm afraid PC Cooper's tied up in interviews presently, likely to be so for a while. Anything I can help you with?'

'I don't know. Is there any news on Darshana, Raj's wife... err, widow?'

'Interesting you ask. The Chief has just put up a missing persons on her. No news so far as I've heard.'

'Was there anything else ma'am?'

'Yes, are you looking for any more people in connection with the recent deaths of Angela Morris and the bodies in Raj's van?'

There was a pause at the end of the line, before Alan replied, 'All lines of enquiry are being pursued… Nothing ruled in and nothing out.'

Ruth worried at this. 'So is… can… Tony Morris consider himself to be safe?'

'Any unemployed youngster like our friend Tony Morris, out wandering the streets of Edmonton, needs to watch out for themselves. He knows how to survive that one. You'd know that better than most ma'am, wouldn't you? And by the way, good effort in church this morning. Sorry Alice and myself couldn't stay on for coffee.'

Ruth couldn't think of anything else to ask and by now it was absolutely clear to Ruth that Alan Dallow wasn't going to be any more forthcoming whether or not he had any further information on the investigations. He'd been polite but not open, so she offered her thanks, said her good bye and ended the call.

'Phil, you probably heard most of that, but I don't feel reassured. It is entirely possible, given what PC Alan Dallow just said that more people are out there beside the two already picked up. Oh, and there's still no more news on

Darshana. You'd think someone would have found out something after all this time.'

'I agree. If she was caught in the shop fire, then forensics would have found something by now I'd guess. They were quickly enough on to Ravi possibly being there. No, I think she's out of it somewhere, probably frightened and hiding. If she's doing that then she'll be thinking that she's still in danger and that adds to your theory that all this may not be over yet.'

'She may not know two people have been picked up?'

'I was looking at the Edmonton live website while you were making your call, for the latest news. That bit's been released. Only that they are saying two men are being questioned under the Terrorism Act for murder and arson. It doesn't say any more. There's a chance she doesn't know that, but I'm convinced she's gone to ground. She's hiding. Last time you saw her she was frightened for her safety, mark my words, she'll be hiding.'

'Let me try calling her.'

A message came back saying the number was not available.

'Could be her mobile is switched off,' offered Ruth.

'Which makes sense if she doesn't want to be tracked down by the police or anyone else.'

An uneasy quiet settled in the kitchen, soon interrupted by the front door bell. A glance out of the kitchen window to check who it might be revealed Tony standing there. Ruth wondered when that Arsenal kit he was wearing last had a wash.

'It's Tony Morris,' she declared as she went to the front door.

'Hi Tony, come on in. Cuppa?'

Phil took himself out of the kitchen to leave the two to have their conversation in the more relaxed surroundings the kitchen offered. Tony took a can of coke, Ruth poured herself the remaining coffee from the cafetière and they sat facing one another across the kitchen table, Tony with his back to the window and the street.

'I was so pleased to see you this morning,' offered Ruth warmly. 'Free again and so pleased that you came to find me.'

'Well, like I said, want you to take Mum's funeral. Don't know who else to ask. Not just that. You knew her.'

'I'd be very happy to Tony, but that is likely to be a while yet. There's still a live police investigation into her death and they don't tend to release a body for a funeral for quite some time in these situations.'

'Nothing urgent then?'

'No, far from it. There will be lots of things to do before then. Are you her only relative? Did she leave a will as to her wishes?'

'Yeh, there's only me. Only ever has been.'

'And do you know if she wrote a will as to her wishes?'

'No, won't have done nothin' like that.'

'So you're going to have to sort out a few things, Tony. All deaths have to be registered and you'll need to do that. Also you'll need an undertaker to handle the funeral side of things in due course.'

'Don't know anyone like that. Do you?'

'Mr Bernard, Fore St, know the place?'

'Yeh, yeh.'

'He'll give you good advice. Nice man. A stand up undertaker, the real thing. Pop in and see him tomorrow if you get chance. He'll tell you what to do and help out. Or I can ring him if you like, just to let him know.'

'I'll call round tomorrow. Know the place.'

'And will you be alright living where you do?'

'Yeh yeh. Mum had my name written into the tenancy, she weren't stupid, I can stay at home.'

'And how will you manage for money?'

'Dunno. Got a few quid for the next few days. Relied on her Disability Benefit. Guess that'll stop. Dunno. I've been running round for her, never had a job.'

'Well, can't do much on that front today, being Sunday, but call tomorrow morning, around 11am, we could make a few calls. And, until you get some income coming in, keep me posted if you need anything, ready meals, that kind of thing, to tide you over, until some money comes in…'

'Thanks. Andy said he'd help. Thing is, his son Drew and I were kind of friends at school. Drew's still at home, but working for some builder geezer down Cheshunt way, but Andy, he's a good guy, asked me to call, drop in. Reckon I will. One thing, I don't have to be running round for Mum anymore. Things are different. I kinda feel free, but guilty at the same time.'

Ruth was anxious to find out if Tony had any idea how the police case was proceeding and asked, 'Did you learn anything while you were in the Police Station as to who killed your Mum?'

'The guys who killed Raj had seen me in the shop before. They'd seen me about on the street. Raj told me they'd been following him and Darshana doing deliveries. They'd followed him to Henley Road. They knew where I lived. They knew my Mum was a friend of Raj. They also wanted to warn me I think. If I spilled the beans, if I grassed them up, then the same would happen to me as happened to Raj, as happened to my Mum… '

'Do you know if there were other people Tony, beside the two they've arrested? People who could still be out there?'

Tony fell silent.

'Yeh. Three more I think and maybe a couple of Raj's friends are trouble too.'

'Are you certain? How do you you know that?'

'They all came into the shop at different times. There was definitely something building between the two sides?'

'Two sides?'

'Yeh Yeh. Two sides, like gangs fighting a turf war. You can soon tell round here if there's a turf war brewing, even before the knives come out. Raj is Hindu, right. The two arrested and the other three I've seen with them at other times, Muslims right; they hated one another big time. I tried to leave or hang around outside the shop when their arguments kicked off. It was bad, scary bad.'

'You saw that?'

'Yeh. Raj had these two friends he told me were from his Temple, who "saw things the right way" and he could always count on these "brothers" to be there if he felt himself in danger. They only lived round the corner in Haselbury Road and would show up real quick if he ever called them. I once asked Raj about it. He told me not to worry, he was going to sort it out. I think he went with his two friends from Haselbury and caught two of the three just before he was killed last weekend. He kept saying "two nil" and smiling when I saw him last Saturday morning. He wouldn't say and I didn't know what he meant, he wasn't giving nothing away, but whist I was in my cell I got to thinking he'd fixed two of the three Muslims. Reckon the third will have run away if he knew what's good for him. I need to go. Things to sort out.'

With that Ruth let him go, but not without telling him to be on his guard and watch out for his own safety, for by Tony's own reckoning there was still at least one dangerous man out there.

It was only after he'd gone she wished she'd asked Tony how much of what he'd told her he'd actually told the police. She didn't know for certain, but she was left with the uncomfortable feeling that she'd been the first person he'd told his story to.

Knowing what she did, what should she do now? She looked over at her phone and decided to await April's overdue call. It couldn't be long in coming. She must phone back soon.

31

By early Sunday evening Ruth was feeling quite unsettled. She was beset with a fidgeting restless. She stood up, she sat down, she went into her study and finally went upstairs to do the usual Sunday evening chores – try to get clean clothes sorted for everyone for the week ahead. Nothing helped.

There was still neither a call from PC April Cooper nor news on Darshana and somewhere out there, Tony Morris was on the street and in danger. Having done what she could with the dry washing and having placed neat piles of school wear ready for Olivia and Paul to put on in the morning, she went back downstairs not knowing what to do next for the best.

Like a prison officer on duty, she twice went round to check the three downstairs outside doors of the vicarage – the front door, a side door and one back door to the garden. With no real cause she could lay her finger on, she checked each one carefully to ensure locks and bolts were securely in place. Mindful of the burglary they'd had a year ago, that experience had left her feeling any intruder could all too easily find their way inside again. An old house like this, bigger than all its neighbours, with so many doors and windows on offer, it was hard to defend.

She spied Phil with a magazine sitting at the kitchen table, his back to the sink. For his part, he seemed on the surface to be quite relaxed, in fact he looked to Ruth like someone who had found himself and she couldn't help herself from passing comment.

'Phil, you seem very chilled for someone recently out of a job,' she said, a certain edginess escaping her lips, the sound of which she didn't much like.

'Guess I am. And, if you don't mind me saying so, Reverend Churchill, you seem quite unable to relax now duty is done for the day,' he replied, coolly. 'Sunday evening is time to chill out in my book,' he added.

'Have you any plans for tomorrow? Monday won't seem quite the same if you're not going to the City.'

'I thought I'd prepare a report for the local vicar here,' he said, glancing in her direction with a mischievous twinkle in his eye.

'What are you planning Mr Churchill? Out with it!' she replied, infuriated by his coy manner.

'Before you say anything, I'm not having a mid-life crisis! However, I do want to work with you, to try to make a difference through the church's presence, here in Edmonton. One thing has become very clear to me, I've come to a conclusion and I've made a decision. I've had quite enough of the City and I'm never going back!'

'You've a got a plan, you schemer. I know you... Out with it...'

'We need a Community Foodbank. I thought I'd put together a report for the Church Council. They're meeting next week and something other than safeguarding and wall building would do very nicely as I see it. I can write reports, please credit me with being able to do that!'

'Yes, I'll give you that. You write very excellent reports.'

'This one will be the best you've ever seen! The cunning plan is that it will give you your Drop In Centre back in all but name. Look, young Tony Morris is the latest one to need food help. What's he going to live off for the next couple of weeks?' The need is there. It's a crime we don't use our church halls to the maximum. What's more, I'm going to make you an offer you won't be able to refuse.'

'What kind of offer? What are you thinking, Philip Churchill?'

'I am offering to personally manage and develop a Foodbank here as a Community Interest Company. We'd get it accredited as part of Foodbanks nationwide, registered through the Trussell Trust and I will make sure it works well.'

'Are you sure?'

'The Diocese can't stop us doing that. As a CIC we can arms length the initiative, tell Mr Archdeacon it's not us, it's the CIC and there's nothing he can do. Lots of churches run them and believe you me it's very much needed. Austerity might be the name of the game in politics, but someone has got to do something to address the fallout, help all the suffering people. Look, mental health provision in the community round here is a nonsense – they're all at your door because there's no one else to go to – many others are going hungry, a Foodbank will give us a platform to provide all kinds of services using the church as a community base. Besides, I can tap into one or two of those City Trusts to kick start our efforts with their sponsorship. There are ways to do this…'

'I don't think we could afford your services, Mr Churchill,' said Ruth teasingly.

'Ah, the small matter of my wages. We need to discuss that…'

'We can offer you nothing… well, maybe you can keep your free lodgings if you behave, but there's little chance of that, behaving I mean,' she said, her mood lightening.

'Done!' he said, grasping her round the waist and pulling her to him.

At that very moment a loud crashing sound came from the utility room by the back door. Both sprang back in alarm and swung their heads round. It sounded like a vicarage back window had been put in. Ruth couldn't move. She heard Phil give instruction in measured tones.

'Get upstairs, call the police, quick! Do it quick!' said Phil, looking around him for anything he might use to defend them. He pulled out the cutlery drawer and grabbed the carving knife. The sight of the knife spurred Ruth into action and her mind turned to Olivia's and Paul's safety; but Phil was standing still now, statuesque, holding the knife. He needed to move too.

'I think someone's trying to get in. Come on, we need to get in the hall, to get the other side of the kitchen door,' said Ruth. 'We can bolt it from the other side.'

They moved quickly into the hallway. The bolts on the kitchen door had never been used before and they didn't know if they even worked. Someone in the diocese, at some time after the previous break in, had had them fitted to improve the family's personal security. Phil swiftly kicked the lower one in place with the heel of his shoe, Ruth slid across the upper and then both were in place. The door was a solid old one, one of the original Edwardian features of the house. It might give them some precious minutes.

'Come on, quick, quick!' she said.

They ran upstairs, Phil now bounding ahead, Ruth stumbling to her knees half way up, Phil then pausing to pull her arm with one hand, the carving knife in the other. Another panic moment.

'Where are the children?' screamed Ruth.

'Olivia, Paul, come here now,' Phil shouted, as Ruth tried to keep up. The two stuck their puzzled heads out of their bedroom doors simultaneously.

'What's all the noise Daddy?' asked Paul.

Protectively, no answer given, they pushed and shepherded the two uncomprehending and confused children ahead of them into the large front bedroom at the far end of the landing, the master bedroom, their own room.

Once in their last place of refuge, Phil explained to the kids there was a burglar downstairs and began issuing instructions to them to help Ruth and himself build a barricade against the bedroom door.

There came another loud crashing from downstairs and the sound of repeated blows being struck. Fury and frustration were being taken out on the kitchen door downstairs. Would it hold?

Ruth's emergency call had been picked up and put through, the calm operator assuring them a police car, was on its way. In the meantime Ruth was told to, "hold the line please" as if this was just another request from a call centre. Ruth could feel palpitations rising in her chest. Calm and silence at the police end, a scary unknown intruder in her home at the other.

She passed the phone to Olivia so she herself could be of some practical help to Phil moving the heaviest furniture to defend them. Ruth noticed Phil had lain the carving knife on the window cill and wondered whether in setting it down he'd had second thoughts and his heart wasn't really into using it, even to defend his family. So how were they to protect themselves now except by building a stronger defensive barrier? She threw herself into the task.

First the double bed was dragged across to the door and then the dressing table and portable wardrobe. Panting from their efforts they heaved all the items as quickly as they could across the room, piling them up, leaning them against the door making it look like it was the corner of some junkyard or church jumble sale. It didn't look to be enough. Could one ever totally protect oneself enough, wondered Ruth, or will they always get you in the end?

The noise downstairs stopped. They all listened intently. Perhaps he'd given up, gone? Something or someone may have distracted, disturbed him? But no, the fearful sound of more glass being broken was heard, this time from the direction of the front of the vicarage, the newly repaired front door perhaps, they guessed. He was looking for another way in.

'Where are the police?' called out Ruth anxiously, clutching at Olivia and Paul.

The intruder was persistent and determined, seemingly completely unconcerned that he or they might have been heard. All went quiet again and they listened hard in the terrifying silence. Only a bus whooshed by somewhere outside.

Olivia handed the phone back back to her Mum. 'She wants to speak to you,' she says. Phone to her ear, the reassuring switchboard officer told Ruth help was now nearby.

'How near? How near? Tell me.' she cried.

'Silver Street,' came the reply, which meant, they were indeed near, but still in the next street and not yet here.

'Do these particular officers know where the vicarage is?' she pleaded.

'Yes, ma'am,' came back the calm voice.

After what seemed like an age, they heard the sound of a siren and then from their upstairs window they saw a police car approaching fast, closely followed by a second, pulling up at the front of the house. Phil forced up and open the sash window calling out, 'Up here, officer, we're up here,' as he saw an officer climb out of his car.

'Someone's got in from the side, down there, couldn't get passed the kitchen door so we think they went next to try another window. Don't know who or how many or where they are now,' he shouted at the top of his voice.

'We're coming in through the front door, it's wide open. Are you all in the one room?'

'Yes.'

'Then stay where you are. Keep it shut,' the officer ordered.

Olivia and Paul both began crying and Ruth clung on to them, trying with a cuddle to reassure them. She looked at Phil and she could see his mind was wrestling. She guessed he was wondering whether or how he would use the carving knife. As if obeying some primeval urge he went to the window and placed his hand on the knife's handle, slowly gripped, lifted and pointed it toward the door, pushing his family back behind him.

They all recoiled when there was a fearful crash against the bedroom door, as if it had been shoulder barged. The upper hinge gave way at the impact, light from the landing beyond could be seen, but the heavy furniture was still doing its job.

Then a metal blade crashed through the flimsy middle door panel. With a squeaking and with difficulty it was withdrawn and with repeated crashing the blade struck again and again, the frenzied attacker expressing their determination to get at them. All turned to see the horrified expressions in each other's faces and simultaneously pulled back back from the bedroom door retreating further into the middle of the bedroom.

There was nothing left to hide behind except each other. Phil's knife, now hanging limply at his side, seemed a woefully inadequate final piece in their line of defence. Ruth found she had been instinctively clutching her new broach and a sharp edge had cut her finger. She sucked the drop of salty blood.

Then there were more noises, running footsteps along the landing and a scuffle could be heard taking place, then a thud to the floor and the clicking sound of what might have been handcuffs being applied. Footsteps and hushed voices could be heard and all gradually became quiet. Holding their breaths and each other in terror, they tried to hear what was happening only feet away.

Then Phil stepped forward and started moving the furniture from on top of the bed, the wardrobe first; then he started pulling the bed itself back from the door.

'Don't move anything. Stay put until I give the word that we have searched and made the whole site secure,' ordered the officer. 'You hear me in there?'

Phil acknowledged and duly complied. By now he had placed the carving knife back on the window cill, putting a distance between the object and himself.

They waited in silence facing the door for what seemed an age. After a while footsteps could once more be heard approaching and pulses raced.

'You can come out now,' the police officer said calmly.

'Yes, will do,' answered Phil quietly.

'Are all the occupants of the house safe with you in there?' the officer asked. 'There's no one else in the house you know of?'

'No, no one.'

The waiting had seemed like an age. It was long after the sound of a resisting man being pulled along the landing and then out to the police car had past, that this same police officer was now outside their bedroom door telling them that although he believed the coast was clear, when they came out, they were to stay with him for the time being and wait on the landing whilst the premises was thoroughly searched.

Phil dragged the bed back and cautiously opened the bedroom door. A long glinting curved knife, more like a sword, quivered in the door as if alive. It was stuck fast and they gave it a wide berth as they stepped in turn onto the landing. All could not help but gaze and be fixated by it. The inescapable truth was the intruder had not come to burgle, he had come to find them and do them harm.

'Don't touch that,' the officer said firmly, meaning the knife. 'We'll have someone along for photos and evidence taking shortly. We'll deal with it.'

Whilst waiting at the top of stairs the officer asked if he could arrange interviews with them and after checking with his colleagues who confirmed the coast really was now clear, they were told it was safe enough for them to head back downstairs where they were led in the direction of the kitchen. Ruth wondered if any of them were up to speaking coherently, let alone being interviewed.

32

The adrenaline still coursing and shaking them, they'd clung tightly to one another as they'd gone downstairs and into the kitchen. Pausing briefly at the foot of the stairs, Ruth observed that the kitchen door had proved remarkably robust, the two bolts had held, scuff marks and dents on the other side were all there was to show for the noisy battering it had received. It was then the familiar face of PC Alice Such appeared. She joined them at the kitchen table and took charge. Tea was made and with everyone sitting down quietly, shock written on all their ashen faces, an initial interview session began.

Brief interviews were conducted by Alice as the follow up police SOCO team moved silently around the vicarage, poking into corners, brushing, dusting, waving plastic bags, clinically gathering their scientific analysis of the crime scene dressed for the task in their white sterile overalls. As Alice spoke, her words floated over their heads as if they themselves were in a trance and Alice often had to repeat herself to bring them back to the question in hand.

Meanwhile an emergency repair handyman had come to make the house secure. Ruth could see it was Greg, the same man from J B Builders who had repaired the door only two days earlier. He gave her a wry smile.

All the police 'processing' meant that they weren't able to be alone as a family until 11pm, well after the children's bedtime, though the terror of lying in bed after what had happened, put any thought of settling down for the night a long way from anyone's mind.

As Greg, who was the last to leave, was finally loading his tool box and taking the unused offcuts of window-boarding timber back to his white van, another police car arrived.

The officer introduced himself as PC Colin Armstrong and told them he'd been detailed to provide them overnight security. He'd be right outside keeping an eye if they needed him. As if to provide a reassuring voice as they closed the front door on him, he touched his hat with a relaxed, 'evenin' all,' as if this was a normal evening and nothing untoward had ever occurred.

Phil was happy to take the kids off upstairs to begin afresh the ritual of getting them to bed. Tonight it had been decided they'd be sleeping on their mattresses in the same room as Mum and Dad.

Then there was another knock at the front door. From the kitchen window could be seen PC April Cooper, looking left and right, her face tired and strained, but wanting to come inside. No doubt she herself looked much the same, weary, drained, just as worn down, Ruth thought.

April joined Ruth in the kitchen, no words being exchanged, whilst Phil took the children upstairs.

'Good decision to go where you did, upstairs. You held him off, stayed safe,' began April, trying to both restore the sense of being in control and give some reassurance.

'It didn't feel like it,' replied Ruth unconvinced.

'We've already learned he was after Darshana, not you. He thought you were hiding her here. It's alright, I came to tell you we've got her safe and the entire cell your burglar was part of, are now either dead or securely held in police custody.'

'Where's Darshana? You say she's OK?'

'Darshana's currently being driven from Edmonton over to her brother Hitesh's place in West London as we speak. She'll be fine there. We've told her to keep her head down and she'll stay there for the foreseeable future. She's nothing left here, their Edmonton shop's finished, utterly destroyed by the fire and it was almost certainly her brother Ravi whose body was found inside. You'll understand that formal identification is going to take a while to process...'

'Yes... So it's over? Are you absolutely certain?' said Ruth anxiously, 'Like, like it wasn't fully over before, was it?'

'It's over. That's it. No more.'

'Let me explain what I know. It may take a while.'

'That's OK. I couldn't sleep right now anyhow.'

'At the heart of all this was the visit Raj made to India way back in 2002 when he visited Gujarat for his Father's funeral. Whether he got caught up in the Hindu mob violence against Muslims willingly or whether he was an instigator we don't know. The experience may have radicalised him as a Hindu or that may have happened later here in England, but at the local Edmonton Temple where he regularly attended, what we do know is he was outspoken when it came to Indian politics, aligning himself with elements considered extreme even within the BJP ruling political party.'

'You know he never once talked to me about his politics.'

'He was pretty discreet, keeping the world of his shop and his Indian politics quite separate. So far as India was concerned, where his first love lay, he was adamant India should be a Hindu country which meant for him the present secular state, as the holder of the ring for all different faiths should be removed. That's what he firmly advocated. From what we've learned from Counter Terrorism in India, when it came to Indian politics, he was totally intolerant of all other religions. So back in 2002 when Hindu pilgrims died at the hand of Muslims, Raj was incensed.'

'It's strange perhaps then to think how nice he was to all his different customers coming to his shop. He was certainly pleasant enough to me. I'd never have thought…'

'However, I'm afraid there's no escaping the fact that he was photographed taking part in the brutal reprisals and massacre of Muslims in India in 2002.'

'But that was all so long ago…'

'Yes, and when a chance visitor to his shop tracked him down recently and identified him from those days, his fate was sealed. Raj was part of a vengeful extremist group that went from house to house systematically seeking out any Muslims they could find and killing them.'

'After tonight, I can now appreciate something of the terror those Muslims must have felt.'

'Indeed. Steps were then taken by a militant Muslim group to take their revenge. We knew of Raj and his radical sympathies some while back and more recently we were tipped off as to the Muslim group's presence, but it wasn't until after Raj's death we connected the two.'

'Raj died when two men from the cell of five came into his shop and stabbed him. Tony was unfortunate enough to witness what happened and got himself caught up in it. He was released from custody by the police early this… err Sunday morning when, by then, we believed we knew who the real killers were, the identity of the two men who had actually killed Raj. Once we held them. We knew Tony was innocent. That's why we let him go.'

'I know. I saw Tony here earlier and he explained,' said Ruth.

'Last weekend, we believe, on the Friday, Raj took steps of his own to perpetrate murder. He took two of his extremist friends from the Temple in his van to near Edmonton Green where they knew they'd probably find their targets after Friday prayers, coming away from the mosque. They spotted two of the five Muslims they were seeking, and once in a quiet side street, they used knives to kill them wrapping their bodies in rugs before putting them in the back of Raj's van where they were left, in Henley Road, outside the Morris's house. There's some CCTV camera footage we've got, it's poor quality but it makes the connections in the events that day clear. Presumably the bodies were to be disposed of somewhere else later. That's when you saw them. We believe Raj's friends set fire to the van, when you were visiting Angela only after they knew Raj had been murdered. It was a clumsy attempt to destroy evidence and we were already on to them. Those two Hindus have also been picked up and are currently being detained by police.'

'And Angela Morris?'

'Having witnessed Raj's murder, Angela Morris died to serve as a warning to Tony Morris to keep his mouth shut. Two further men, here on visas from Gujarat, were arrested earlier tonight and will be charged with arson in respect of Raj's shop, the murder of Ravi and the murder of Angela.'

'That's the Hindu's accounted for, Raj and his two accomplices you now hold, together with the two who burned the van. So, have I got it right? Then, two Muslims found dead in the van, and two others are in custody. That leaves one remaining of the five?' asked Ruth.

'Yes, and he tried to come and find Raj's wife Darshana, whom he believed to be staying here with you as she had nowhere else to go. His motive was vengeance, pure and simple. How he found out she might be here, we're not yet sure. Perhaps he followed her earlier and then bided his time until it seemed quieter.'

'And that's the end, can you be certain it's the end of it?'

'Yes, though in my work, terrorism keeps rearing its head and one has to be ever vigilant. Sadly in these matters the reality is there's never an end. We all need to remain vigilant.'

'Thanks for filling me in April. I'd better rejoin Phil with the kids. They were very upset by it. We all were...'

'We'll need to take further statements from you Ruth... can I see you first thing? I'll call you.'

With that April excused herself. Ruth made her way upstairs thinking that in spite of the reassurances, the putting of everything into place, no one would be settling down quite just yet, least of all, herself. After showing April out, she slowly climbed the stairs with a thankful heart. Her family were safe at last, thank God. One hand clutched the banister, the other touched her new broach.

33

Several weeks later, October in Dubai was hot, scorchingly hot. Adam and Raqiyah had not insisted Ruth robe in full clerical attire for their wedding blessing, nonetheless she did robe up to conduct an open air ceremony at a plush beachside hotel. In a sauna-like temperature, the breath-stealing, hot and humid air drifted in off the azure sea.

They'd said they wanted a quietly traditional occasion. So finding herself wilting in around 40°C Ruth smiled at having agreed to turn out in what she thought was appropriate attire, her new broach worn proudly pinned to her clerical scarf. With perspiration rolling down her face her robes clinging to her like a wet bath towel, she nonetheless considered herself to be fortunate indeed to be part of such a happy occasion. There were many tears of joy and just a few of sadness, the latter mainly when thinking of absent family and friends.

Adam and Raqiyah for their part looked radiant. Adam, was beautifully kitted out and splendidly handsome in a grey and blue morning dress. Raqiyah wore a traditional Omani gold trim vermillion silk full length wedding dress.

After her uncle, Abdul Zayed, had proudly brought her to stand beside Adam, she then wore her long, dark brown hair loose, uncovered. Abdul's children alongside Ruth's provided a suitable younger escort and with one of Adam's oldest Muswell Hill friends as best man, Raqiyah invited a friend from her university course to be her bridesmaid. In sum it was a small and intimate gathering added to only by the presence of a young female photographer doing her best to capture the occasion without too much intrusion upon everyone's enjoyment.

Ceremony and photographs over, as the sun began to drop in the sky without appearing to lose any of its penetrating heat, the guests moved slowly away from the bright sunlight of the sandy beach front into the hotel behind them with its ever so welcome blast of cool air conditioning to greet them.

Being a small group, the party occupied four tables in a room with other groups beginning to gather for an evening meal. Looking at the feast before them, Ruth remembered her recent visit to see her doctor who had advised that her blood results suggested Type 2 diabetes. It had been a wake up call. After this evening's banquet, she was determined to take her nutrition in hand.

The visit to the doctor's surgery had happened on the same day that Archdeacon Stephen Nicholls had publicly announced he was moving from London to Walsingham, Norfolk, by the end of the year. His few days there earlier in the week had been part of the process of transition now made public. Bad and good news often came along simultaneously, she thought.

Later in the evening, as people were finishing their meals, the wedding party settling into relaxed quiet conversations in groups of twos and threes. It was then Adam and Raqiyah came over to speak to Ruth.

'Thanks so much Aunt Ruth for today. You've no idea how much it means to us both, it was exactly what we'd hoped for,' said Adam.

'My pleasure Adam. What are your plans now? Will you both be travelling? A honeymoon perhaps?'

'No, nothing like that yet,' said Raqiyah. 'I need to finish my course first and then we'll see what transpires. We've no firm plans. Adam never quite knows where he'll be next, but that suits him. He chases where the action and the stories are and the arrangement is fine for now. He loves his job as a correspondent and believes that the freedom of the press is the first step on the road toward democracy and human rights.'

Adam scowled in jest. 'Well that's what he tells me!' she added, pushing against him playfully.

Adam's phone vibrated in his pocket and he couldn't resist the temptation to look at it. His face dropped.

'You'll never guess what! Harry McNamara, the shadiest MP in Parliament, is visiting Dubai from next Saturday to promote arms sales. My newspaper editor's texting me, today of all days, to tell me I'm just the man to get the real story out of him! That's my job for next week sorted. There's bound to be mud Harry's brought from England, dirt sticking to him, like ticks on a rat. I just need to find out what he's been up to! This is going to be fun.'

His phone vibrated again and this time Adam broke into a grin. 'It's him again! He also says congratulations and have a great day!'

It was two days later, when the family were on the plane back to London Heathrow, Ruth saw something that made her think.

Circling above north London waiting for clearance to land, she thought she saw her parish far below in the sprawl of north London's urban development. Ruth spotted in one glimpse the place where she was needed. For one thing, Tony Morris needed her to bury his Mum, Angela, in a few days time since permission had now come through. Her heart still full of the joys of a wedding blessing it would have to turn full circle to embrace Tony's sadness. She recalled Angela and all her strange mystical ways, glad now to have met her and therefore well placed to try to do Tony proud when it came to saying a final farewell.

Right now, high above London, contemplating all the ups and downs of ministry, she really believed she was just the right person for her job. The archdeacon was finally off her back, Phil happily running the Foodbank, and the plans for a church wall consigned to the waste paper basket.

The Revd. Ruth Churchill would be arriving back at her vicarage later today and she had absolutely no plans to leave Edmonton any time soon.

Afterword

My original vision was to write a contemporary trilogy with the themes of cultural diversity and political extremism to the fore. In giving a serious treatment of these together with several other societal themes set in the genre of thriller I believe these novels to be unique. As sometimes happens with authors, once embarked on a course, it becomes hard to stop and ideas for further books based around the characters familiar to author and reader.

Beginning with the stories of Adam, Ali and Kaylah, the reader is introduced in **Flashbacks** to what has sadly become a reality – terror on city streets. The book's climax is set in the centre of London on Armistice Day. Aspects of the storyline have been disturbingly prophetic.

Flashbacks was followed by **IStanbul**. It was a privilege for me to spend time in the beautiful historic city of Istanbul in the spring of 2016. Turkey has become a country to watch. It lies in the borderlands of east and west and has seen recent political upheaval and religious revival replacing Ataturk's secular republic. **IStanbul** imagines a possible future scenario in which an attempt is made to destabilised the country. In the course of events a visiting England football supporter, Harry McNamara, makes an appearance.

Harry is central to **Harry's England**, a novel which considers the possibility of an extreme right wing candidate being elected to parliament in the South West of England. I found historian Todd Gray's well researched book, 'Blackshirts in Devon', looking at local right wing extremism in the 1930s fascinating and it inspired me to ask the question, could it happen today? Indeed what would happen if the populace became fearful through terrorist activity? Might someone like Harry be elected?

In 2018 I was fortunate to make a visit to Oman in which the whole of the next book **Domain** is set. My reason for going there was to respond to an invitation offered me to visit when I helped host an Omani group in Leicester a few years ago. I had been impressed by what I heard from them about the Omani tradition of 'tolerance' and the Ibadi Muslim culture in that country. So I wanted to see the place for myself. Once there I discovered an amazingly dramatic and challenging land and a welcoming people. When I learned of the political situation in the country and added a little imagination of my own, I found Oman promised to be a fabulous setting for **Domain**.

As the title suggests, a major theme is the person and their relationship with place. It operates in the novel on a number of levels. This is a universal theme and not a matter that solely concerns Oman and Omanis. Characters in the story also have their personal domain issues. Key characters from the earlier books, are Adam Taylor and Raqiyah Nahari. Raqiyah's family, in particular her father Abdul Aziz Nahari, feature. There is a diversity theme, once again operating in **Domain** at a number of levels. Other characters who play significant roles are Raqiyah's mother, Maryam and her brother, Hassim. Rather differently from my earlier books, **Domain** covers a longer period of time, taking the reader back to stories that certainly, as the author, I found so fascinating.

TRUTH takes the reader back to connect with the Revd. Ruth Churchill whose north London Drop-In project inadvertently provided support for the terrorist Ali Muhammed. After the furore his attack created, a Church

Report subsequently forces the Drop-In to close and places Ruth herself under close scrutiny. This novel covers the intense period of little more than one week at the end of August. When a knife attack in the parish takes place, all is not what it at first appears and as pressures mount on Ruth herself, both she and her family take centre stage in a story which has deep roots in India.

The novel **TRUTH** addresses some new themes, in particular the demands women in church ministry can face. It reveals the varied and different pressures that can come to bear when one is exposed to life in the community. The novel raises questions as to what authentic religious experience is and what is truth; and the call for walls to be built to make places, including religious buildings safe. This is but one example of several contemporary themes that can be found in the pages of this in many ways, a both claustrophobic and liberating thriller.

In the course of writing I have been fortunate to have bent the ear of so many people and to have gained from their support and encouragement. Writers in Ottery St Mary and in the Exeter Authors Association have energised and advised. Editors and friends, amongst whom are Jeni Braund, Steve Chapman, Simon Cornish, Angela Harvey, Mary Hewlett, Chris King, Jill Rose, Ruth Ward, Margaret Whitlock and Shirley-Ann Williams all kindly advised on the various texts – the remaining errors are mine!

I am immensely grateful to Exeter University student Jack Kerslake who spent hours of his time on developing the cover design when I was stumped. Many other people answered my obscure questions, friends and former colleagues in the inter-faith, mental health, policing and

Prevent worlds offered their insights – you know who you are and thank you!

One thing I must underline is that all my novels and their characters are fiction. There is no attempt to demonise anyone or besmirch reputations of countries, cities or religion and belief. Sadly though, the subjects of extremism, terrorism and political instability mean these stories deal with challenges that are deeply felt and reflect the reality that all too many people's lives are damaged by such events.

Many of the parish experiences of Ruth Churchill are loosely based upon my own parish and probation service experiences and fiction is a way to anonymously allow them to surface and be given expression.

In writing my hope is that these books serve to prompt helpful discussion, provide safe places to air ideas and explore societal issues, but most of all give everyone a good read!

I am always willing to hear from readers and reply to any questions. Please contact me through my website:

http://jehallauthor.com

Suggested
Book Group Questions

1.   Ruth Churchill is the central character in this novel. What do you make of her?

2.   The story begins with a knife wielding young man. What impact do you think his presence has?

3.   Do you find Angela and Tony Morris believable characters? Does Angela's religious dimension have any similarities or differences with that of Ruth's?

4.   Are walls to defend countries, churches, schools and homes effective? What do you think of Julie's suggestion that the safeguarding of Ruth, her family and the congregation are best addressed by building a high wall and adding other security features?

5.   Is Archdeacon Stephen Nicholls a good guy or a bad guy?

6.   Do women ministers in the church have to contend with more than men? Do they fall into two categories – those who can't cope and those who have to be super-managers?

7.   Raj and Dashana's world is shown to have links with events in Gujarat back in 2002. Can grievances get carried across national boundaries and through extensive periods of time? Can such extremism lead to terrorist acts and retain their lethal potency?

8.   Did it surprise you that the church was the focus for so many social concerns – climate change, Rohingya

Muslims, mental illness, foodbanks, pastoral care, funerals and bereavement, etc.....? Which of these themes appealed to you? Facing so many demands, where do you think Ruth should have best focussed her energies?

9.   What's your take on Ruth and Phil's marriage and family life?

10.   Did Ruth change? If so, how and when do you think things turned a corner for her? Why do you think the broach was important?

11.   How did you feel the story line developed and did the ending satisfy you? What do you think Ruth did next?

12.   What does the reader take away from this book?

Flashbacks

J E Hall

This, the author's first novel, introduces the characters featured in subsequent books.

In Flashbacks, Adam Taylor from Muswell Hill, north London, goes on an adventurous solo cycle ride across Europe to the Middle East before going to University. It ends unexpectedly. Is his life over?

Ali Muhammed is haunted by flashbacks since seeing his father shot before his eyes. He is subsequently trained by IS and is sent to London as a jihadist.

Kaylah Kone has Afro-Caribbean cultural roots. A business studies student in London, she finds her life becomes tangled up with Ali.

All three characters and those around them are drawn into a terrorist plot to attack an Armistice Day parade outside Parliament. Can Ali be stopped and tragedy averted?

'Controversially current, intense and compelling debut thriller, grappling with themes and issues pertinent for contemporary societies'

Dr Irene Pérez-Fernández
University of Oviedo
Spain

IStanbul

J E Hall

This novel is a sequel to Flashbacks.

Ali Muhammed's lone-wolf attack in London on Armistice Day is followed by plans for a new and ambitious terrorist initiative in Turkey. Forces are mobilised. Ali travels from Mosul to Istanbul, and with local help, he hopes IS can destabilise the country.

Adam Taylor, traumatised by the events of the previous year, begins a new life as a student. He is determined to understand Islam better. At the end of his first year he goes to Istanbul with three other students to explore and learn from this great city.

Kaylah Kone, in new circumstances agrees to help the security services.

Unimaginable tension and life-changing events in Istanbul take the reader on a compelling adventure.

'In the context of our multi-faith world and with a mix of the familiar and unfamiliar this drama succeeds in both entertaining and challenging the reader.'

Rt Rev Dame Sarah Mullally
Bishop of London

Harry's England

J E Hall

Harry McNamara is from Plymouth in the South West of England. A young man with ideals, not ones you'd probably agree with, but he can be very persuasive.

When he declares his intention to stand as an extreme right wing candidate for his parliamentary seat, after a slow start, his campaign suddenly gains momentum.

There are unknown sinister forces at work behind the scenes and Harry is suddenly on a roll.

Terrorist attacks in Exeter and Plymouth unsettle the population. Might these turn things Harry's way?

Adam Taylor, Raqiyah Nahari and Clive Kone don't like Harry one bit, but what can they do?

In the background the police and security services have a job on their hands.

Will Harry get elected?

'A novel of our times with all the twists of an accomplished thriller'

Ann Widdecombe

Domain

J E Hall

When Raqiyah Nahari and Adam Taylor finish their university courses in the UK they fly out to Oman together.

As their plane from London lands Oman's ruler, the Sultan, dies.

Raqiyah's family and the country fall into a time of crisis.

Her father Abdul Aziz is in trouble.

What is his story?

Troubles mount. Raqiyah and Adam flee to the interior making their situation even more dangerous.

Can Raqiyah's mysterious brother Hassim help?

This personal family story set in the context of a contemporary political thriller will grip the reader.

'A thriller that has it all…
a fast pace, political intrigue and interfaith love'

Dr Irene Pérez-Fernández
University of Oviedo
Spain

What's Next?

J E Hall is working on his sixth novel
which is set in south west England

It is due to be published in 2020

See the author's website for further details, for reviews and
anticipated date of publication:

http://jehallauthor.com